The Collected Stories of María Cristina Mena

Recovering the U.S. Hispanic Literary Heritage

The Collected Stories of María Cristina Mena

Edited, with an Introduction,
by Amy Doherty

Recovering the U.S. Hispanic Literary Heritage
Arte Público Press
Houston, Texas
1997

gh grants from the National
agency), Andrew W. Mellon
r's Digest Fund and the City
s Council of Houston, Harris

Recovering the past, creating the future

Arte Público Press
University of Houston
Houston, Texas 77204-2090

Cover design by Mark Piñon

Mena, María Cristina, 1893-1965.
[Short Stories]
The collected stories of María Cristina Mena / María Cristina Mena ; edited by Amy Doherty.
p. cm. — (Recovering the U.S. Hispanic literary heritage)
Includes bibliographical references.
ISBN 1-55885-211-5 (alk. paper)
1. Mexico—Social life and customs—Fiction. I. Doherty, Amy. II. Title. III. Series: Recovering the U.S. Hispanic Literary Heritage Project publication.

PS3525.E39A6 1997
813'.52—dc21 97-22174
CIP

The paper used in this publication meets the requirements of the American National Standard for Permanence of Paper for Printed Library Materials Z39.48-1984.

Contents

Acknowledgments

In recent years, thanks to the Recovering the U.S. Hispanic Literary Heritage project sponsored by the University of Houston, many Mexican-American women writers who would have remained unread have been recovered for scholarship. This project represents one of the many that they have encouraged through their annual Grants-in-Aid. Without their help, I could not have undertaken this work. I am deeply appreciative of their support and their continued work in recovering this literature.

I am also indebted to The Rare Books and Manuscripts Division of the New York Public Library for allowing me to research the Century Company Records for Mena's letters, and to the Department of Special Collections, Stanford University Library, and the Harry Ransom Humanities Research Center, University of Texas at Austin, for use of the letters of D. H. Lawrence. I would also like to thank Elizabeth Ammons, Professor of English and of American Studies at Tufts University, for introducing me to Mena's short stories and for her advice throughout this project. For providing valuable research assistance, I would like to thank Asa Rubenstein, research librarian at the New York Public Library; Everette Larson and Reynaldo Aguirre of the Hispanic Division of the Library of Congress; Jean McManus, Reference librarian at Tufts University; and those who have offered support and encouragement in many ways: Tiffany Ana López, Amelia Katanski, Valerie Rohy, Julia Lisella, Sara Eddy, Min Song, Kimberly Hébert, and Dawn Mendoza; my parents, Paul and Beth, for always being there for me; and Joe, for more than I can say.

Introduction

Born in Mexico City, María Cristina Mena (1893-1965) emigrated to New York City at the age of fourteen before the Mexican Revolution of 1910 (Simmen 39). In the United States, she later published a series of short stories in English in prominent U.S. magazines. Although Mena's fiction has been analyzed in literary publications and dissertations, studied in classes, discussed at conferences, and included in anthologies and criticism of early twentieth century Chicana literature, her stories have not been collected until now. This anthology includes her narratives in *American Magazine* and *The Century Magazine*, as well as stories recently recovered from *Cosmopolitan* and *The Household Magazine*. Because she wrote for a critical group of editors who expected an appealing version of life in Mexico, her stories were largely dismissed in studies of Chicano literature.[1] However, more recent readings by Chicana theorists and literary critics, particularly those who recuperate traditional Mexican figures such as La Malinche and Coatlicue, provide a new theoretical lens through which to read Mena's stories. She was not only a "local color" writer in the canonical sense of the term; she artfully responded to contemporary political and social issues.[2] In particular, her charac-

[1] For example, see Paredes 49-50 and Tatum 33.

[2] In *Chicano Literature,* Tatum characterizes Mena as a "local color" writer and criticizes her "obsequious" characters: "María Cristina Mena is a fine writer whose short stories and sketches appeared early in this century in the *Century* and *American* magazines. Unfortunately, her talents are undermined by her tendency to create obsequious Mexican characters who fit comfortably within the American reader's expectations. This results in trivial and condescending stories" (33). For a revisionist reading of multicultural "local color writers," including Mena, see Ammons and Rohy.

ters reveal the changing roles of women in relation to U.S. commercialism, Mexican social codes, Mexican archetypes such as the Virgin of Guadalupe and Coatlicue, and the Mexican Revolution. With tropes of vision and mirroring, Mena suggests alternative roles for women and confronts her U.S. readers with their own prejudices.

Mena writes from a distinctly privileged vantage point compared with other recently recovered Chicana writers who lived in the southwestern United States during the Mexican Revolution. Her upper-class background allowed her family to send her to New York City to live with family friends before the onset of the Mexican Revolution. There, she began publishing at the age of twenty-one, married Henry Kellett Chambers, a playwright of Australian descent, befriended D.H. Lawrence, became active in literary and service clubs, and went on to write children's books in her later years (Simmen 39-40). In her writing and in her life, Mena moved easily in Anglo society, yet maintained her memories of and her loyalty to her Mexican heritage.

In her stories, Mena describes disparate aspects of life in Mexico at the turn of the century, such as class oppression under the Díaz regime, the influence of U.S. capitalism on Mexico, and the increasingly active role of women during the Mexican Revolution. Her first short stories were published in November 1913: "The Gold Vanity Set" in *American Magazine* and "John of God, the Water-Carrier" in *The Century Magazine*, which was chosen for *The Best Short Stories of 1928* following its reprinting in *The Monthly Criterion*, edited by T.S. Eliot.[3] Although Mena presents a stereotypical image of Mexican Indians in both stories, she also demonstrates the implicit role of U.S. capitalism in Mexico's modernization. As will be discussed regarding her negotiations with her *Century* editors, her inclusion of the Virgin of Guadalupe was crucial to both stories.

Mena often uses the vehicle of romance to discuss gender roles, colonialism, and immigration. For example, in "The Emotions of María Concepción" (*Century,* January 1914), she warns Anglo readers against a "misreading" of María's passions, an admonition which speaks to *Century*'s stereotypical portrayals

[3] O'Brien 77-93 and *The Monthly Criterion* (1927): 312-330.

of Mexican women. "The Education of Popo" (*Century*, March 1914) depicts the intertwined and exploitative relationship between the U.S. and Mexico when a young Mexican boy falls in love with an older American woman who seduces him and then leaves him for her wealthy ex-husband. Mena's characters often evade such exploitation, as in "The Vine-Leaf" (*Century*, December 1914), where the *marquesa* eludes the grasp of those who attempt to "frame" her in a single interpretation. Similarly, in "Marriage by Miracle" (*Century*, March 1916), Mena questions the colonizer, figured as the U.S. doctor, who believes too strongly in his own power. In "The Birth of the God of War" (*Century*, May 1914), she offers an alternative to feminine role models such as the Virgin of Guadalupe or romantic heroines. In this story, the narrator's grandmother recounts the legend of Coatlicue, recuperated in contemporary Chicana theory for her life-giving and spiritual capacities. Mena returns to Aztec legend as the grandmother reminds her granddaughter that the village cathedral was built on an Aztec temple. In each of these fictions, Mena contributes to a vision of Mexico as a community independent of U.S. projections of its own desires and ideals.

Although all of Mena's stories for *Century* take place in Mexico, she turned to the U.S. in a story for *Cosmopolitan,* "The Soul of Hilda Brunel" (December 1916), in which a clairvoyant opera singer recalls her immigrant past. Although this fiction seems removed from Mena's life in Mexico, Hilda's memories may suggest the author's own experience as a foreigner in the U.S.: in the background of the sophisticated opera singer lies the lonely experience of immigration. In a sense, Hilda Brunel shifts worlds by returning in memory to a former life, and one might ask if Mena too felt that "successive waves of the hand" would reveal layers of a life transformed over time by migrations to different regions of the world. In all of her stories, she shows that women are not easily captured in a single role; her powerful female protagonists move fluidly across boundaries of class, race, and nationality.

Class hierarchy and revolution are important in "Doña Rita's Rivals" (*Century*, September 1914), "The Sorcerer and General Bisco" (*Century*, April 1915), and "A Son of the Tropics" (*Household*, January 1931). In "Doña Rita's Rivals," Mena illustrates the strict class divides governing Doña Rita's life, ultimately leading to revolution. Mena turns directly to the Mexican Revolution of 1910 in "The Sorcerer and General Bisco," where two revolutionaries, Carmelita and Aquiles, flee from a ruthless patrician, Don Baltazar, who hypnotizes their military leader, General Bisco. Carmelita uses her clairvoyant powers to play a significant role in the murder of Don Baltazar. Mena's most overt narrative of class friction and revolution, "A Son of the Tropics" was published in *Household Magazine* in January 1931. Ironically appearing in a magazine devoted to housekeeping, "A Son of the Tropics" does not couch the Mexican Revolution in romance. Instead, Mena portrays women's roles in war: a *soldadera*, Tula, inadvertently fashions the means of Rosario's suicide, a doorknob-turned-bomb. In this story, she strips the romantic veils of her earlier stories and turns to a smoldering core of prejudices and self-delusions. Superficially, the plots of these stories emphasize the popular and recurrent themes of lost love, binding tradition, U.S. and European influence on Mexico, class stratification, and political intrigue. However, at a deeper level, her stories also reveal her characters' complex identities and their misguided presumptions about themselves and each other.

Because Mena's stories shift between Mexican and Anglo-American perspectives, readers have had contradictory reactions to her work.[4] On one hand, critics of Chicana literature praise her strong female characters. For example, Tiffany Ana López states that Mena "revises the La Malinche reading to depict women as sexually assertive and communally productive—rather than destructive—individuals" (34). On the other hand, her stories have been criticized as "trivial and condescending" (Tatum 33). Although Raymond Paredes describes Mena as a "talented storyteller" in *Three American Literatures* (49), he concludes his brief analysis by stating that "Mena's portrayals are ultimately obsequious, and if one can appreciate the weight of popular attitudes on Mena's consciousness, one can also say that a braver, more perceptive writer would have confronted the life of her culture more forcefully" (50). While it is significant that Mena was mentioned

[4] To explore this conflict in Mena's fiction, Velásquez-Treviño draws a parallel between W.E.B. DuBois's term "double consciousness," which describes the African-American experience in the U.S., and "cultural ambivalence," which "characterizes the dual consciousness of Chicanos as they mediate between the values of the dominant culture and those of the minority group" (140, 146).

in Paredes's chapter on "The Evolution of Chicano Literature," his commentary suggests that overt confrontation is traditionally more highly regarded than Mena's coded interplay of cultures.[5]

As a struggling writer in New York City, Mena had to deal with the standards of the magazines in which she published. Also, because she emigrated from Mexico at a young age, she would have been susceptible to the influence of U.S. stereotypes of Mexicans. However, her writing shows her critical ability to acknowledge those stereotypes and confront them while still maintaining her audience. Mena had a dual purpose in writing: first, to entertain a privileged, conservative, Anglo audience with a passion for travel and the exotic, an audience which sought a pre-packaged version of another country. Second, it was her purpose to comment on the meeting of U.S. and Mexican cultures both as an "interpreter" and as a critic, a role which she plays most subtly in her fiction.

In her short stories, Mena is critical both of the U.S. and of the elite of Mexico. During the time she lived in Mexico, President Porfirio Díaz, with the complicity of U.S. corporate investors, carried out his plan of modernization on the backs of dispossessed laborers and indigenous Mexicans. In her fiction, Mena becomes increasingly critical of the U.S. and supportive of the Mexican revolutionaries who rebelled against such injustice. After setting the stage with more stereotypical characters in her early stories in *American Magazine* and *Century*, she moves toward revolution with characters who reject their upper-class background to join the militant underclass. Mena wrote from a difficult, if not contradictory, position on two counts. First, as a Mexican woman expected to produce exotic, picturesque stories of romance and intrigue, she attempted to present the Mexican Revolution to U.S. readers. Second, she wrote about Mexican revolutionaries and native Mexicans after having lived an elite childhood in Mexico City. Given the fact that her increasing interest in the Revolution represents her social sympathies rather than her personal background, those characters, such as Carmelita in "The Sorcerer and General Bisco," who reject their upper-class background may symbolize Mena's own wishful projection.

[5] See Garza-Falcón-Sánchez 187-90.

Biography

In her life and in her writing, María Cristina Mena literally and figuratively crossed borders of race, class, and nationality. Born on April 3, 1893, to "a Spanish mother and Yucatecan father of European blood" (Simmen 39), she lived the life of a privileged person, well-educated, and fluent in Spanish, English, French, and Italian. A precocious child who began writing poetry at the age of ten, she later recalled "with pleasant memories how she liked to hide in corners and write verses which no one ever saw."[6] She was educated at the Hijas de María, an "elite convent school" in Mexico City, and "later at an English boarding school." Her "politically powerful and socially prominent" father was a "partner with several Americans in a variety of businesses during the last two decades of the rule of Porfirio Díaz, renown general and president of Mexico" (Simmen 39). This background played a large role in her writing, both in her depiction of upper-class women in Mexico and in the rebellion of several of her characters against their own privileged families.

During the tumultuous period leading up to the Mexican Revolution, Mena emigrated to New York City, where she lived with family friends, continued her education, and began sending manuscripts to the editors of well-known magazines (Simmen 39). Six years after arriving in the U.S., she published her first short stories in *Century* and *American Magazine* in 1913, and later in *Cosmopolitan* and *Household*, where she was described as "the foremost interpreter of Mexican life" (137). Mena clearly built a name for herself as a writer early in the twentieth century, but despite that fact, most of her stories would lie dormant in back issues of those magazines for decades.

Although her short stories do not include characters who emigrated from Mexico to the U.S., Mena did plan to tell a story close to her own experience. In 1914, she responded enthusiastically to *Century* editor Douglas Zabriske Doty's suggestion of "transplanting a Spanish character to this country; that is to say, using a

[6] Hoehn 118. Hoehn also writes that "Mrs. Chambers' stories have been translated into Spanish by the famous Mexican author and poet, Manuel Sales Cepeda, of Yucatan" (119). This reference suggests that her work appealed to audiences in Mexico and the U.S.; however, the translations have not been located at this time.

Mexican character with an American background."[7] The following excerpt from her letter to Doty sheds light on her personal development during her transition from Mexico to the U.S.:

> I have in outline the personalities of a family of wealthy refugees from Mexico, with possibilities of rich comedy in their contact with American life, especially in relation to the gradual emancipation of their daughter, who in spite of the efforts of her parents to keep her in pious subjection in accordance with Mexican tradition, takes to American freedom like a duck to water and blossoms into an ardently independent young woman, with, of course, a suitable romance to crown her adventures—the whole story to be unfolded in a succession of amusing letters from the different personages to their friends at home. For all this I have a rich store of material to draw from, and the work would not take me very long if I could only give all my time to it. [November 1914]

Certainly, the "rich store of material" was Mena's life in New York City. Although she was not commissioned to write this work during the "lean times" of World War I,[8] she increasingly questioned traditional codes of gender and class in her later short stories.

During the early decades of the twentieth century, Mena established her literary career and developed relationships with other writers. She shared her love of literature with her husband, playwright and journalist Henry Kellett Chambers, whose plays included *Butterfly,* starring Lillian Russell, and *An American Wedding,* later filmed with Ethel Barrymore in the leading role ("Henry K. Chambers"). Mena and Chambers, "a divorced man twenty-six years her senior," were married in 1916.[9] As she built her own literary reputation, she cultivated a friendship with D.H. Lawrence, who frequently travelled to Mexico and the Southwest during the 1920's and wrote several works inspired by his journeys, including *The Plumed Serpent*, *Mornings in Mexico*, and "The Woman Who Rode Away" (Gunn 123-44). He and Mena exchanged letters from 1927, after the republication of "John of God, the Water-Carrier" in *The Monthly Criterion,* until several

[7] Douglas Zabriske Doty, letter to María Cristina Mena, 28 September 1914, Century Company Records, New York Public Library, New York.

[8] Doty, letter to Mena, 19 November 1914

[9] Simmen 39. After 1916, Mena published under her married name, María Cristina Chambers.

months before his death in 1930.[10] Their friendship culminated in her two-week visit, along with Aldous and María Huxley, to the Lawrence villa in Forte dei Marmi, Italy, in the summer of 1929. Mena recalls this visit in an essay, "Afternoons in Italy with D.H. Lawrence," written for *The Texas Quarterly* in 1964, the year before her death (114-20). In this piece, she describes her support of Lawrence's controversial *Lady Chatterley's Lover*, as well as their treasured friendship.

She fondly reminisces: "And yet, whether speaking or laughing with Lawrence, he made one feel 'in touch,' as he called that implicit something which makes some people one with the flowers, the trees, with life itself" ("Afternoons in Italy" 114). Of the "life implicit," she recalls a letter from Lawrence, "so full of hope and enthusiasm for *Lady Chatterley's Lover*." Lawrence had written,

> 'It is nice of you to set about my novel. . . In my opinion my novel is worth working a bit for. I think you and I instinctively turn to the same thing, the life implicit instead of the life explicit. And the life implicit is embodied and has touch: and the life explicit is only ideas, and is bodiless. And my novel is an attempt to be in touch, to give the throb of the implicit life.'[11]

In the context of her writing for *Century*, it is interesting to consider how Mena encoded the clash of Mexican and American cultures as embodying an implicit life, unspoken but vibrant with meaning.

As one of Lawrence's supporters when *Lady Chatterley's Lover* was censored in the U.S., Mena wrote to Lawrence, in a letter discovered in 1991, offering to sell volumes of the book to booksellers in New York: "Am not afraid of *la cárcel*. And am free to do as I like. Let *me* sell the books and let them [the booksellers] all come to me and pay for them, if they want them" (9 August 1928). Years later, in an interview for *The Brooklyn Eagle* in 1960, the year after Lawrence's novel was first published in its unabridged form in the U.S., Mrs. Chambers remembers "with

[10] D.H. Lawrence Papers, M116, Department of Special Collections, Stanford University Libraries, Stanford, California. Quoted by permission.

[11] Lawrence, 24 April 1928, qtd. in "Afternoons in Italy": 115. Also see letter 4403, Boulton 377.

more amusement than resentment, the horrified reactions of her friends 30 years ago when the book she had sold to them, sight unseen, slipped by U.S. customs officials and was delivered." The interview reveals a vital woman with a sense of humor: "'There was no more playing bridge with me,' she reminisces, her dark eyes laughing" ("Heights Woman"). Although Lawrence warned Mena not "to go round talking to booksellers. . . The quieter one keeps the better" (25 August 1928), this episode demonstrates the industrious, ambitious, and bold personality behind the often genteel characters of her short stories.

Although Mena's writing has been criticized as "incapable of warming the reader's blood" (Paredes 49), she shared with D.H. Lawrence an openness about sexuality which appears in her fiction. As she notes in the 1960 interview for *The Brooklyn Eagle*, "'Americans, you know . . . have very strange conceptions about sex'" (11). She depicts these "strange conceptions" in "The Education of Popo," when Alicia Cherry, the recently divorced daughter of a U.S. businessman, seduces Popo Arriola, the adolescent son of a Mexican governor. Similarly confronting her U.S. audience in "The Emotions of María Concepción," she criticizes "the North's" misreading of Mexican women as sultry and seductive (39). While these authors differ in many ways, the literary and philosophical interests they shared apparently led Mena to support Lawrence's paean to the "natural." Lawrence, finding a friend and confidante in Mena, who disagreed with the initial reaction to *Lady Chatterley's Lover*, wrote to her, "Many of my friends are mortally offended by the openness of the novel—but many, on the other hand, seem really grateful for it. By their reactions shall ye know them. Those that are offended show their own dirtiness, or their own deadness. There are so many living dead" (25 August 1928). Such divulgences suggest that Lawrence included Mena among the true friends who understood his writing, a role she relished in her memories of their relationship.

Lawrence's letters and Mena's own recollection of her visit to Forte dei Marmi reveal a brooding Lawrence with a characteristically critical view of Mena's writing, as demonstrated in one letter: "The story was nearly first-rate—but the gods didn't want you to be a writer: at least of fiction: they refused to put the bright spark at the point of your pen" (18 February 1928). However, his continued correspondence and the invitation to visit him and Frieda in Italy suggest the distinguished and ailing author's admiration. Because Mena sent one last essay to *The Texas Quarterly* regarding her friendship with Lawrence in the year before her death, we can surmise that she valued this friendship and wanted to commemorate it in her later years.

Information about Mena's life as a writer in New York City lends insight into her literary accomplishments after she published her short stories. Years after her husband died of a paralytic stroke in 1935 at the age of sixty-eight ("Henry K. Chambers"), she wrote five children's books: *The Water-Carrier's Secrets* (1942), *The Two Eagles* (1943), *The Bullfighter's Son* (1944), *The Three Kings* (1946), and *Boy Heroes of Chapultepec: A Story of the Mexican War* (1953).[12] She was devoted to recreating her short stories, and other narratives from Mexican history and legend, into fiction for young people.[13] In her later years, she wrote and bound her own books in her apartment on Joralemon Street in Brooklyn. She also began transcribing these books into Braille as part of her own dedicated work with the blind, which included learning Braille herself ("Author Writes Book in Braille"). She attended the regular meetings of the Catholic Library Association and the Author's Guild of New York, where, as Simmen writes, "she was able to continue her friendships with editors, librarians, educators, and other writers, such as Clare Booth Luce, Theodore Maynard, and Wilfred Sheed, and where she made new friends such as Covelle Newcomb, a promising young writer from San Antonio" (40). Looking back on her writing career, Mena offered the following observation on her work:

> I have never read, much less studied, the so-called 'methods' for learning how to write. I do not believe an aspirant for authorship needs any more than to learn from observation and much reading of good authors; that writing is something that is born and grows naturally through much working at it and particularly from one's own original and very personal feeling and thinking. (Hoehn 119)

[12] Mena published her children's fiction under her married name, María Cristina Chambers.

[13] According to biographical records, María Cristina and Henry Kellett Chambers did not have children. María Cristina Chambers, Last Will and Testament [1950]; Petition to Open Premises (Aug. 17, 1965). Both documents are on file with King's County Surrogate's Court, Brooklyn, NY.

In her writing, both published and unpublished, she lived up to her own definition of the writing life.

Although Mena became a "virtual shut-in" in her later years (Simmen 40), she did publish the final essay reflecting on her friendship with D.H. Lawrence mentioned earlier. She died on August 3, 1965, at the age of seventy-two. As her obituary in *The New York Times* states, she "dedicated her work 'to bringing to the American public the life of the Mexican people'" ("Mrs. Henry Chambers"). Her letters to *Century*, recovered for the first time in this edition, show her struggle to mediate between her editors' vision and her own. Because she was far removed from relatives who may have saved other letters and manuscripts after her death, the most telling unpublished documents remaining appear to be her letters to *Century*. These letters, as well as her short stories and children's books, provide an account of her life as a writer translating her experience into short stories.

The Century Magazine

In writing for *The Century Magazine*, Mena published in one of the most well-known periodicals of her day, a magazine which spoke to the concerns of the Anglo-American middle- and upper-class. In *Magazines in the Early Twentieth Century*, Theodore Peterson writes:

> In 1890, educated readers of substance, readers who could easily afford magazines, had a place on their library tables for perhaps only *Century*, *Harper's*, and *Scribner's*. In artistic and literary quality, in volume of respected advertising, in sales, these three magazines were the leading general monthly periodicals. Their editors edited not for the great mass of the population . . . but for gentlefolk of means. (3)

Peterson further notes of these magazines, "Concerned as they were with editorial fare for the genteel, the magazines in retrospect seem curiously remote from the dramatic changes then taking place in American life. Literature, art, manners, travel, and history got their attention, and their editors often seemed to have had their eyes more closely on Europe than on America" (3). In *Century*, articles such as "Is our Art Distinctively American?" by John W. Alexander, President of the National Academy of Design (April 1914), reveal this turn-of-the-century American anxiety. In answering the questions posed by the essay's title, *Century*'s editors respond to their readership's fears of the foreign in the struggle for a distinctive and "common" "American" identity. The editorial "Topics of the Time" suggests the search for a "common quality" in the October 1913 issue of *Century*, which announces an increase in fictional pieces starting with the November 1913 issue, the first issue in which Mena published. Stating that "this is, in a real and vital sense, the very age of fiction," the editorial depicts *Century*'s intended audience through their reading tastes:

> There must be fiction for all kinds of cultivated readers, for the lovers of artistry and subtlety and the fine distinctions of human nature and for those who revel in plot and climax. There must be fiction for the laughter-loving and fiction for those for whom fiction seriously interprets life. But whatever its kind it must all possess a common quality, and this, we realize, it will take long to attain consistently.[14]

As *Century* struggled to maintain a "common quality" in its fiction, Mena was commissioned to contribute to this literary project, which, in inviting her, opened the doors to a wider variety of fiction but still sought to appeal to a "cultivated" white audience.

As the definition of "society" itself shifted with the influx of European and Mexican immigrants during the early twentieth century, the editors struggled to define *Century*'s audience and its mission as a literary magazine. Editor Hewitt H. Howland enumerates these changes:

> The feminist movement, the uprising of labor, the surging of innumerable socialistic currents, can mean nothing else than the certain readjustment of social levels. The demand of the people for the heritage of the bosses is not short of revolution. The rebellious din of frantic impressionistic groups is nothing if not strenuous protest

[14] "Topics of the Time," *Century Magazine* Oct. 1913: 951-952. Although the editor's name is not included in the essay nor the index of *Century*, the description of the Century Company Records indicates that Hewitt H. Howland was the editor from 1912-30, and thus would have written "Topics of the Time." Valerie Wingfield, Rare Books and Manuscript Division, New York Public Library, New York.

> against a frozen art. The changed Sabbath and the tempered sermon mark the coldly critical appraisement of religious creeds. And science, meantime, straining and sweating under the lash of progress, is passing from wonder unto wonder.[15]

This period of social transformation in the U.S., particularly the revolution against "the bosses" and scientific progress, mirrored the early uprisings in Mexico during the same historical period, a topic which would soon be addressed in *Century*.

The articles in *Century* reveal an overt bias against immigrants coming to the U.S., and the possible dangers they posed to Anglo-American culture. In a series on "The Old World in the New," Edward Alsworth Ross, a well-known sociologist, enumerates his concerns in an essay titled "American and Immigrant Blood: A Study of the Social Effects of Immigration"(December 1913); specifically, he disparages Southern and Eastern European immigrants with inflammatory subheadings, such as "Illiteracy," "Peonage," "The Position of Women," "Vice," "Insanity among the Foreign Born," and "Social Decline." While the fear of invasion is omnipresent, the article presents itself as a sociological treatise, underscored by Ross's title, "Professor of Sociology, University of Wisconsin" (225-32). To the editors of *Century*, Mexican immigrants may not have seemed as threatening as those from Southern and Eastern Europe during this period of economic depression. However, the Mexican Revolution was at hand: hundreds of thousands of Mexican immigrants were fleeing North from the depressed economy and loss of land brought on by social upheaval, lured to the U.S. by the promise of work in agriculture, industry, and railroad construction. Fearing that Mexican immigrants might become a "public charge"[16] during the economic depression of 1913, Rodolfo Acuña writes, "The North American press from the start whipped up anti-Mexican sentiments" ([1988] 159). The articles, illustrations, and advertising in *Century* demonstrate Anglo-American fears of those crossing their self-inscribed

[15] "Topics of the Time," *Century Magazine* Sept. 1913: 790. In this anonymous editorial, the author refers to himself as the "fourth editor," after Dr. J.G. Holland, Richard Watson Gilder, and Robert Underwood Johnson. As stated above, the editor was most likely Hewitt H. Howland.

[16] U.S. Department of Labor, "Report of the Commissioner General of Immigration," *Report of the Department of Labor* (Washington, D.C.: Government Printing Office, 1913) 337, cited in Acuña, 3rd ed., 158.

borders, particularly in the magazine's distancing or subordination of "the foreign" inside the U.S.

Although *Century* initially focussed on Southern and Eastern European immigrants, the editors later turned to Mexican subjects as the Mexican Revolution led to more interest in Mexico. The stories and articles presented Mexico as exotic and quaint. For example, a photographic essay titled "Unfamiliar Mexico" (September 1915), depicts churches, a "water-carrier," and several street scenes of daily life, with Mexicans mostly surprised by or turned away from the camera (McArthur 729-36). The photographs, stories, and illustrations often focus on the stereotypes of the inept lower-class Mexican *peón* or the seductive, inscrutable upper-class Mexican woman. For example, "The Transformation of Angelita López" (August 1914), written by Gertrude B. Millard, tells the story of a young Mexican, Angelita, a servant of a wealthy family in California. Angelita speaks in broken, almost nonsensical, English, and the narrative describes her relationship with Antonio, a stereotypically lazy, drunken Mexican who loses his job after Angelita bears their child. Angelita is deferential, dependent on the "Puritan, common-sense, ex-New Englander" (547) Miss Jane for her livelihood and advice concerning her unmotivated husband. Here, the Mexican man, Antonio, is portrayed as shifty, unwilling to work, and unable to hold down a job or maintain his family. Angelita is childlike, and her inability to communicate clearly in English diminishes her few moments of self-assertion. The Anglo author distorts their language to ridicule her Mexican subjects. The stereotypical "low-down greaser," as Antonio's boss calls Antonio (553), and his dependent Angelita, signify the Anglo author's vision of the "authentic" Mexican. Similarly, in "Creole Beauties and Some Passionate Pilgrims" (February 1914), Julius Miller attempts to come to terms with the mysterious, sheltered women of the Caribbean who bewitch him with their eyes, rarely speaking, seeming to seduce and repel at once. Miller's entire article is a meditation on the women's beauty, and those wayward American men who attempt to break through their impervious shells. These texts describe a gendered relationship with the Latina woman which reflects the authors' desires for either a dependent servant or a passionate romance.

In her reading of the cultural construction of "Mexicans, women, and people of color" in *Century*, Tiffany Ana López reads Mena's stories in the context of the magazine's racialized imagery (27). For example, in an advertisement for the Santa Fe Railroad in the publication (November 1912), López analyzes the implied "system of service": the railroad, the Mexican laborers, and those Mexicans viewed by the Anglo passengers as "part of the service to be received." Explaining Mena's position as a writer for *Century*, López states, "Mena herself was implicated in this system of service for the pleasure of Anglo viewers in her role as a commissioned 'authentic' Mexican voice. Significantly, she was asked to write stories that translated Mexican culture for the same audience that would be buying their tickets for Santa Fe based on images of the Southwest like those in the preceding ad [for the Santa Fe Railroad]" (28). Because this audience expected that a Mexican writer would conform to this code of service, as López notes, they would not have considered that she may have been "writing in resistance" (29). In her reading of trickster discourse in "The Vine-Leaf" and "The Sorcerer and General Bisco," López shows how Mena writes against the expectations of her white audience.

Unlike López, some readers have criticized Mena for apparently supporting *Century*'s demeaning perspective of Mexicans. However, Mena's letters to *Century*'s editors provide further insight into her struggle to confront such stereotypes, the demands on her writing, how much she was allowed to show her audience, and the negotiations behind the published texts. Although her stories evidently possessed the "common quality" which the *Century* editors sought, she struggled with her editors to present her own vision of Mexico, fighting against a white male editorial board which supported *Century* as a bastion of the Anglo-American literary elite.[17]

Initially, Mena was thrilled with her inclusion in the magazine, writing to Robert Underwood Johnson, "Still your wonderful

[17] While Mena struggled with the *Century* editors, she writes that an "all-too-flattering article" was written about her in the *Revista Universal*, a magazine published in New York for the Spanish-speaking community. Mena writes that Dr. Lara y Pardo, the author of the article, "has a very solid reputation as a literary critic in the Spanish-reading world" (Mena, letter to Doty, [October 1914]).

praises ring in my ear, and the afternoon I passed in your office remains in my memory as a moment of enchantment in a life that has not always been as happy as it is now" (20 March 1913). However, her correspondence prior to the publication of "John of God, the Water-Carrier" reveals her struggle to maintain the integrity of her first published story: "I felt as if I had foisted a white elephant upon an amiable friend, who now begged my permission to make the creature more conformable by amputating its legs, trunk and tail—not forgetting its ears." She accuses the editors of wanting to de-emphasize her story because of its focus on a Mexican Indian. "Could it be that the water carrier's lowly station in life made him a literary undesirable? Then what of Maupassant's Norman peasants, Kipling's soldiers and low-caste Hindoos, Myra Kelly's tenement children, and many other social nobodies of successful fiction?" (letter to Yard, [March 1913]) Mena's statement calls attention to a racialized literary hierarchy, which includes a corresponding caste system of "literary undesirables."

Although Mena forcefully argues for keeping her detailed description of John of God's pilgrimage to Guadalupe, she softens her argument by revealing her own upper-class bias.

> I expect to write more stories of Inditos than of any other class in Mexico. They form the majority; the issue of their rights and wrongs, their aspirations and possibilities, is at the root of the present situation in my unhappy country, and will become more and more prominent when the immense work of national regeneration shall have fairly begun; and I believe that American readers, with their intense interest in Mexico, are ripe for a true picture of a people so near to them, so intrinsically picturesque, so misrepresented in current fiction, and so well worthy of being known and loved, in all their ignorance. (letter to Yard, [March 1913])

While her reference to "their ignorance" echoes the *Century* articles on immigration, Mena subtly supports her argument: she compares the reactions of two friends, a Mexican and an American, to her short story. Her juxtaposition illustrates the values of reading audiences from different cultures and speaks to the *Century* editors who expect her work to meet standards solely derived from European literature:

> The other night I read "John of God" to some friends, among whom were an exiled countryman of mine—author, editor and patriot—and an American man of letters associated with a prominent publishing firm. The American said, among other things: 'Your water-carrier is a primitive saint. He has a rugged spiritual grandeur that suggests Turgenief.' The Mexican said: 'Divided between those brothers, Juan de Dios and Tiburcio, I feel the absolute soul of the Indito, dissected with precision into its contrasting elements of John the Baptist and Sancho Panza.' For the future of my work they made predictions which I dare not repeat, but which have given me courage to ask you to sweep away, as I know you can, whatever technical difficulties may oppose the publishing of my story as it stands—no, not exactly as it stands, for I will gladly undertake to cut out a few hundred words, if you will kindly send me a clean set of proofs for that purpose. (letter to Yard, [March 1913])

This anecdote clearly suggests that the *Century* editors lack knowledge of *her* culture. Further illustrating the point, in her response to editorial suggestions, Mena emphasizes the importance of the pilgrimage scenes:

"Another passage marked for cutting out was the one telling of the pilgrims eating blessed earth and drinking blessed water and buying blessed tortillas with chile sauce, and tortillas of the Virgin, which are small and sweet and dyed in many colors—a passage that I would almost defend with my life!" (letter to Johnson, 4 April 1913).

Although Mena's retort may sound "picturesque," she argues to save the signs of her culture; she will not let these important details be lost in translation. Finally, the editors allowed her to keep the details of the pilgrimage to Guadalupe which they had suggested she strike from her copy. Significantly, in the final version of "John of God, the Water-Carrier," she suggests that the indigenous Mexicans' faith in the Virgin of Guadalupe provides strength against U.S. capitalism.

Although Mena does not overtly describe the atrocities against the Mexican Indians in stories such as "John of God, the Water-Carrier," she does suggest their struggles during the turbulent Díaz regime. Dispossession of the Indians' land and their enslavement were just becoming known to the U.S. In *Barbarous Mexico*, written in 1910, John Kenneth Turner graphically depicts the Díaz regime's enslavement of the Yaqui and Mayo Indians and asserts

U.S. complicity in Mexican slavery because of U.S. corporate investment in Mexico and governmental support of Díaz (219). However, *Century*'s stance toward Mexico in the later years of the revolution was less informed and more conservative than Turner's account. In their more recent reading of the treatment of the Mexican Indians, Camín and Meyer state:

> Additionally, the struggle against the Indians in the North during the Porfiriato included the "pacification" of the Mayo and Yaqui Indians of Sonora, a bloody war that disrupted the organizational forms of both tribes, rejected their ancient rights, and transferred their lands to white domination—the richest lands of the Northwest, fertilized by the only two rivers with a quasi-permanent waterflow in the arid Sonorense plains.

Camín and Meyer also note that the Yaquis played a significant role in the Revolution: "the Yaqui resistance to the occupation remained alive, irreducible, and uninterrupted during the whole period of the Porfiriato and the Revolution, part of which was fought with Yaqui troops and part in Sonora against Yaqui insurgents" (5). Although Mena does not address the specific injustices against the Mexican Indians, nor their insurrection, she shows their oppression as well as their vital role in Mexican culture.[18]

In "John of God, the Water-Carrier" and "The Gold Vanity Set," the Virgin of Guadalupe is a figure of mediation. As Tey Diana Rebolledo explains, "the first dark Mestiza Virgin," the Virgin of Guadalupe, "represents the merging of European and Indian culture since she is, in some senses, a transformation or 'rebirth' of the native goddesses."[19] In important ways, the Virgin watches over Petra of "The Gold Vanity Set" and Juan de Dios of "John of God, the Water-Carrier."

[18] Mena also wrote an article about a Mexican composer of native Mexican heritage entitled "Julian Carrillo: The Herald of a Musical Monroe Doctrine," *Century* Mar. 1915: 753-59. In response to a letter from the editor suggesting that it may be "too remote from our interests" (Doty, 7 December 1914), Mena replied, "it will print itself somewhere, very soon — so new is it, so true, so inspiring, so intensely of Today, so sublimely of Tomorrow . . . I send it to you first as a matter of course, only begin you to fulfil your most amiable promise of a very quick reading" (Mena, letter to Doty, [December 1914]).

[19] In *Women Singing in the Snow,* Rebellodo writes that "the Virgin appeared in an area known to be the sacred worshipping place of an important pre-Columbian Nahuatl goddess, Tonantzín" (50).

In "The Gold Vanity Set," Petra places Miss Young's vanity set among the objects in the shrine to the Virgin, believing its "magic" responsible for Manuelo's vow never to beat her again. The narrator interprets this scene for the reader: "The gold vanity set, imposing respect, asking for prayers, testifying the gratitude of an Indian girl for the kindness of her beloved" (11). Following this description, Mena turns to Miss Young's self-centered reaction: "'Well, if it saves that nice girl from ever getting another beating, the saint is perfectly welcome to my vanity set'"(11). In this portrayal of Miss Young, Mena challenges the Northern reader's likely dismissal of the Virgin of Guadalupe. Does the reader want to "read" like Miss Young? Mena offers an alternative: she shows Petra's reworking of the significance of the vanity set, "wrapped in a dry corn husk, covered with a stone" (5), and carried to the Virgin in gratitude. Undermining the Anglo woman's reading of him as a "wife-beater," Manuelo concludes the story in a plaintive song: "'Into the sea, because it is deep, / I always throw / The sorrows that this life / So often gives me" (11). In this song, Mena alludes to the injustices described in her letter to *Century*, although Miss Young, caught up in her "snapshot" perspective of Petra, does not hear Manuelo's song. These narrations may be read as either positive or derogatory portrayals of the Indians; each story includes elements of both perspectives. Petra, Juan de Dios, and their faith in the Virgin of Guadalupe contrast with those characters who "buy into" materialism, such as Miss Young and Tiburcio. By attaching these narratives to an important cultural symbol, the Virgin of Guadalupe, Mena centers a disrupted community.

As a translator, Mena suggests several incarnations of the goddess in Mexico, offering new models to Anglo and Chicana readers alike. As Gloria Anzaldúa writes in *Borderlands/La Frontera,* various figures are linked: "*Coatlicue-Cihuacoatl-Tlazolteotl-Tonantzin-Coatlalopeuh-Guadalupe*—they are one" (50). After describing the faith in Guadalupe in her first stories, Mena turns to the ancient Aztec goddess, Coatlicue. Rebolledo explains, "Coatlicue is an extremely complex goddess of many aspects, transformations, and features, and she is considered to be probably the most ancient of the Nahuatl deities."[20] In "The Birth of the God

[20] Ferdinand Anton, *Women in Pre-Columbian America* (New York: Abner Schram, 1973), cited in Rebolledo 50.

of War," Mena describes the birth of Huitzilopochtli by Coatlicue, and narrates the events prior to that conception and birth. In a dialogue between grandmother and granddaughter, she reminds the reader of Coatlicue's foundational role in Mexican culture before the onset of Christianity. In doing so, she presents a fusion between the Mexican upper class and the native Mexicans, a connection missing in her earlier stories.

In "The Birth of the God of War," Mena offers a new model for women readers similar to, though less radical than, more recent readings of Coatlicue, Tonantsín, La Malinche, and La Llorona. She distinguishes between Coatlicue and the Virgin Mary in the granddaughter's reaction to the story: "Once I voiced the infantile view that the fate of Coatlicue was much more charming than that of the Virgin Mary, who had remained on this sad earth as the wife of a carpenter" (69). Although careful to admonish her granddaughter for her "sin," the grandmother also distinguishes the legend from Catholicism. She reminds her granddaughter of the past buried beneath the signs of conquest:

> Such, attentive little daughter mine, is the legend narrated to the Aztec priests by the forests, the waters, and the birds. And on Sunday, when *papacíto* carries thee to the cathedral, fix it in thy mind that the porch, foundation, and courtyard of that saintly edifice remain from the great temple built by our warrior ancestors for the worship of the god Huitzilopochtli. Edifice immense and majestic, it extended to what today is called the Street of the Silversmiths, and that of the Old Bishop's House, and on the north embraced the streets of the Incarnation, Santa Teresa, and Monte Alegre. (69)

Here, Mena's recounting of Aztec legend is not distancing, not merely picturesque, not "superstitious." As she writes, "It was not mythology to me" (64); instead, it was her cherished heritage. In her series of stories, she works tirelessly to dispel U.S. myths about Mexican culture, ending "The Birth of the God of War," for example, with the grandmother's admission, "I am a little fatigued, *chiquita*. Rock thy little old one to sleep" (69). By narrating the grandmother's story, Mena becomes the voice which perpetuates the Aztec legend in *Century*.

In "The Birth of the God of War," Mena uses folklore, Spanish, and literal translation to convey her experience. As Mary Louise

Pratt explains in "The Short Story: The Long and the Short of It," short stories often function as a repository "where oral and non-standard speech, popular and regional culture, and marginal experience, have some tradition of being at home, and the form best-suited to reproducing the length of most oral speech events" (190). Mena's distinctive use of language "to capture in English the sound and feeling of Spanish" (Paredes 50) illustrates the use of the short story as a vehicle for, as Pratt puts it, "oral and non-standard speech" (190). Paredes writes that Mena and Josephina Niggli "simulated the flavor of Spanish by reproducing in English its syntactical and idiomatic qualities" (55). For example, Mena directly translates Spanish to English in idiomatic phrases, such as "playing the bear" ("Marriage by Miracle" 114), or in exclamations such as "What roses or what pumpkins!" ("A Son of the Tropics" 141). She also skillfully shuttles between various dialects and voices in English and Spanish. For example, the narrative voice of Alicia Cherry in "The Education of Popo" ironically explains, "she did beg the privilege, however unprecedented, of promenading with a young gentleman at her side, and showing the inhabitants how such things were managed in America—beg pardon, the United States" (50). In addition to the ironic voice of the U.S. tourist in Mexico, Mena's polyphonic narrations also signify class status: the simple, formal, sincere English of "John of God, the Water-Carrier," the complex, heavily descriptive, dramatic sentences of the upper-class Mexican family of "The Emotions of María Concepción," as well as the more informal upper-class American phrases of Alicia Cherry and Edward Winterbottom in "The Education of Popo." Speaking in various registers of Spanish and English, Mena's language, in itself, crosses borders.

In "The Birth of the God of War," Mena speaks directly about her inclusion of Spanish. She inserts some phrases in Spanish, such as *"ruge éste por la vez postrera,"* and literally translates "roars this for the last time" (65), explaining that "I render the construction literally because it seems to carry more of the perfume that came with those phrases as I heard them by the blue-tiled fountain" (65). For her, linking the past and the present, translating oral legend from Spanish to "sober English," means confronting the difficulties of mediating between two cultures. Evidently, she had to gain permission from her editors to include Spanish words in her short stories. For example, in a letter to Douglas Zabriske Doty, she comments on the editor's suggested changes for "The Son of His Master," a story which was not accepted for publication in *Century*, noting that she "cut out many of the Spanish words—but I must make a special plea for the few that remain, all of them having a definite value of humor, irony, local color, or what not" ([November/December 1914]). In a statement applicable to Mena, Roberto González Echevarría explains the dilemma of the Latin American author, "writing in a language supposedly alien to the realities portrayed, unsure of his own situation as transcriber, torn between languages that betray him" (26). As translator of life in Mexico for an English-speaking audience, Mena uses Spanish and English to portray both the class status and nationalities of her characters. Stories such as "John of God, the Water-Carrier" and "The Birth of the God of War," based on oral tradition,[21] implicitly and explicitly represent the conflicts, values, and legends of her culture.

Mary Louise Pratt's analysis of the relationship between the short story and "marginal subjects" is significant to Mena's position as a writer in the U.S.:

> Obviously, whether a given subject matter is central or peripheral, established or new in a literature has a great deal to do with what is central and peripheral in the community outside its literature, a great deal to do, that is, with values, and with socioeconomic, political and cultural realities. In some cases at least, there seem to develop dialectical correspondences between minor or marginal genres and what are evaluated as minor or marginal subjects. (Pratt 188)

Initially, Mena's role was to show readers a glimpse of the world south of the U.S. border, to write about subjects marginalized by the predominantly upper-class Anglo culture of *Century*; because of the marginalized status of the author, subject, and genre, critics have denied the artistry and intricate politics of her work for decades. As Pratt states, "The short story's status as craft rather than art is hugely overdetermined of course. Its connections with folklore, with speech, humor, children's literature, with didacticism, the very notion of lack that goes with shortness, all conspire to deny it the status of art" (191). The *Century* editors expected that

[21] Velásquez-Treviño notes that "John of God, the Water-Carrier" is "based on a religious folktale" (29).

Mena's short stories and their folkloric, orally-based content would provide readers with an exotic glimpse of another culture. Mena, however, went beyond the magazine's mission, and in the pages she was allowed for each story, created intricate plots, complex interactions between characters, and as discussed above, argued with her editors to keep many of the cultural and linguistic elements of her stories. Her letters to *Century* exemplify Pratt's observation about editorial control: "Magazine stories are made to order, their tone, subject matter, language, length controlled in advance by the other more powerful discourses in whose company they appear" (192). Although Mena's short stories were influenced by "more powerful discourses," she argued forcefully for her words, and through folklore and oral tradition, she used the short story to introduce Mexican culture to an American audience.

Although undervalued as art, short stories are a useful vehicle for telling various tales, showing many different aspects of a society. In her stories, Mena develops intricate relationships between classes, genders, and nations. She weaves back and forth between the U.S. and Mexico, revealing misconceptions, presenting legends, and showing her readers a different version of reality. She was writing a vision of the borderlands, a site of definition, confrontation, and difference, before it became a popular theoretical methodology. As Barbara Harlow writes, "Borders . . . function as a site of confrontation between popular and official interpretations of the historical narrative" (152). Using the short story as her venue, Mena offered readers an alternative to the dominant culture's historical narrative presented in *Century*.

The Downfall of the *Porfiriato*

Although Mena was a child in Mexico City during Díaz's reign, she would have been familiar with the wealthy lifestyle of those in Díaz's favor, as she portrays in "The Emotions of María Concepción" and "The Education of Popo." However, her letters to *Century* and her short stories, particularly "The Sorcerer and General Bisco" and "A Son of the Tropics," demonstrate her awareness of the atrocities of the Díaz regime, as well as the changing roles of women in Mexico during this volatile period. As part of pre-revolutionary Mexican society, Mena would have been raised as a Porfirian woman, where "the parameters of feminine morality and immorality were established by masculine judgment" (Lomas xxxiv), as she describes in "The Emotions of María Concepción," "The Vine-Leaf," and "Marriage by Miracle." As Shirlene Soto writes, "Prior to the Revolution, Mexican women lived in virtual seclusion. Only 8.82 percent of Mexican women were gainfully employed in 1910; marriage, family life, and the Catholic Church dominated their existence" (Soto 31). However, women played various roles in the Revolution:

> Upper-class women generally served the Revolution by donating their time to such health organizations as the Red Cross or White Cross; middle-class women served the revolutionary cause by working in a broad range of skilled and semi-skilled capacities; and thousands of lower-class women worked at unskilled jobs heretofore closed to them. Some women even followed their men into battle, serving the cause as *soldaderas.* (Soto 32)

Mena's stories informed *Century*'s historical narrative by demonstrating the shifts in gender roles during the Mexican Revolution.

Mena lived in Mexico City during the *Porfiriato,* the thirty-four year period during which Porfirio Díaz ruled Mexico as president.[22] These years were characterized by "great modernization and industrial progress," including increased growth in railroads and mining (Soto 7). Although this progress may seem positive from a capitalistic perspective, Mexico was unprepared for this rapid growth, and Díaz's optimistic doctrine of "orden, paz y progreso" ("order, peace and progress") had disastrous results for the poor and middle classes. Specifically, "the law of vacant and idle lands" allowed those in power to wrest land from owners who could not produce titles to property which had been in their family for generations.[23] Furthermore, Díaz's plan for "agricultural modernization consolidated an extraordinarily dynamic sector, but it contributed to the destruction of the peasant economy, usurped the rights of the rural towns and communities, and thrust its inhabitants into the inclemency of the market, hunger, peonage, and migration" (Camín and Meyer 3). Many displaced peasants entered a

[22] Porfirio Díaz's presidential terms were 1877-1880 and 1884-1911 (Lomas 232).
[23] Camin and Meyer 4 and Turner 128.

system of peonage (labor for debt), from which they could not extricate themselves (Turner 14).

The U.S. played a significant role in this social and economic turmoil. As Rodolfo Acuña explains in *Occupied America* (1981), the "preferential treatment" Díaz gave to foreign (particularly U.S.) investors helped the U.S. gain control over capital.

> By 1910 foreign investors controlled 76 percent of all corporations, 95 percent of mining, 89 percent of industry, 100 percent of oil, and 96 percent of agriculture. The United States owned 38 percent of this investment, Britain 29 percent, and France 27 percent.[24]

This exponential increase in foreign investment left Mexicans dispossessed of their land, as Acuña states: "97.1 percent of the families in Guanajuato were without land, 96.2 percent in Jalisco, 99.5 percent in Mexico (state), and 99.3 percent in Pueblo."[25] Because of the increased dependence on foreign markets, industrialization, and the creation of the railroad system, hundreds of thousands of displaced Mexicans migrated to the U.S. to find work in mining, agriculture, and railroad construction.[26]

Mena depicts the capitalistic influence of the U.S. on Mexico in "The Gold Vanity Set," "John of God, the Water-Carrier," and "The Education of Popo." In "The Gold Vanity Set," she presents the infiltration of U.S. ideals; for example, Miss Young's vanity set, a cosmetic mirror and "caskets" of powder, changes Petra's self-image. "Two things startled her—the largeness of her eyes, the paleness of her cheeks" (4). When Petra defines the vanity set as a sign from the Virgin of Guadalupe and Miss Young "misreads" Petra's inclusion of the vanity set in her shrine, Mena plays on the Anglo woman's self-centered perspective. Similarly, in "John of God, the Water Carrier," Mena addresses the implicit influence of

[24] Peter Baird and Ed McCaughan, "Labor and Imperialism in Mexico's Electrical Industry," *NACLA Report on the Americas* 6.6 (1977): 5. Cited in Acuña, 2nd ed., 126.

[25] Lawrence Anthony Cardoso, "Mexican Emigration to the United States, 1900-1930: An Analysis of Socio-Economic Causes," diss., University of Connecticut, 1974, 18, 57; Ed McCaughan and Peter Baird, "Harvest of Anger: Agro-Imperialism in Mexico's Northwest," *NACLA Latin America and Empire Report* 10.6 (1976): 5, cited in Acuña, 2nd ed., 127.

[26] Acuña, 3rd ed., 152-156. In the 1981 edition of *Occupied America*, Acuña writes that "officially 222,000 entered by 1910, but experts estimate that that number may have been as high as 500,000." Jorge A. Bustamante, "Mexican Immigration and the Social Relations of Capitalism," diss., University of Notre Dame, 1976, 50; Cardoso, 60, cited in Acuña, 2nd ed., 127.

the U.S. on Mexico's modernization with the displaced water-carrier, Juan de Dios, refusing to use "the highly painted and patented American force-pumps" (19-20) and playing a communal role in carrying water to the city-dwellers, while his more materialistic brother, Tiburcio, pumps water and gains popularity in the city. As a water-carrier for the pilgrims to the Villa de Guadalupe, the legendary "John of God" implicitly rebels against capitalism's inherent competition. Although Mena's stereotype of the "quaint" Indian may appeal to her U.S. audience, she also shows the reader the detrimental effects of U.S. capitalism.

In "The Education of Popo," Mena directly contrasts the U.S. and Mexican families by having the narrator explain that the "admirable Señor Montague Cherry of the United States . . . was manipulating the extension of certain important concessions in the State of which Don Fernando was governor." The governor's family prepares for their U.S. visitors with "unusual preparations" of canned soups, "ready-to-serve cereals, ready-to-drink cocktails, a great variety of pickles, and much other cheer of American manufacture" (47). In her tongue-in-cheek style, Mena writes, "By such amiable extremities it was designed to insure the ladies Cherry against all danger of going hungry or thirsty for lack of conformable aliment or sufficiently frigid liquids" (47). The Cherrys are the "ugly American tourists" expecting to be served, refusing to speak Spanish, seeing every object as "picturesque," and using the Mexicans for their own pleasure.

In the exploitative relationship between Alicia Cherry and Don Fernando's son, Popo Arriola, Alicia represents a "consume and dispose" attitude. Although she sees herself as a "confirmed matinée girl" (56) having a "summer flirtation" (59), Alicia becomes a ridiculous and even contemptible figure. She teases the fourteen-year-old Popo, infatuated with the "woman with hair like daffodils, eyes like violets, and a complexion of coral and porcelain" (49), then abandons him when her ex-husband, Edward Winterbottom, is sufficiently jealous. To her surprise, Popo condemns Alicia Cherry: "And he wound up with a burst of denunciation in which he called me by a name which ought not to be applied to any lady in any language" (61). With a humorous plot that shifts from the Mexican family's conforming to their visitors' desires to rejecting their self-centered guests, Mena both entertains and criticizes the reader/tourist.

Besides the U.S. influence on Mexico, Mena focuses on the transformation of the Mexican class hierarchy and traditional gender codes. The seismic shifts in social structure during the final years of the *Porfiriato* resulted in restless and segregated citizens with only despair in common. Historians Camín and Meyer describe the various displaced sectors of Mexican society as:

> landowners with tradition but without future, communities that resisted the usurpation of their lands, professionals without positions, teachers burned out by the misery and the heroic halo of the history of the homeland, unemployed politicians, and military officers. And that crucial provincial petite bourgeoisie: the shopkeepers, pharmacists, anxious ranchers, small farmers, and sharecroppers, all dragged down by the double yoke of their local aspirations and the credit- and social-worthlessness of their modest enterprises. (17)

As Mena shows in her stories, the old elite struggled to maintain some semblance of dignity while U.S. investors, riding on the faith of Díaz and the Mexican capitalists (Acuña [1981] 126), contributed to undermining their former status. In the marginalized sectors of society, *campesinos* and Indians struggled to keep their land and adjust to increasing industrialism. Similarly, women raised with traditional expectations of domesticity were challenged to join in the revolution.

Mena presents the shift from a colonial tradition of class hierarchy to rebellion against that tradition in "Marriage by Miracle." Doña Rosalía craftily evades the marriage of her young, attractive daughter, Clarita, to Don Luis, the son of a flashy Spaniard, by claiming that Clarita can marry him only if the ugly (unmarriageable) elder sister, Ernestina, is married first. Although Doña Rosalía wants to ensure the purity of her unidentified lineage, Mena reveals the fissures in her construction of privilege. "The House of Colors [Doña Rosalía's home] had its nickname from the blue and yellow tiles covering the whole of its facade in a gay design which passing centuries had blemished with cracks and gaps" (113). Mena develops this metaphor of erosion in her depiction of Doña Rosalía's attempts to "fool the neighbors" with apparent luxury despite their dependence on tenants "not nearly as well-born" as themselves (113). The House of Colors becomes something of a madhouse, a house of mirrors, as the servants go through the house pretending to serve the meals of more luxurious days. This formerly powerful upper-class Mexican family loses its superiority when wealth is no longer ensured by inheritance.

In "Doña Rita's Rivals," Mena further describes the strict codification of class. In this narrative, families are divided into three categories: *de sombrero* (of hat), *de tápalo* (of shawl), or *de rebozo* (a long, narrow, woven material "capable of being draped in a variety of graceful and significant ways"). Mena writes,

> No maid or matron of shawl would demean her respectable shoulders with the rebozo . . . but, contrariwise, young ladies of hat, authentic *señoritas*, to whom the mere contact of a shawl would impart "flesh of chicken," delight by wearing it coquettishly at country feasts. Persons of rebozo—one never speaks of "families" so far down the social scale—are the women of petty tradespeople, servants, artisans. They, in their turn, have consolation. (70)

Those lowest on the social scale, the "consolation of the unregarded persons of rebozo," are the *enredados* ("literally 'the wrapped-ups'" [73]). Mena explains, "The social superstructure, with its mines, plantations, and railroads, its treasure-house cathedrals, and its admired palace of government, rests on their backs—for they are the people, prolific of labor and taxes—but otherwise they do not count, unless it be with God" (73). As the story moves toward the class struggle of the Mexican revolution, she reveals the deeper significance of the seemingly superficial distinctions between classes.

Doña Rita's son, Jesús María, rebels against his elitist background: formerly a member of the "Young Scientifics" (79), he shows his support for the *enredados* in his "songs of revolution" (85). The "Young Scientifics" signifies the *científicos,* "the group of men under the *Porfiriato* who first set out to create a plan for Mexico's modernization, economic, and political stability" (Calvert 17). However, as Shirlene Soto writes, the *científicos*

> viewed themselves as naturally selected elites in a Darwinian evolutionary process; and, under Díaz, they took advantage of every

> opportunity to enrich themselves. . . In addition to economic exploitation and unjust treatment of the masses, the *científicos* ignored the plight of the Indian population (considering Indians to be inferior). They turned their backs on indigenous Mexican cultures while openly emulating European and North American cultural styles. (7-8)

Doña Rita's attitude toward the indigenous Mexicans demonstrates her affinities with the old order of Porfirio Díaz. Underestimating her son's aversion to her ideology,

> she chose a vein of sympathy . . . varied by occasional sprightly darts to a semi-skeptical point of view, as by pointing out the indolent and pious resignation of the dear Inditos, and wondering naïvely whether education, property rights, and an audible voice in government might not spoil their Arcadian virtues and dispel their truly delightful picturesqueness. (77-78)

This reference to the Indians' picturesqueness echoes Mena's own letter to *Century*, as mentioned above, in which she describes the Indians as "so intrinsically picturesque . . . so well worthy of being known and loved, in all their ignorance" (Mena, letter to Yard, [March, 1913]). However, in the story, Mena switches voices from Doña Rita's racial prejudice to Jesús María's support of the lower classes, showing him cross class boundaries in his love for Alegría, a "woman of shawl" (72). When he joins the revolution, he breaks his ties to the aristocratic Díaz regime.

Doña Rita's son is her only hope for the continuation of her aristocratic existence. "He, son of a general immortalized equestrianly in bronze, student at the military college, sole surviving hope of a line the perspective of which vanished among the lords and priests of an extinct civilization—he, Jesús María Ixtlan y Azpe, to be imperiling his future by concerning himself about the base fortunes of *los enredados!"* (73). To her despair, Doña Rita's loyalties provoke Jesús-María's rebellion: "But even from his mother's lips Jesús María could not endure to hear the cant with which ramparted feudalism masks its crimes" (78). After being expelled from a military college, Jesús María begins his personal transformation, writing "songs of revolution so disguised as to deceive the authorities" (85), a phrase suggestive of Mena's own disguised "songs of revolution." Ironically like Mena, an upper-class Mexican writing of revolution from New York City, Jesús María, the son of a general, will lead the "uplift" of the *enredados*. Doña Rita's demise, "her face serene in the inviolable aristocracy of death" (86), signals an end to upper-class complacency; her son's metamorphosis from a "Young Scientific" to a revolutionary suggest the implosion of the class hierarchy.

The Mexican Revolution

Mena's stories illustrate the increasing chaos and violence of the Mexican Revolution, from the downfall of the dictatorial Porfirio Díaz and the uprising of his successor, Francisco I. Madero in 1911, through the factional shifts in power following Victoriano Huerta's uprising against Madero in 1913. Madero, the son of a wealthy land-owning family, first challenged Díaz in his treatise *La sucesión presidencial en 1910* (The Presidential Succession in 1910), in which he "condemned the Porfirian political system, called for free elections, and declared himself a candidate for the presidency" (Soto 33). Díaz had Madero imprisoned, but Madero escaped. Although the overwhelming revolutionary support for Madero led to Díaz's resignation and exile in Europe in 1911, Madero did not produce the expected social reform in his own presidency, but focussed instead on democracy. As Camín and Meyer write, his "political character was adequately summed up in one of the slogans of his campaign: 'The people do not want bread, but liberty'" (16). The increasingly volatile political and social climate led to the uprising of General Victoriano Huerta: "Conspiring with Henry Lane Wilson, the US ambassador to Mexico, and General Aureliano Blanquet, he [Huerta] arrested President Madero and Vice-President Pino Suárez and forced their resignations" (Lomas xxiv). Madero and Suárez were murdered by officers under Huerta's command on February 22, 1913 (Camín and Meyer 35). U.S. President Woodrow Wilson, who took office shortly after Madero's assassination, decided there should be a new policy toward Mexico. "He wanted as a neighboring country a stable nation, based on free enterprise and parliamentary democracy" (Camín and Meyer 44). Wilson did not follow through forcefully enough with his plan to depose Huerta, causing impatience among U.S. citizens concerned about their unruly neighbors south of the border.

The U.S. struggled with the question of intervening in Mexican politics during Huerta's takeover. In the January 1914 issue of *Century*, in an article titled "The Mexican Menace," W. Morgan Shuster writes that "the Mexican question" was becoming a popular topic of conversation, "along with the tariff, currency legislation, the business outlook, and the weather" (593). Shuster questioned the issue of deposing Huerta: acting alone, the U.S. could incite a "war between the Mexican and American peoples." He writes:

> Suffice it to indicate that we should not be fighting to kill Huerta and his clique of congenial power-tasters, but thousands of ignorant and blameless peons, Indians, and other Mexican citizens who would be found bearing a gun in Huerta's or other ranks either through misguided patriotism, because above them would fly their country's flag, or through being pressed into military service under pain of death. For fear of the vengeance of his own people, no rebel leader or even bandit chief in Mexico would dare ally his men with United States troops, and a war entered into with the best and highest motives would speedily lapse into a long-drawn-out guerrilla struggle, with the usual degenerating effect on both sides engaged. (599)

Shuster wants Huerta, who seized executive power from Madero, to be held responsible for his murder, which occurred four days after Huerta's *coup d'état.* This author argues that the United States, along with European powers, should intervene in Mexico—but only with outside help. "Acting alone in Mexico, the American nation will only soil its hands in a useless, aimless, inglorious struggle with a weaker, if misguided, people" (602). Mena searched for a middle ground from which to portray life in Mexico as her commission requested, and, at the same time, to comment on U.S. intervention in Mexico, which was close to her personal experience.

Mena not only portrays the uprisings in Mexico but also the changing roles of women during the Mexican Revolution. While her early works concentrate on upper-class Mexican women ("The Emotions of María Concepción") and women from the U.S. in Mexico ("The Education of Popo," "The Gold Vanity Set"), her later works include the *soldaderas*, the women who accompanied the revolutionary troops. Shirlene Soto describes women's various roles during the Mexican Revolution:

> Women from all socioeconomic backgrounds were joining resistance groups; publishing revolutionary newspapers and magazines; serving as teachers and nurses; founding hospitals and health organizations; purchasing, smuggling, and selling arms; fighting on the battlefields; and collaborating in the planning and drafting of revolutionary documents. (31)

Mena begins breaking barriers with bold characters who appear to live a traditional life, such as the *marquesa* in "The Vine Leaf." In her later stories, she depicts ever more overtly revolutionary characters, such as Carmelita, in her transformation from wife of a *hacendado* to revolutionary-in-a-ripped-dress in "The Sorcerer and General Bisco" and Tula, a proletarian revolutionary who fashions bombs from doorknobs in "A Son of the Tropics."

Translating Women

Mena's women characters of Mexican descent creatively undermine hierarchical dichotomies of man/woman, American/Mexican, and science/religion. Theoretical works such as Gloria Anzaldúa's *Borderlands/La Frontera*, Tey Diana Rebolledo's *Women Singing in the Snow*, Paula Gunn Allen's *Sacred Hoop*, and Trinh T. Minh-ha's *Woman, Native, Other* are particularly useful for thinking about Mena and her characters as creative, dynamic, and potentially subversive. While "border-crossing" has become a popular theoretical term for disparate projects, Mena's stories represent the literary, linguistic, and cultural significance of border-crossing from Mexico to the United States in the early twentieth century. Writing decades before contemporary readings of La Malinche, La Llorona, Coatlicue, and the Virgin of Guadalupe, Mena reappropriates these images in diverse personifications: translator, clairvoyant, rebel, mother, sister, daughter, and lover. In her short stories, Mena offers a vision of the Mexican woman as cultural mediator, translator, and revolutionary.

Illustrating this transformation of Mexican society from the *Porfiriato* through the Mexican Revolution, Mena's stories at first depict the domestic roles of daughter and wife, as in "The Emotions of María Concepción," as well as the diplomatic roles of master of ceremonies and hostess in "The Education of Popo." In "The Vine-Leaf" and "The Sorcerer and General Bisco," her characters become increasingly rebellious in subtle and overt ways, disrupting social categories of gender, class, race, and nationality. She uses gender relations and romantic plots as vehicles to explore the power relationship between Mexico and the U.S. in "The Gold Vanity Set," "The Education of Popo," and "Marriage by Miracle." As she takes more risks in her writing, Mexican women play increasingly revolutionary roles, from the seemingly subservient women in "John of God" and "The Gold Vanity Set," to the internally rebellious in "The Emotions of María Concepción" and subtly subversive in "The Vine-Leaf," to the revolutionaries in "The Sorcerer and General Bisco" and "A Son of the Tropics."

Many times in Mena's stories, border-crossing women are associated with the conqueror in his various guises: the *hacendado*, European, scientist, doctor, *marqués*. For example, in "The Emotions of María Concepción," the tension lies between the European and the Mexican. The drama unfolds through conflicting desires, the widowed Senator Montes de Oca's admiration of the matador and his need for his daughter's companionship (31), the matador's desire for María and his dependency on the crowd's reverence, and María's loyalty to her father and her admiration of the matador. Her alternatives are to be a dutiful daughter or the mistress of a matador. Mena foreshadows María's decision to the U.S. reader:

> She loved without a hope of ever touching her lover's hand; and the thought of contact with his lips would have troubled her with a sense of passion desecrated—passion all powerful, but also all delicate, immaterial, and remote compared with that which the North too confidently assumes to read in the smoldering eyes of the South. (39)

Although the reader may expect a consummation of desire, Mena foregoes this plot contrivance and returns María to her community. Even though the daughter desires the Spanish matador, she rejects him when he insults the plebeian crowd "in the sun." In a sense, the matador is a conquistador, reminiscent of those who originally conquered Mexico. By returning María to her father, Mena not only shows the importance of the Mexican community; she also depicts its patriarchal structure, one which "could not pinion her soul" (44). With the artistry of a bullfight, "The Emotions of María Concepción" illustrates the tensions between feminine rebellion and conformity.

"Marriage by Miracle" and "The Vine-Leaf" address a different form of colonialism, as European and American cosmetic surgeons operate on upper-class Mexican women. In both of these stories, Mena contradicts the readers' expectations with surprise endings. In "Marriage by Miracle," the famous surgeon from New York City gives Ernestina a surgically enhanced spiritual countenance: a "pale and symmetrical face, as smooth as an egg" (121). However, the "magic" of the surgery shifts from miraculous to ominous when the surgeon robs Ernestina of her smile. In his hollow reassurance, the doctor confirms his link with colonial powers: "English immobility was in the latest mode cultivated by the most fashionable *señoras*" (122). Ironically, Ernestina decides she has risen above marriage: "From the rarefied heights on which she now dwelt a descent to the banality of marriage was out of the question" (123). With an ironic twist on the surgeon's "solution," Mena reveals the strangeness of a woman surgically altering her face at the expense of her smile.

In "The Vine-Leaf," Mena writes a story close to her own experience as a Mexican woman writer struggling to make herself heard. The *marquesa* craftily resists the surgeon's demand of "confession," as well as her husband's desire to capture her, like her portrait, in a domestic frame. In recent criticism of Mena's work, including Elizabeth Ammons's analysis of "The Vine-Leaf" in her volume *Conflicting Stories*, and Tiffany Ana López's "María Cristina Mena: Turn-of-the-Century La Malinche, and Other Tales of Cultural (Re)Construction," "The Vine-Leaf" stands out as the most popular and deeply analyzed of the *Century* collection; it is Mena's most intricate story. The fiction received *Century*'s editorial praise: "It is an exquisite thing, worthy of de Maupassant, both for style and treatment" (Doty, letter to Mena, 28 September 1914). Mena replied that "The Vine-Leaf" was "a great favorite of my own, between you and me!" (letter to Doty, [October 1914]).

Certainly, this story represents her desire for linguistic and artistic control in her publishing career.

In "The Vine-Leaf," Mena artfully portrays the *marquesa's* rebellion against dominant masculine figures, such as the European doctor, Dr. Malsufrido, and her husband, the *marqués*. Dr. Malsufrido, the surgeon, insists on confessions from women whose bodies are literally in his hands. However, Mena plays on his authority, and, through inversion, displaces his class position. The narrative voice builds on Dr. Malsufrido's inflated identity: he knows the "family secrets of the rich," he had been "dosing good Mexicans for half a century," and he was "forgiven for being a Spaniard on account of a legend that he physicked royalty in his time" (87). However, in response to Dr. Malsufrido's pompous treatment of "good Mexicans," the *marquesa* asserts: "'To you I come, *Señor* Doctor, because no one knows you'" (88). In Mena's artful narration, Dr. Malsufrido's self-created reality becomes *incredible*. He represents those Europeans and Anglo-Americans who separate themselves from "bad Mexicans"—in other words, those who may not believe in his medicine nor accept his appropriation of their "secrets."

As the *marquesa* resists Dr. Malsufrido's proprietary and violating perspective, Mena enacts the subversion of science and class through magical realism. He says of the vine leaf, "'My science tells me that it must be seen before it can be well removed'" (89). "My science" suggests an imperialistic relationship to the "foreign" body; the demand that the object "must be seen" illustrates the importance of the empirical to modern science. Instead of confirming the doctor's possession of her secret, the removal of the *marquesa's* vine leaf allows for the proliferation of a reality beyond the doctor's empiricism. The vine leaf is magically removed: "'Neither the cutting nor the stitching brought a murmur from her'" (89) and no scar remains. Mena contrasts Dr. Malsufrido's religion based on confession and a science founded on the visible, with so-called "superstition," an Anglo-European view of Mexican beliefs. While confirming a stereotype of "feminine intuition" or irrationality, the *marquesa* also plays on the doctor's language. When Dr. Malsufrido defines the vine leaf as a "blessed stigma," the *marquesa* replies, "Fix yourself that I am superstitious" ("The Vine-Leaf" 89). The *marquesa*'s reference to "superstition" apparently confirms the doctor's expectations, but the events of the story subtly contradict empiricism. The magic of the vine leaf unravels the doctor's colonializing logic, his association of touching with knowing, seeing with controlling, hearing with possessing. In "The Vine-Leaf," magical realism operates outside the grasp of the reader who would claim interpretive mastery.

The concealed power of feminine sexuality, the unexpected potency of the regenerative vine leaf, arises again in the "story within the story" of the artist and the *marquesa*. Like the doctor and the *marquesa's* husband, who considers the portrait of his wife's back to be one of "the curiosities" (90) of his collection, the European artist, Andrade, also objectifies the *marquesa*. Andrade mirrors her image in the portrait of her back, in the reflection of her face, and in the "excrescence" (92) of the vine leaf. However, Mena refuses to allow the vine leaf to be an identifying mark. The artist's portrait of the *marquesa's* face in the mirror is effaced: "The figure was finished, but there was no vine-leaf, and the mirror was empty of all but a groundwork of paint, with a mere luminous suggestion of a face'" (92). The woman refuses to be bound to her signifying blemish. Finally, the artist mirrors the *marquesa*: the knife sticking between Andrade's shoulders reflects the "stain" on Alegre's back. The *marquesa* seizes control of those who attempt to make her, a feminine and Mexican subject, their mirror.

Mena suggests the *marquesa's* almost supernatural powers in this story, in her ability to sustain the removal of the vine leaf without a sound, in her eerie presence, veiled at the doctor's office, and, in a sense, "unveiled" in her husband's "museum." Mena mirrors the gaze of the conqueror in the *marqués's* collections, the artist's portrait, and the doctor's surgery, then undermines their perspectives. Writer, narrator, and protagonist merge in the *marquesa's* rhetorical question, "Can you blame me for not loving this questionable lady of the vine-leaf, of whom my husband is such a gallant accomplice?" (93). This "questionable lady of the vine leaf" resists interpretation. The reader never knows if the *marquesa* or her husband actually murdered the artist, whether the *marquesa* was having an affair with the artist, or the extent of her husband's knowledge of their relationship. The plot leads in many directions simultaneously; it refuses to be captured in a single interpretation. In a succession of "frames," Mena's story builds outward from Dr. Malsufrido, to his female patient, to the *marquesa*, and finally, to Mena; each character overlaps and pushes the interpretation a little further. *Century* also frames the story with a nude portrait facing the title page, objectifying the *marquesa* and sensationalizing Mena's story. However, even in *Century*'s "portrait," the *marquesa*'s identity, concealed from the mirror, is not revealed to the viewer. By shifting the tensions of the romance to the woman who holds the key to the mystery, Mena mediates between text and reader, image and viewer. She plays on the false view of the "conquerors" and collectors who attempt to capture the *marquesa*'s identity.

In "The Sorcerer and General Bisco," Mena's writing becomes more overtly political. Carmelita, rebelling against the social dictates of marriage and domesticity, represents the increasingly active role of women from varied classes in the Mexican Revolution. As Don Baltazar's wife-turned-revolutionary, she mediates between Don Baltazar and General Bisco, who captures Don Baltazar in his own hacienda. The narrator suggests that Don Baltazar murdered his first wife in order to receive "a large part of the inheritence of her young brother, Aquiles de la Vega, of whom the law had appointed him guardian." Carmelita, Don Baltazar's second wife, is the "young daughter of a family *muy distinguida* which had been despoiled by Rascón and compelled to give him its cherished lamb in marriage" (102). Carmelita leaves Don Baltazar, runs off with Aquiles, and joins the revolution. She plays a clairvoyant role, dreaming of danger at the hacienda where, in actuality, General Bisco falls prey to Balthazar's hypnotic suggestions to execute his own followers, Aquiles and Carmelita. She breaks the spell, convincing General Bisco that Don Baltazar is using him for his own ends. As in "Marriage by Miracle" and "The Vine-Leaf," Mena demonstrates Don Baltazar's arrogant and misguided belief in his own science, symbolized by the microscope, an "instrument of sorcery," (103), as well as his "hypnotic art" of psychic suggestion (106). In this story, Carmelita plays a crucial role in revealing the truth to General Bisco so that he turns against Don Baltazar.

Mena contrasts Don Baltazar's artificial "clairvoyance" with Carmelita's ability to "see through" the situation. She reveals her secret to El Bisco: "While you looked into the crystal he made himself your master, as he is master of many others, as he was of me until I freed myself and learned to use his own arts to spy upon him—I, little and weak as you see me, with no power but love" (109). In this one sentence, Carmelita confirms her own power and belittles it by naming her feminine charm: "love." Although Mena lends this woman certain power, she also romanticizes Carmelita. However, while Carmelita denounces herself as "little and weak," her intimate knowledge of the enemy allows her to "translate" for El Bisco, who has been duped by Don Baltazar's "art." In the end, thanks to Carmelita's assertions, El Bisco becomes "a practical man with a magazine pistol" (111), killing Don Baltazar. When Carmelita reveals to El Bisco that Baltazar "stole away your will, your understanding, all your natural feelings" (110), she transforms her own role from "Malinchista" to "*curandera,*" a healer. As López notes in her study of "The Vine-Leaf" and "The Sorcerer and General Bisco," Mena "signifies on the La Malinche and La Llorona myths in order to pass on to readers new kinds of tales of cultural survival that take into account the importance of women's roles in the survival of culture and community" (23). In the face of a misguided trust in "science," Carmelita restores El Bisco's humanity, as shown in the vicissitudes of the final paragraphs—the fear of the tarantula and the murder of a tyrant.

Unlike "The Sorcerer and General Bisco," "A Son of the Tropics" is not built on a foundation of romance. It is a story of revolution, of the demise of the class hierarchy. Rosario, the leader of the Revolutionary Encampment of the Morning Star, is ironically, the son of Don Rómulo, the owner of the hacienda La Paloma. Don Rómulo returns to his estate twenty years after he and his servant, Remedios, conceived Rosario, and the plot revolves around the revelation of Rosario's identity as "the son of his master."[27] In the voice of a laborer, the narrative explicitly states the reasons for the *peónes'* revolution against "the master": "the wrongs of the people, dating from the time when their lands had been ravished from them under the placid but infamous régime of Don Porfirio, and themselves reduced to a state of virtual slavery at the mercy of the masters" (146-47). Class and race fit together uneasily here, as sig-

[27]Mena's wrote an earlier story called "The Son of His Master," which she submitted to *Century*. Her revisions to this story, particularly the "new and dramatic" end (Mena, letter to Doty, [November/December 1914]) suggest that this was an early version of "A Son of the Tropics," published in *Cosmopolitan* in 1931. "The Son of His Master" was never published in *Century*.

nified in Tula's response to Rosario's reverence for Julius Caesar: "And this Don Julius César, did he kill many masters, or were they all gringos?" (145). Rosario wants to believe he is "of the people," but the revelation of his father's identity as a *hacendado* confirms his own link with tyranny. Shattered by this knowledge, he recalls his image of his mother: "In all the *peón* population of the *hacienda*, she had been the only woman of shawl, and he in his childhood had imagined that she was permitted that distinction as a testimony of her peculiar excellence. Now he understood the true reason" (149). They both try to escape a past they would rather avoid; for Don Rómulo, an affair with Remedios, for Rosario, the father as master. Even though they each reject their past, they recognize the other in themselves, as Rómulo notes: "the passionate face of Rosario recalled a revered family portrait, that of Beltrán Salgado, Don Rómulo's great-great-grandfather, a statesman, poet, and soldier, who had played a telling role in the overthrow of the Spanish dominion" (148). Don Rómulo's ancestors conquered the Spanish dominion, but he rejected this past to live a life of ease. Rosario's literacy and reverence for Julius Caesar suggest his upper-class past, which he rejects in suicide. Published years after the Mexican Revolution, "A Son of the Tropics" not only demonstrates the downfall of the old order and its system of inheritance, but also dramatizes the Revolution's deconstruction of fixed identities.

In "A Son of the Tropics," Mena turns from the realm of the romantic to the material, as shown in the instrument of Rosario's suicide—a doorknob filled with dynamite. Tula, the barber's daughter, creates this weapon of self-destruction. As a *soldadera*, a militant revolutionary, she stands in direct contrast to upper-class women, such as Carmelita in "The Sorcerer and General Bisco," who joined the revolution with a sense of adventure and romance:

> Carmelita laughed with sympathy, and then laughed again at the transformation of her own once fearful and fastidious self. Scratched and sunburned, soaked to the knees in black swamp-ooze, her dress torn, her bosom laboring from the exertion of the march, she wove a wreath of narcissus for her loosened hair; and when Aquiles showed fatigue she enticed him on with snatches of song. (98)

In contrast to Carmelita, Tula represents the laborers and their children who rebel against the upper-class citizens of Mena's earlier stories. Of Dorotea, Rómulo's daughter captured while seeking "the Chair of the Devil," Tula remarks, "The *señorita* has no valor . . . the *señorita* is afraid of dynamite." Emphasizing the material aspect of their revolution, Tula's father responds to Rosario's idealistic praise of Julius Caesar's military victories: "If thou canst make thy machine answer me where this Don Julio César found a million cartridges growing on the trees, let us march there quickly" (145). As women play more direct and violent roles in the Revolution, Mena repositions her characters from a domestic to a revolutionary context. Ultimately, Tula determines General Rosario's fate: when he learns his true identity as his master's son, Rosario commits suicide with Tula's bombs made from doorknobs, a sign of domesticity turned to revolution.

The Mirror Image

Writing of Mexican society for a U.S. readership, Mena uses mirror images in her stories to deflect the viewers' possible readings and provide alternative perspectives and interpretations. The mirror image halts penetration, mimics the readers' attempts to come to a definitive reading, and provides endlessly reflective readings. With mirror images and magical realism, Mena reveals her characters' complex identities and counters the presumptions each makes about the other and about themselves. For example, although the reader may see differences between characters such as Rosario and Don Rómulo, Mena holds up the mirror to their similarities. And, although a U.S. reader may project his/her own vision onto Mexico, Mena obstructs such self-imposing reading. The mirror may be aesthetic or material, as in the vanity mirror reflecting the U.S. in "The Gold Vanity Set," the mirror held by the woman in the portrait of "The Vine-Leaf," or the crystal ball of "The Sorcerer and General Bisco." In these stories, Mena uses the mirror to flash the image back at the reader, evade the viewer's interpretation, and show the limits of psychological comprehension.

Mirrors are important in part because Mena depicts the problems which occur internationally and domestically because of misinterpretation. Internationally, projection can create a violent, manipulative view of those outside the "imagined community."[28] For example, in "The Education of Popo," Alicia and Popo see their romantic ideals in each other: to Popo, Alicia is "an image of the Virgin," and to Alicia, Popo is the passionate Latino who "makes love" to her "in a foreign language." Alicia interprets, "although the inhabitants have a deluded idea that blue eyes are intensely spiritual, they get exactly the same Adam-and-Eve palpitations from them that we do from the lustrous black orbs of the languishing tropics."[29] This projection of desire becomes destructive when Popo does not perceive Alicia's shallow character. In contrast, when Alicia and Edward Winterbottom mirror each other, Mena emphasizes that their striking appearances are equally superficial. Like Alicia's Anglo version of "beauty," Edward is the masculine "ideal toward which their [Anglo] race is striving." Edward's handsomeness, like Alicia's, is linked to its commercial value:

> A thousand conscientious draftsmen, with that national ideal in their subconsciousness, were always hard at work portraying his particular type in various romantic capacities, as those of foot-ball hero, triumphant engineer, "well-known clubman," and pleased patron of the latest collar, cigarette, sauce, or mineral water. (58)

Alicia and Edward both represent the values of an image-conscious society. Mrs. Cherry's misgivings about Alicia's divorce, and her suggestion of Edward's own infidelity, also illustrate the U.S. double-standard. Furthermore, Mrs. Cherry's engineering of their reunion shows her fears of Alicia's "going native" in her relationship with Popo, as suggested in her retort: "If you continue studying the language . . . as industrially as you have been doing to-night, my dear, you will soon be speaking it like a native" (51). This fear of the foreign suggests similar attitudes presented in *Century Magazine*. Mena's use of projection and mirroring clearly shows the dangers of misperception, of devotion to a materialistic ideal, and of enthnocentricity.

[28] This term derives from Benedict Anderson, *Imagined Communities: Reflections on the Origin and Spread of Nationalism*.

[29] 59-60. In her analysis of "The Education of Popo," Garza-Falcón-Sánchez notes that "people, right or wrong, imagine others in other cultures in ways which bring their mirror-images of each other so close as to be in certain respects interchangeable" (206).

Mena questions the determinacy of empirical vision; she suggests the powers of intuitive "vision" used for the good of the community rather than individual gain. For instance, the downfall of the toreador in "The Emotions of María Concepción" occurs when he turns his back on "the masses," focussing instead on the upper class; his lack of vision, or connection with the people, is one reason María Concepción rejects him. She also must remain her widowed father's "companion and consolation" during his "remaining years on earth" (31). In contrast to María, who must remain faithful to her father, her twin brother, Enrique, roams freely in society. In this story, Mena deflects a romantic reading to emphasize community; she also uses the mirror image to suggest an alternative to María Concepción's traditional role.

Through mirroring, Mena dupes those who trust their vision too much. For example, in "Doña Rita's Rivals," Doña Rita relies on distinguishing hierarchically between women *de sombrero* (of hat), *de tápalo* (of shawl), and *de rebozo*. When she is confronted by the mirror image of her son's girlfriend, whom she rejected because of the girl's lower-class status, Doña Rita dies because she is not able to readjust her perspective of class hierarchies. Although the disenfranchised women in this story, Alegría and Piedad, are more like mirages than fully developed characters, they not only magically reflect each other, but also ignite Jesús María's activism. Because they splinter the carefully constructed social structure, Alegría and Piedad deviate from hereditary class domination. Alegría's death results in Piedad's resurrection: with her nameless, lost, and double identity, she can infiltrate upper class society and empower those without names.

With definitive vision in question, the women in Mena's stories close off determined readings. In "The Vine-Leaf," the *marquesa* plays on the empirical assumptions of the doctor, artist, and *marqués*. The *marquesa* stands for the woman artist who defies objectification: she will not be captured with a mark, scar, portrait, or interpretation. In a twist on the same topic, Hilda Brunel, the apparently "soulless" opera singer in "The Soul of Hilda Brunel," surprises the artist of her portrait, Walter Standish, with her clairvoyant awareness of his love. Brunel reveals the "mirrors" of their past lives, which predict disaster for the present consummation of their love. Again, the woman character holds a magically strong intuition which obstructs a predictable conclusion, and challenges the viewer's initial presumptions. Similarly, in the unpredictable plots of "The Sorcerer and General Bisco," Don Baltazar's ability to hypnotize General Bisco is undermined by Carmelita's intuitive strength. When Don Baltazar tries to project his own image of Carmelita and Aquiles onto General Bisco, Carmelita shatters this vision. Likewise, in "A Son of the Tropics," Mena reveals the mirroring pasts of Don Rómulo and Rosario which result in Rosario's self-destruction. In each story, Mena gives the characters a projection or a mirror of themselves, a vision of an alternative life, the tantalizing possibility of meaning, or the enjambment of signification by an image that cannot be captured or finally penetrated.

In *Borderlands/La Frontera,* Gloria Anzaldúa describes the mirror as an "ambivalent symbol." She writes, "Not only does it reproduce images (the twins that stand for thesis and antithesis);[30] it contains and absorbs them" (42). Ancient civilizations in Mexico used obsidian as a mirror; their "absorption" into the glassy surface resulted in visionary revelations. Although seeing may construct barriers ("Subject and object, I and she"), Anzaldúa emphasizes that "in a glance also lies awareness, knowledge" (42). As Mena unsettles the distinction between subject and object for her characters and her readers, she introduces knowledge to those who demanded difference.

Trinh T. Minh-ha's analysis of the mirror is also suggestive for thinking about Mena's works:

> In the dual relation of subject to subject or subject to object, the mirror is the symbol of an unaltered vision of things. It reveals to me my double, my ghost, my perfections as well as my flaws. Considered an instrument of self-knowledge, one in which I have total faith, it also bears a magical character that has always transcended its functional nature. In this encounter of I with I, the power of identification is often such that reality and appearance merge while the tool itself becomes invisible. . . From mirage to mirage, the subject/object takes flight and loses its existence. Trying to grasp it amounts to stopping a mirror from mirroring. It is encountering the void. (22-23)

Interpreting Mena's texts, then, means trying to account for one's own relation to her work. Where is she mirroring her audience?

[30] Marius Schneider, *El origen musical de los animales-símbolos en la mitología y la escultura antiguas* (Barcelona, 1946), cited in Anzaldúa 42.

Which interpretations does she allow? Which does she prevent? In encountering "the void" in Mena's endless reflections, we need not despair of "a lack" but rather we must recognize the void's creative potential. As Paula Gunn Allen states, "the position of power for a true Warrior is the Void. . . The work of women of color arises out of the creative void in a multitude of voices, a complex of modes, and most of these women are quite aware of their connection to the dark grandmother of human wisdom" (304-5). This "dark grandmother of human wisdom" is a central image for studying Mena's texts. Meaning, for her, is signified through gender, the creativity of women in accomplishing their aims, the increasing empowerment of women in her work, and her own life as a writer. As she builds her reading audience, she "bewitches" them in her own way, through stories of Mexico, through romance, and through magical realism. Mena uses magical realism to portray Mexican culture and to portray the "real" of the dominant culture as just another mythology.

The Gold Vanity Set

When Petra was too big to be carried on her mother's back she was put on the ground, and soon taught herself to walk. In time she learned to fetch water from the public fountain and to grind the boiled corn for the tortillas which her mother made every day, and later to carry her father his dinner—a task which required great intelligence, for her father was a donkey-driver and one never knew at what corner he might be lolling in the shade while awaiting a whistle from someone who might require a service of himself and his little animal.

She grew tall and slender, as strong as wire, with a small head and extremely delicate features, and her skin was the color of new leather. Her eyes were wonderful, even in a land of wonderful eyes. They were large and mysterious, heavily shaded with lashes which had a trick of quivering nervously, half lowered in an evasive, fixed, sidelong look when anyone spoke to her. The irises were amber-colored, but always looked darker. Her voice was like a ghost, distant, dying away at the ends of sentences as if in fear, yet with all its tenderness holding a hint of barbaric roughness. The dissimulation lurking in that low voice and those melting eyes was characteristic of a race among whom the frankness of the Spaniard is criticized as unpolished.

At the age of fourteen Petra married, and married well. Her bridegroom was no barefooted donkey-driver in white trousers and shirt, with riata coiled over his shoulder. No, indeed! Manuelo wore shoes—dazzling yellow shoes which creaked—and colored clothes, and he had a profession, most adorable of professions, playing the miniature guitar made by the Mexican Indians, and singing lively and tender airs in drinkshops and public places wherever a few coins were to be gathered by a handsome fellow with music in his fingers. Most Mexicans, to be sure, have music in their fingers, but Manuelo was enabled to follow the career artistic by the good fortune of his father's being the owner of a prosperous inn for *peons*.[1]

Petra's attractions made her useful to her father-in-law, who was a widower. At the sight of her coming in from the well, as straight as a palm, carrying a large earthen pot of water on her head, the *peons* who were killing time there would suddenly find themselves hungry or thirsty and would call for *pulque*[2] or something to eat. And so she began to wait on customers, and soon she would awake in the morning with no other thought than to twist her long, black hair into a pair of braids which, interwoven with narrow green ribbon, looked like children's toy whips, then to take her husband his *aguardiente*,[3] the little jug of brandy that begins the day, and then to seat herself at the door of the inn, watching for customers beneath trembling lashes, while bending over the coarse cloth whose threads she was drawing.

In six months she had formed the habit of all that surrounded her life. The oaths no longer sounded so disagreeable to her, the occasional fights so terrifying. Manuelo might lose his temper and strike her, but a few minutes later he would be dancing with her. Her last memory going to sleep was sometimes a blow, "Because he is my husband," as she explained it to herself, and sometimes a kiss, "Because he loves me." Only one thing disturbed her: she did not like to see her handsome Manuelo made inflamed and foolish by the milk-white *pulque*, and she burned many candles to the Virgin of Guadalupe[4] that she might be granted the "beneficio"[5] of a more frequently sober husband.

One afternoon the pueblo resounded with foreign phrases and foreign laughter in foreign voices. As a flock of birds the visitors kept together, and as a flock of birds appeared their chatter and their vivacity to the astonished inhabitants. American fashion, they

[1] Members of the landless laboring class, or persons in compulsory servitude.
[2] A fermented drink.
[3] Liquor.
[4] Patron saint of Mexico.
[5] Favor.

were led by a woman. She was young, decisive, and carried a camera and guide book. Catching sight of Petra at the door she exclaimed: "Oh, what a beautiful girl! I must get her picture."

But when Petra saw the little black instrument pointing at her she started like a frightened rabbit and ran inside. The American girl uttered a cry of chagrin, at which Don Ramón came forward. Don Ramón, the planter, had undertaken to escort these, his guests, through the pueblo, but had found himself patiently bringing up the rear of the procession.

"These are tenants of mine," he said with an indifferent gesture. "The house is yours, Miss Young."

"Girls, do you hear that?" she cried. "This is my house—and I invite you all in."

Immediately the inn was invaded, the men following the women. Manuelo, his father, and the *peons* in the place formed two welcoming ranks, and the *Patrón's* entrance was hailed with a respectful: "Viva Don Ramón!"

Manuelo's father looked a little resentful at these inquisitive strangers occupying the benches of his regular customers, who obsequiously folded up their limbs on straw mats along the walls. To be sure, much silver would accrue to the establishment from the invasion, but business in the Mexican mind is dominated by sentiment.

Don Ramón, reading his mind, tapped him on the shoulder with a sharp: "Quick, to serve the *señores*!"[6]

Then he clapped his hands for Petra, who came in from the back with oblique looks, and soon the guests were taking experimental sips of strange liquors, especially *aguamiel*, the sweet unfermented juice of the *maguey*[7] plant. Manuelo tuned up his instrument and launched into an elaborate and apparently endless improvisation in honor of the *Patrón*, standing on one foot with the other toe poised, and swaying his body quite alarmingly—for he had drunk much *pulque* that day. As for Petra, she was followed by the admiring looks of women and men as she moved back and forth, her naked feet plashing softly on the red brick floor.

"I positively must have her picture!" exclaimed Miss Young.

"Of course—at your disposition," murmured Don Ramón.

[6] Gentlemen.

[7] Any of various fleshy-leaved agaves, esp. the American aloe.

But the matter was not so simple. Petra rebelled—rebelled with the dumb obstinacy of the Indian, even to weeping and sitting on the floor. Manuelo, scandalized at such contumacy before the *Patrón*, pulled her to her feet and gave her a push which sent her against the wall. A shiver and murmur passed through the American ranks, and Don Ramón addressed to the young *peón* a vibrant speech in which the words "*bruto*"[8] and "*imbécil*"[9] were refreshingly distinguishable. Miss Young, closing her camera with a snap, gave her companions the signal for departure, and they obeyed her as always. Don Ramón gave the innkeeper a careless handful of coins and followed his guests, while the innkeeper and his customers ceremoniously pursued him for some distance down the street, with repeated bows and voluble "*Gracias*"[10] and "*Benediciónes*"[11] over the *Patrón*, his wife, his children, his house, his crops and all his goods. But Manuelo threw himself upon a mat and fell asleep.

Miss Young had left her guide book on the table, and Petra pounced upon it as a kitten upon a leaf. Some object in the midst of its pages held it partly open. It was a beautiful thing of gold, a trinity of delicate caskets depending by chains from a ring of a size for one's finger. With one quick glance at the unconscious Manuelo she stuck it into the green sash that tightly encompassed her little waist. The book, in which she had lost interest, she put in a drawer of the table. Then she ran outside and climbed the ladder by which one reached the flat stone roof.

Wiping the palms of her hands on her skirt, she extracted the treasure. Of the three pendants she examined the largest first. It opened and a mirror shone softly from its golden nest. A mirror! Novelty of novelties to Petra! Two things startled her—the largeness of her eyes, the paleness of her cheeks. She had always imagined that she had red cheeks, like the girls in Manuelo's songs, some of whom even had cheeks like poppies. Feeling saddened, she opened one of the smaller caskets. It contained a little powder of ivory tint and a puff which delighted her with its unheard-of delicacy. She caressed the back of her hand with it, perceived an

[8] Stupid.
[9] Idiot.
[10] Thanks.
[11] Blessings.

esthetic improvement, and ended by carefully powdering the backs of both hands, even to the finger nails.

And then the third box. A red paste. It reddened the tip of her nose when she sniffed its delicate perfume. She rubbed the spot off with her finger and transferred it to one cheek, then rouged a large patch on that cheek, then one on the other, with a nice discretion partly influenced by her memory of the brilliant cheeks of the American *señorita* of the brave looks, the black box, and the golden treasure.

Thus did Petra discover the secret of the vanity set. But her concept of it was not simple, like Miss Young's. Its practical idea became a mere nucleus in her mind for a fantasy dimly symbolic and religious.

Her eyes—how much larger they were, and how much brighter! She looked into them, laughed into them, broke off to leap and dance, looked again in many ways, sidelong, droopingly, coquettishly, as she would look at Manuelo. Truly the gold treasure was blessed and the red paste was as holy as its smell, which reminded her of church.

Where should she hide it, the treasure? She would bury it in the earth. But no; Manuelo had the habit of burying things—foolish, Indian things—and in his digging he might find her talisman. Better to leave it on the roof. And she did, wrapped in a dry corn husk, covered with a stone.

The afternoon was falling when she went down from the roof. Manuelo slept noisily on the same mat, his father peacefully on an adjacent one. Wild to be looked at, Petra lifted her husband's arm by the sleeve and shook it, but he jerked it free with childish petulance and cuddled into a deeper sleep. She laughed and, inspired with a thought of further embellishment, ran out of the house, too excited even to notice the distant approach of a storm, which at any other time would have kept her indoors praying her rosary. When she returned she was crowned with yellow jonquils, their stems wet from the brook, and in her hand was a long stalk of spikenard with which to awaken Manuelo. But first she would make light, for it was already dusk in the inn. So she lit the antique iron lanterns which hung by chains from wooden arms at the front and back doors, and two candles, one of which she placed on a window ledge and the other on the floor near Manuelo's face, and she squatted in front of the second one and held the spikenard beneath his nose, mystically tracing with it in the air the sign of the cross, until its intoxicating incense pierced his consciousness and he opened his eyes.

He blinked at the light, then blindly caught her hand and smiled with a flash of white teeth as he inhaled luxuriously with the flower against his nostrils. Then, as he was thirsty, she fetched him a jug of water, and at last he saw the jonquil wreath, and the eyes beneath them, and those cheeks of flame.

He did not speak, but looked at her for a moment, and then, with the abrupt and graceful movement that she knew so well slung forward his guitar—it never left his shoulder by day—and the words he sang to her in passionate Spanish softened by Indian melancholy were these:

> "Whether thou lovest me I know not;
> Thou knowest it.
> I only know that I die
> Where thou art not."

He had not sung her that since the night of his serenades outside her father's adobe hut, and even then his tones had not pulsed with the magic tenderness that was in them now as he stared at her in the candle light. She crept along the floor to him and he caught her under his arm, pulling his poncho over her head, and cuddled her to him with protecting caresses which she received with the trembling joy of a spaniel too seldom petted. They were startled by a voice exclaiming:

"That our sainted Mother of Guadalupe might permit that you should always be like this, my children!"

It was the old man, whom the music had awakened. Manuelo quickly kissed the medal that hung at his waist, stamped with the image of the patron saint of Mexico. No other saint so intimately rules the hearts and lives of a people nor rewards their love with so many miracles and apparitions, and the falling of her name at that instant of love tinged with a half-felt remorse, produced a powerful effect upon the young husband. He scrambled to his feet, lifting Petra with him, and cried:

"Yes, yes, yes, my father, that the blessed Mother of our Country may hear thee!"

As he looked upward, a murmur of thunder made them all jump. They crossed themselves, and their voices mingled in a tremulous chorus of fear and piety. Manuelo, pale as a ghost, seized Petra's hand and led her with bended body before the old man.

"Thy benediction—give us thy benediction, Father mine, while I make a vow." He shook with sobs as he and the girl knelt beneath the father's benediction, and a louder rumble sounded in the sky. "I promise our blessed Mother, the Virgin of Guadalupe, that I will never again maltreat my Petrita, and if I keep not this promise may she send a thunder to fall on me!"

Petra uttered a wail of terror, and just then a withering light flashed on the world and a deafening blast of thunder shook the building and sent the three on their faces, where they remained in an ecstasy of devotion until long after the storm god had rolled the last of his chariots across the reverberating platform of the sky.

And it was by the miracle of Manuelo's vow and its answer from the heavens that Petra's mind grasped the unalterable faith that the golden treasure was a blessed thing, most pleasing to the Mother of Guadalupe.

Next morning the planter was driving his guests through the pueblo, and they were talking of many things, including the loss of Miss Young's vanity set, when they saw Petra coming toward them in the direction of her home, her great eyes looking out like an Egyptian's from between the folds of her scarf. The joy of her heart shone in her face and her native shyness almost vanished as she pulled the scarf down from her chin to give them her graceful "*¡Buenos días!*" which they acknowledged with smiles. And Petra ran on singing like a bird—singing of the exceeding richness of American *señoritas* who can lose golden treasure of miracle-producing potency and still smile.

"One thing I'm convinced of," said Miss Young to the planter as they drove on. "That girl hasn't got my vanity set. She looked me straight in the face."

"You don't know my people, Miss Young," returned the *Patrón* with a heavy sigh—he was anguished because of his guest's loss. "The girl has an innocent heart—yes; but that proves nothing. These are children of the youth of the world, before the limits of 'mine' and 'thine' had been fixed. When an *Indito*[12] finds lost treasure he believes that he receives a gift from God."

"It's a mighty comfortable belief, and not confined to Mexico," declared the American. "Well, if those cheeks of hers weren't their own natural color this morning, I must say that her complexion makes a stunning blend with my rouge."

Don Ramón trembled at her frankness. Not for worlds would he have smiled, or mentioned her vanity set by name. "How original!" he reflected, epitomizing the thought of all his people when they meet the people of the North.

"But why not have put the question to her right straight out?" pursued Miss Young.

"It was wiser to put her off her guard," he replied. "If these people have your—your ornament, it is probably buried in the earth. Now it is likely to be brought to light, and when I go to the inn—"

"You will take me with you?"

"I beg you not to trouble yourself. It may be painful. I—"

But she insisted, and when dinner was over at the hacienda, Don Ramón sacrificed his siesta to drive with her to Petra's home. Taking a leaf from Mexican tactics, Miss Young allowed the *Patrón* to precede her, and received with dignified apathy the greetings of the natives who, like marionettes pulled by one string, scrambled into rank as a reception committee. Don Ramón ushered her through the house to the courtyard and seated her there, assigning Petra to defend her from mosquitos with a feather fan. That was part of his plan. With *Inditos* one must employ maneuvers. Reentering the inn, he caused it to be cleared of strangers. The innkeeper and his son, questioned concerning the missing gold, professed profoundest surprise and ignorance. Without ceremony the *Patrón* searched them. Feeling a foreign object beneath Manuelo's sash he drew forth Miss Young's guide book, which Manuelo had found in the drawer—a thing of no apparent utility, but a treasure of a sort, possibly of occult virtue.

This discovery, while unexpected, fell in with the *Patrón's* plan, which was to stir Petra's fears through her husband—his instinct telling him that she was the key to the problem. And

[12] Diminutive of *Indian*.

Petra's feather fan fluttered to the earth when she heard the *Patrón's* stern voice raised in the ringing command to accompany him to the prefecture.

In a flash she was inside, crying in Manuelo's arms. Her Manuelo—to be led as a sacrifice into the ominous precincts of justice, there to be interrogated amid terrors unknown! No, no!

"No, no, Don Ramón! My Manuelo did not find the gold! It was I—I found it!"

She sobbed, almost choking with grief. The *Patrón* allowed a few minutes for her emotion to spend itself before commanding her to restore to the American *señorita* her property. With a piteous look she shook her head. *¡Caramba!*[13] What did she mean? Her answer was a fresh outburst, so violent, protracted and crescendo that Miss Young, disturbed by visions of medieval torture, ran in to protest against further inhumanity in her name. And Petra groveled at the American's feet, wetting the bricks with her tears for a long time. At last a resolve came to her and with face swollen but calm she picked herself up, turned to Manuelo and his father and motioned them toward the courtyard.

When they had gone out she shut the door. Then with bent head, speaking to the *Patrón* but looking beneath fluttering eyelids at a button on Miss Young's duster, she told the story of the miracle—of how the golden treasure had yielded that which had made her lovely in the eyes of her beloved, of how the blessed Virgin of Guadalupe had inspired him to vow that he would never again maltreat her as yesterday he had before the eyes of the *Americanos*, of how the saint had acknowledged his vow with much thunder, as the *señorita* must have heard for herself, and of how Manuelo was so impressed with the peril of breaking a vow thus formidably recognized that he had drunk no *pulque* that day and had resolved earnestly to become temperate in his use of that beverage for the rest of his life.

All of which Don Ramón translated to Miss Young, who looked puzzled and remarked: "Well, I just love the temperance cause, but does she want to keep my danglums to make sure of this Manuelo staying on the water wagon?"

[13] How strange!

"Certainly not!" declared the *Patrón*, and turning to Petra abruptly demanded the production of the gold.

She turned pale—so pale that the rouge stood out in islands streaked with rivercourses of tears, and Miss Young looked away with a shuddering prayer that she herself might never turn pale except in the privacy of her chamber. And now Petra spoke. The gold was not in this house. She would conduct the *Patrón* and the *señorita* to where it was.

So it was that a pilgrimage in quest of the vanity set sallied forth, Petra leading the way on the back of the burro, the surrey following slowly with Miss Young and her escort. Manuelo and his guitar formed a distant and inquisitive rear guard. It passed, the pilgrimage, into the populous heart of the pueblo.

"Have you any idea where we're going?" inquired Miss Young.

"No," returned the planter. "The ways of the Indito are past conjecture, except that he is always governed by emotion."

He was nervous, sensitively anxious about the impressions of his guest from the North.

"You may observe that we always speak of them as *Inditos,* never as Indios," he said. "We use the diminutive because we love them. They are our blood. With their passion, their melancholy, their music and their superstition they have passed without transition from the feudalism of the Aztecs into the world of today, which ignores them; but we never forget that it was their valor and love of country which won our independence."

"They certainly are picturesque," pronounced Miss Young judicially, "and it's great fun to run into the twelfth or some other old century one day out from Austin."

Petra halted at the dark, ancient front of the Chapel of the Virgin of Guadalupe, where was inscribed in choice Spanish the history of how the saint had made an apparition to her people stamped upon a cactus plant, together with other miraculous matters. Dismounting from the burro the girl passed among the beggars and sellers of "miracles" and entered the church, uncovering her head. Don Ramón and Miss Young followed her. She knelt before a shrine at which stood the benignant figure of the national saint, almost hidden by the gifts of the faithful—"miracles" of silver, of wax, of feather, of silk—and among these, its opened mirror reflecting the blaze of innumerable candles, the gold vanity set shone at her breast, most splendid of her ornaments. The gold vanity set, imposing respect, asking for prayers, testifying the gratitude of an Indian girl for the kindness of her beloved.

Don Ramón fell on his knees. Miss Young, unused to the observances of such a place, bowed her head and choked a little, fumbling for her handkerchief.

"Well, if it saves that nice girl from ever getting another beating, the saint is perfectly welcome to my vanity set," she assured herself as she left the chapel. And Manuelo, leaning against the burro, perceiving by her expression that all was well, cuddled his guitar and sang:

> "Into the sea, because it is deep,
> I always throw
> The sorrows that his life
> So often gives me."

[November 1913]

John of God, the Water-Carrier

Most of the inhabitants were still on their knees in the middle of the street, praying that there might be no repetition of the trembler. Others were searching anxiously for divine symbolism in the earthquake's handwriting of crossed and zigzagged crackings in adobe walls. It had come without warning. Through the ground had passed a series of shudders, like those of a dying animal, with a twitching of houses, a spilling of fountains, and a quick sickness to people's brains.

Several horses from a burning stable were running wild through the streets. An Indian boy who had just risen from his knees unslung his *lazo*[1] and tried to catch one that galloped past him, but it swerved from the flung noose and charged through an open cabin, striking down a kneeling woman in the doorway. The boy ran to her and lifted her head, then lowered it quickly and crossed himself. Beneath the wetted hair, where a hoof had struck, he had felt the grate of a fractured edge of bone.

Suddenly he was driven at one bound into the street by a thin cry inside the hut.

"*Mamá!*" said the voice, and then, "*Mamacíta!*"[2] with a drawling petulance on the diminutive.

The boy moved a little nearer, calling: "Come out, *muchachita!*"

But the unseen raised her voice and replied that she could not come out without her *mamá*, being a little bad with fever. Also, her name was Dolores and she did not desire to be called "*muchachita,*" and she was thirsty, and where was her *mamá*?

[1] Lasso.

[2] Mommy.

"I will come to thee, Dolores," the boy replied in a shaking voice.

As he stepped past the dead woman he turned his head aside with a prayer. There in a corner was the child, swaddled in coarse cloth, lying on a straw mat. Her head was tied up with fresh leaves of rosemary and mallow, which are sovereign for fever if allowed to wither on the skin. He gave her drink from a water-jug, and then she sucked her lips and looked at him searchingly from eyes like balls of black onyx.

"Who art thou?" she demanded.

"I am Juan de Dios, son of Pancho the *aguador*."[3]

Baptismal names of sacred meaning are in high favor with the *Inditos*,[4] and in "John of God" there was nothing uncommon except the solemnity of the youth's tone as he announced himself to the wondering child.

"And thou," he added, "what age hast thou?"

"Five Aprils," she replied impatiently, "Where is my *mamá*?"

"Perhaps with thy *papá*."

"That cannot be. My *papá* is dead." And then, raising herself on one elbow to see him better, "Why dost thou weep?"

"There is dust in my eyes," said Juan de Dios. "Tell me—thou hast brothers and sisters?"

"I have none."

"Grandparents?"

"*¿Quién sabe?*"[5]

"How *'¿quién sabe?'* Hast thou no one?"

"Foolish one! My *mamá* is enough. Where is my *mamá?*"

"Perhaps at the church. We have had a trembler."

"*Santa Bárbara bendita!*[6] Then it woke me!"

"It was a very strong trembler, and if we should have another—"

"Take me out, Juan de Dios!" she cried, holding out her arms to be lifted.

He wrapped her in a blanket, covering her face so that she might not see her mother, and carried her out. An unnoticed figure in that agitated hour, he walked, he stopped, he ran a few steps, he looked around wildly. At last, discerning a closed carriage

[3] Water-carrier.

[4] Diminutive of *Indian.*

[5] Who knows?

[6] Blessed, holy.

approaching soberly, he dropped to his knees, uncovering the child's head and his own. The black curtains over the carriage windows were partly drawn, but not sufficiently to hide from view the gold chalice[7] covered with an embroidered cloth which an acolyte in red and white held steadily before a black-robed ecclesiastic. Poor and rich, old and young, kneeled in the dust as it passed, for this was the carriage of Our Master— "*Nuestro Amo*" —and the whole *pueblo* felt blessed, comforted, and protected by the divine Mystery which it bore among the people. The boy after its passing rose with a light heart and continued on his way, uplifted by what seemed to him a personal message of pardon and peace. The little girl, who a few moments earlier had said, "Why dost thou weep, Juan de Dios?" now said, "Why dost thou smile, Juan de Dios?" He only replied, "*Nuestro Amo* has passed." And she fell asleep, and the warmth of her little body filled him with a troubled tenderness.

His parents ran to meet him, thanking the saints for having preserved their first-born.

"But what thing bringest thou?" said his father, looking at the bundle in his arms.

"A little sick one," said Juan de Dios, displaying the green herbs that crowned his protégé and permitting her sleeping face to make its own appeal. It was the face of a toast-colored cherub.

"*¡Qué bonita!*"[8] exclaimed his mother, admiringly. "But of whom is she, son of mine?"

And he told them in a whisper how the child's mother had been killed, not mentioning the unluckily thrown *lazo* and his own blood-remorse, but adding simply that *Nuestro Amo* had sent him the thought to take care of the little orphan.

"Be it so, son of ours!" exclaimed the water-carrier and his wife in one voice; and Juan de Dios, who still looked at the face of the sleeping child, added:

"The *chiquita*[9] will grow fat and strong for helping, and when she has taken her first communion I will marry her."

And so it was settled. No one else claimed the orphan, and the priest saw no reason why Pancho, the water-carrier, should not add a ninth young mouth to the eight that already busied themselves at

[7] A wine cup used in Communion service.
[8] How pretty!
[9] Young girl.

feeding-time beneath the flat roof of his adobe cabin. After Juan de Dios, who was twelve, came Tiburcio, two years younger, and then a mixed rabble of barefooted infancy, in which the new-comer took a middle place and proved able to hold her own. The new home was a counterpart of the old one, except that it was more populous and amusing. The *tortillas* were just as warm and as grateful to little stomachs; there wasn't a pin to choose between the niceness of the beans, black and red, or of the sauces that would sometimes bite little tongues; and as for the *chilitos verdes*—little green peppers just the size of her fingers—Juan de Dios would bring them to her in handfuls, knowing that she adored to crunch them between her sharp little teeth. She developed a strong affection for the household altar which stood in one corner and was touched by no one but Juan de Dios. It consisted of an image of the Virgin of Guadalupe stamped on a large piece of leather and decorated with delicate white plumes, at its feet an earthen dish of oil in which a butterfly was always burning—not a real butterfly, of course, but one of those little contrivances of a short wick stuck in a float called by the same name, *mariposa*.

A month after his adoption of Dolores, Juan de Dios was a different person. By parting with certain property, to wit, one carved leather belt, one knife, one *lazo*, fashioned in a superior manner with fancy knots and stained in bright colors, one flute, which he had made from a piece of sugar-cane, and one veteran fighting-cock with a bamboo leg, he had raised enough money to buy an income-earning equipment consisting of two water-jugs suspended at either end of a long pole which he balanced on his shoulder. So burdened, he embarked in business in a small way, delivering water to households of the humbler sort, and earning about three *reales*[10] a week. And he was soon rich enough to buy Dolores three white shirts, three skirts of gaily striped and figured baize, much green cotton ribbon for her hair, a medal of their Mother the Virgin of Guadalupe, and scapularies[11] of Santa Barbara, who protects from thunder, the Virgin of the Conception, who defends chastity, and the Archangel Gabriel, who watches over little children.

[10] One-quarter of a peso.

[11] Symbol of affiliation to an ecclesiastical order, consisting of two strips of cloth hanging down the breast and back and joined across the shoulder.

When his day's work was over Dolores would beg for a story; and sitting cross-legged, with their backs against the sun-warmed cabin wall, he would tell her stories of the miracles and apparitions of saints, and she would catch her breath and stretch the rims of her eyes at the exciting parts, just as children of the northern land do over the deeds of giants and fairies.

And she would tell him the events of her day. She had spread the clothes on the rocks to dry for the *mamacíta* washing at the brook; she had fetched holy water from the church; she had gathered wild jasmine, pink and white, and made a basket of posies which she had taken to the station with Tiburcio and some of the sisters, and the passengers in the trains had given her many *centavos*, which she had tied in a corner of her *rebozo*[12] to keep them from Tiburcio, who was as full of tricks as a monkey.

Sometimes Juan de Dios would remonstrate with Tiburcio for teasing the little motherless one; and then Tiburcio, taking the scolding in good part, would make Dolores laugh with his comical grimaces. He had bright, impudent eyes and a mole under his mouth which gave him a laughing look and earned him many gracious glances from the *señores* on the trains when they bought his pomegranates or purple passion-fruit.

Juan de Dios saved enough money in the course of a year to discard his long pole, which caused the *porteros*[13] of the better residences to exclude him from their patios, and provide himself with a mature *aguador's* outfit like his father's. Thenceforward he bore a very large jug on his back, balanced by a smaller one on his breast, and his knees bent more than ever, and he was very proud. No other Indito was so alert in undertaking small errands or so faithful in performing them. And at last it fell out that some of the oldest families in the *pueblo*, lifelong patrons of the deliberate Pancho, would ask him in emergencies for the services of his son. Now, Pancho loved his son, but he also had his proper pride, and one day he said to Juan de Dios: "Son of my life, comfort of my soul, thou art now a man and mayest choose thine occupation."

"Choose my occupation?" stammered the astonished youth. "But your honor knows that I have chosen it these four years."

[12] Cloak.
[13] Doormen.

"Not so," replied Pancho, positively. "Of *aguador*, sufficient with thy father. Better that thou be a donkey-driver. It is my wish, thou consolation of my miseries; and the day of thy saint I will give thee a burro—and may God accompany thee!"

Juan de Dios was silent. The thought of changing his occupation filled his heart with anguish. Was he not sixteen, and long settled in life? Did not all the world know him as Juan de Dios, the *aguador*?

That evening at twilight, as he and Dolores squatted against the wall, he said to her: "To-morrow we will go to early mass, and after we will speak to the padre about thy confirmation. I have to leave thee, Dolores."

"To leave me!" Incredulity and indignant protest struggled with a very lively curiosity.

"Even as I say. I have a weight in my heart, Dolores, but all is for the best. I am going to work for thee a few years in the capital."

She looked at him with mingled terror and admiration, for in the imagination of the Indian of the *pueblos* the City of Mexico is enveloped in formidable and sinister mystery. With the same feeling in his heart, and a sudden surge of loneliness, Juan de Dios wept. She tried to comfort him, begging him not to go, but he stammered: "The road of the glory is sown with thorns. I will go. Resign thyself, little daughter. When I return we shall receive the benediction of the padre, and thou shalt be my little wife."

"Yes, yes, Juan de Dios!" She joined her bronze hands flatly as in prayer, bowed her forehead on the finger-tips, and then threw back her head with a heavenward glance of mild ecstasy. "Yes, yes! I shall be very big when thou comest back, and thou wilt take me to my own little cabin—oh, what enchantment!"

She kissed his hand reverentially, and her heart was filled with the great calm that assurance of protection gives to the weak and ignorant.

And so a morning arrived when Juan de Dios departed from his birthplace, accompanying a party of donkey-drivers who were taking various wares to sell in the capital. It was a morning of farewells, promises, benedictions, and tears. The capital was only two days' easy march distant, but it seemed to all that Juan de Dios, the confidant and comforter, whose daily blessing of the hut had carried an unnameable gentle charm, was embarking into dark distances full of dangers.

The capital, as sensitive of its reputation as an elegant woman, has a code of manners for *Inditos* and enforces it in times of peace, peremptorily though kindly. Juan de Dios learned that in the City of Mexico one may no longer enjoy the comfort of going barefoot, and dutifully he taught his feet to endure the encumbrance of leather sandals. He learned that the city *aguador* may not blow his whistle to halt the traffic while he gravely crosses the street, but must wait for the passing of many vehicles, some with horses and some outlandishly without. From early morn to the fall of the afternoon he would go from fountain to fountain and from portal to portal, his lean body so accustomed to bending that he never thought of straightening it, his head bowed as if in prayer.

On the first day of each month he visited a little shop in the street of San Felipe Neri, where a good old widow sold tobacco and snuff, candles for the poor, for the rich, and for the church; flags of silver and gold paper stuck in dry oranges to adorn altars; toys, candies, lottery-tickets, and many other necessaries. With her Juan de Dios understood himself very well. She would change his mountain of centavos into silver pesos, and from her he would buy his meager supplies for the month, including his lottery-ticket, with which he never won a prize although he never neglected to have it blessed by holding it up in church at the moment of benediction. Very happy, he would jog home, the heavy silver pieces in his leather pockets making a discreet and dulcet "*trink-trak*" between his jugs and his body. He lived with a charcoal-seller in one room at the back of a *bodega*,[14] where the odors of dried fish and vats of wine mingled with the dust of the charcoal nightly swept into the farthest corner of the soft earth floor to make place for his sleeping-mat.

When his first jugs had worn out—the sweet-scented, porous red clay becomes perforated in time—he had buried them to their necks in the corner where he slept, and they were now his treasury. On returning home from the widow's he would uncover them and drop his coins one by one into their depths, receiving a separate

[14] Cellar or shop selling wine and food.

thrill of satisfaction at the piquant echo of each one from the hollow of its prison.

Once in a year or so he received word from his family by the mouth of some donkey-driver or pilgrim. They were well. They sent him benedictions. And he, as opportunity offered, sent them gifts for their saint-days.

It was the month of June, which always makes the heart restless. During his five years in the capital Juan de Dios had treated himself to fewer holidays than most *peons*[15]—not celebrating the days of more than ten or a dozen favorite saints each year—and now his spirit rebelled at many things. The rainy season was, as usual, depriving him of the *centavos* which at other times accrued from the sprinkling of the streets in front of his customers' houses, as ordained by law. And then there was a new and mischievous spirit in the air, a spirit named "modern improvement," and it now possessed and agitated one of the houses on his route, a three-patio building inhabited by fifteen families of the middle class. The plumber—worker of evil and oppressor of God's poor—had been exercising his malign spells. Was it the will of God that water should run upstairs, except in jugs sustained by the proper legs of a man? Was the roof of a building a fit place for a large and unsightly tank? Was it reasonable to suppose that a man could fill such a reservoir with water by see-sawing laboriously an erect stake of painted iron, as tall as his breast, which had sprouted diabolically in a patio at the margin of the fountain? Or that the tenants could supply themselves with water by no more than turning a stick of brass not as large as an honest man's finger? Was it for him, Juan de Dios, to become a confederate in these mysteries by hauling and thrusting that painted stake, instead of making many sociable trips between the fountain and the kitchens of his customers? No! He would not so endanger his soul. With firmness he had refused to serve the strange gods of the plumber. And the owner and tenants of the building, liking well their patient and apostolic-looking *aguador*, and understanding perfectly his prejudices, had murmured "*¡Mañana!*"[16] and allowed the highly painted

[15] Members of the landless laboring class, or persons in compulsory servitude.

[16] Tomorrow!

and patented American force-pumps in the three patios to rust in unlovely idleness.

But the incident had given Juan de Dios a shock and turned his heart toward the simplicity and piety of the *pueblo*. His Dolores was fourteen now, and ready for marriage. He had saved enough money. He could build a little hut and buy a *burro*, and lead an easy and blessed existence with his chattering little squirrel of a wife, and the babies that would crawl in the sunshine at their cabin door.

Meanwhile the excellent business which he had built up in the capital should not be lost to the family, for Tiburcio should succeed to it. That part of it had already been arranged; it only remained to send him word that the time had come.

Then came many days of patient waiting and of serious preparation—days, too, of fasting and prayer—until one afternoon there dawned upon his vision at the public fountain which he had appointed as their meeting-place a radiant young spark whom he would not have identified as the weeping boy he had left in the road except for the eloquent mole under the still-laughing mouth. He wore leather trousers, wondrously tight-fitting, and laced up the sides from foot to hip between double rows of brass buttons; a white shirt, without a collar, but with a large, flowing scarlet bow sewed to the middle of the bosom; a leather belt hung with a fancy knife, a plain knife, and other decorative items; from his neck a religious medal which clashed cheerfully against the metal of the knives; on his feet heavy shoes of wine-colored leather, much overlaid and ornamented in punctured designs; on his head a cheap straw *sombrero* heavily bound to its very apex with silver rope, richly knotted.

Tiburcio saw his brother trotting along with head bended as of old, and moved to meet him; and with many simple ejaculations of joy and affection they placed each his hands on the other's shoulders, with smiles and graceful bendings of heads, and strokings and pattings, like a pair of friendly ants. Thus they remained, regardless of the disorganized traffic, until a *gendarme,*[17] himself an *Indito*, ran to them and in a friendly fashion moved them on. And at length Juan de Dios permitted himself to take cognizance of Tiburcio's elegance.

[17] Soldier employed in police duties.

"But, brother of my soul," he protested, "thou appearest a Judas!"

Tiburcio hung his head in shame at this allusion to the garishly bedizened effigies of Judas which are hanged in the streets and plazas on Saturday of Glory and burned amid festive mockery and the sputtering of fire-crackers. Fortunately he had working garments tied up in his blanket, and the *portero* of a neighboring house where Juan de Dios was known allowed him to change there and emerge in the simple habit that God had undoubtedly ordained for water-carriers. And not until then did he remember to impart to his brother a piece of important news. Laughing, he said:

"Brother, with all thy scoldings thou didst put it away from my memory to tell thee that Lola is here."

"Lola?" repeated Juan de Dios, not understanding.

"Dolores—she came with me."

"Protect me, Saint of my name! Dolores here—but for what? And where is she?

"While I found thee I left her at the cathedral."

"Well chosen the place! But I beat my brains to comprehend. Did I not tell her to wait for me in the *pueblo?* And now —*¡Ay! ¡Ay!* What sinful impatience that she must come to meet me here! What sad fortune that I could not have embraced her as I always wished, in the cabin where I left her!" He wagged his bended head with a heavy sigh at this upsetting of his plans. Tiburcio looked uncomfortable and opened his mouth to speak, but Juan de Dios, having eased himself of his pique, began to rejoice: "But since God wishes it to come sooner, the pleasure, so much better. She is here, my young woman! What little moments we will pass! *¡Uy, újule!*"

And with that liquid cry of joy he unharnessed himself, pulling over his head the shoulder-straps, with the leather breast-and-back plates and head-piece, and the heavy jugs, and proceeded to harness his brother, saying: "Do me this service, Tiburcio. Carry on this street five journeys to number fourteen, six to number eighteen, three to number twenty, and eight to the principal patio in number twenty-two. Take care not to touch the pots of flowers in the corridors, and where the cages of birds hang be sure to bend lest thou knock them down. If the parrots speak to thee, answer them not, for the *señoras* like them not to learn our manner of expressing ourselves. If thou seest a melon or a bunch of flowers swimming in a patron's water-jar, touch them not, for after thou hast poured the water they will but dance a little and come up again. Here are my colorines." He passed over a leather bag filled with scarlet beans. "With these count thy journeys, leaving one each time with the servant of the house. Conduct thyself well, and that God may accompany thee. I go to the cathedral to find my Dolores. *¡Adios! ¡Adios!*"

The new *aguador* attracted the attention of a lady and gentleman sitting in the principal patio, and they asked him about Juan de Dios. Tiburcio explained everything with great care, and added in a confident and winning manner that he expected to give just as good service as his brother, if not a little bit better. And the lady in some excitement whispered to her husband: "Perhaps this youth will agitate the pump, and by the grace of God we can utilize at last our porcelain bath!"

The lady's husband, who was the owner of the house, jumped at the idea, and Tiburcio was conducted to the pump. He rolled his eyes at it distrustfully, and seemed to regard the *señor's* explanation of its *raison d'être* as a rather lame one; but when the *señor* himself grasped the lever and moved it sturdily back and forth without suffering any other penalty than a shortness of breath—for he was a fat and not younger *señor*—the youth recovered his courage.

"Lend here, *Patrón*," he said; and getting free of his jugs and rolling up his trousers he attacked the business with confidence. The proprietor and his wife put heart into him at intervals by remarking what a strong fellow he was and how the capital was the proper place for him; and although Tiburcio's muscles were not hardened to such labor he kept at it, his spirit swimming in the ether of pride and praise, for half an hour. Meanwhile the news that an *aguador* who would pump was on the premises had spread to the second and third patios, and so flattering were the overtures made to him that Tiburcio, concealing his fatigue, addressed himself with zeal to the other two force-pumps. When his arms failed him he continued by employing the weight of his body, the forward plunge pulling a quart of water from the fountain and the backward fall projecting it toward the roof—for it is the ungracious nature of a force-pump to work equally hard both ways. On abandoning the third pump Tiburcio felt a weight in his chest, and his legs bent under him like green twigs; but he was wonderfully happy as he took the silver pieces that he had earned by the sweat of his body, and with them made the sign of the cross on his brow, his eyes, his mouth, and his breast. After which he rolled himself in a straw mat in a shady corner, and abandoned himself like a tired child to his well-earned *siesta.*[18]

Juan de Dios and Dolores met under the trees of the plaza in front of the cathedral—a new Dolores, almost as tall as himself, with dove's eyes and a sad little voice, very desirable—and they embraced just as he and Tiburcio had embraced, hands on shoulders, with the same little glances and bendings and soft ejaculations. And she called him "*Padrino,*"[19] as of old, at which he protested playfully, "*¿Que padrino ni qué calabazas?*"

"What godfather nor what pumpkins? Not thy *padrino*, but thy husband, who forgives thee for coming to him."

At that she was troubled, and abruptly withdrew her hands from his shoulders, averting her face. That gesture smote him with the knowledge that an evil had come between them. Trembling with anger, he exclaimed: "What thing is this I see? What thing? What thing?"

His voice pitched higher and higher. Her hands flew to her downcast face. He seized her wrists and shook them, making her whole body reel like a palm in a hurricane.

"Don't beat me, don't beat me!" she sobbed. "Where is Bucho?"

The endearing diminutive of his brother's name, or the tone of instinct in which it was uttered, told him all. He fetched a great sobbing breath and struck her in the face with the back of his hand, and then again with the palm, and then rained blows on her head and shoulders; and she, being a woman and born of blood impressed with the proverb "Who well loves thee will make thee weep," snuggled against him, whimpering. While beating her he swore many oaths, such as "Lightnings and chains of fire!" and spoke bitter reproaches of ingratitude and perfidy, weeping all the while. They were near the central terminus of trolley-lines, and a crowd gathered about them, and there were calls for a gendarme. Hearing that, Juan de Dios turned her about and gave her a push to make her walk in front of him.

[18] Afternoon nap.

[19] Godfather.

Tiburcio had not been seen at number fourteen, nor eighteen, nor twenty, but in the principal patio of twenty-two Dolores heard snores which she recognized, and they found Tiburcio curled in slumber.

Deeply curled, for it required several kicks from his brother to awaken him, and even then his fatigue pressed upon him so heavily that he stared up at them with a vague smile, unconscious of the fury in one face and the fear in the other. Soon, however, it dawned on his sluggish senses that Juan de Dios was declaiming angrily, then that Lola was weeping, then that her love and his own was the cause of the outburst, and then that the girl had thrown herself between them with upraised arms, crying to Juan de Dios: "Don't curse him! Don't curse Bucho! Bucho, speak to him!"

"Lightnings!" shouted Juan de Dios, his voice muffled with foam. "For his sorceries with which he hath bewitched thee, that God may cripple him!"

Dolores gave a gasp of horror. Tiburcio, his face suddenly bleaching to a waxen yellow, tried to rise to his knees for prayer, but at the first movement an intense pain shot through his back between the shoulders and he tumbled over on his face, howling: "Crippled! God favor me, miserable sinner that I am! Brother, brother, thy words have fallen over me! I am crippled truly! I cannot move! *¡Ay-ay-ay!*"

In a series of shrieks he described the progress of his affliction, which extended to all the muscles that he had brought into unwonted action during his intemperate exertions with the force-pumps. Dolores screamed for help, sputtered incoherencies at the *portero*, and ran round the patio like a wild animal, kneeling at intervals to pray but not daring to go near Tiburcio from fear of the demon that possessed him. Shudder after shudder convulsed him as he sprawled with his forehead on the pavement, the poison of terror augmenting that of fatigue. From the house emerged many servants, male and female, asking questions, offering advice, chattering and crossing themselves, afraid to approach.

It was important to get Tiburcio away. Juan de Dios lifted him to his feet at last, despite his piteous moans. It appeared that he could use his legs, although feebly, but from loins to neck he seemed paralyzed. Supported by his brother and Dolores, and uttering cries at each step, he traversed the streets to the charcoal-seller's and was laid on a mat. Juan de Dios rubbed his body with holy water, sprinkling what was left of it all over the room to frighten away evil spirits.

Night fell over the anguish of the three, but without abating it. Toward Juan de Dios and his prayers the other two deferred in a spirit of humility and anxious expectancy, while he performed such prodigies of spiritual concentration that he shook as with an ague and his tears lost their identity among the drops of sweat that rolled down his contorted visage. They would not believe that he could pray in vain—he, the blessed one, he at whose curse the punishment had fallen! And yet, soon after the great clock of the palace had boomed out eleven, Tiburcio reported to Dolores in a whisper that he seemed to be breaking into two pieces. She wailed loudly, and in desperation demanded of Juan de Dios what thing she could do, or he and she together, that would incline the good God to show mercy to Bucho. Since He was angry at the broken troth, might it not appease Him if she renounced her love of Tiburcio and became the little wife of Juan de Dios? Tiburcio from his mat begged that the efficacy of that method of cure might be tested. Juan de Dios said nothing, but his eyes burned as he looked at Dolores, and shortly afterward he abruptly went out into the rain. From the door she could see him dimly, by the light of a distant street lamp, sitting motionless under the sky with his knees to his breast, his face upturned in submission and inquiry.

Hours passed before he returned, and then he was alight with resolve. Making a sign to Dolores that she should help him, he uncovered the buried jugs and removed by handfuls all his savings, which they packed in two leather bags. Soon afterward the three set forth into the dark and rain-swept night, Tiburcio traveling as a passenger on his brother's back, partly sustained by a leather band which passed across the other's forehead, and inadequately counterpoised by the two bags of silver pesos which alternately patted Juan de Dios's chest as he trotted. They traversed unfrequented streets until they reached the outskirts, and then struck the road along which a trolley-line runs to the Villa de Guadalupe,[20] the Mecca of the Mexicans. Tiburcio suffered severely from the jolting and straining of sore muscles; but the knowledge of his destinations so filled him with hope that he suppressed his groans.

[20] Site where the Virgin of Guadalupe first appeared to the Indio Juan Diego on December 9, 1531.

The sun was rising when they reached the Villa de Guadalupe. Juan de Dios stretched his brother on one of the heavy iron benches in the plaza at the foot of the hill. Tiburcio seemed a little easier, which was not to be wondered at, for many miracles had been known to follow the mere arrival of the sufferer within the precincts of the sacred *pueblo*. To Juan de Dios the very air was sensibly impregnated with sanctity, and he breathed it with rapture. Faint incense instilled it, bells trembled in it, some as remote voices imploring faith, others strong and impatient mandates to repentance. *Padres*[21] in long black cassocks flitted hither and thither from church to church and from chapel to chapel. Their houses loomed somberly above gardens which seemed thronging congregations of flowers. Even the rag awnings fluttering here and there under the old trees of the plaza played their part in the enchantment, for beneath them were exposed for sale every imaginable aid to devotion—rosaries, images, ribbons of saints, and many other objects, even to little dark papers of blessed earth, the virtue of which is notorious all over Mexico. Juan de Dios bought some of the earth and all three devoured it, as is the way of the faithful, Tiburcio receiving the largest share. It was a natural transition to blessed water. This they obtained from the sacred well at the foot of the hill in the center of a little ancient domed temple, by casting into its rocky depths a heavy, conical cup of iron attached to a chain. Tiburcio drank of the water as much as he could, its abominable flavor strengthening his faith in its miraculous powers. Also his brother poured a cup of it over him.

And now Juan de Dios was ready for the pilgrimage proper. Shading his eyes with his hand, he traced the course of the stone stairway mounting heavenward from his feet, flight after flight, at first shaded by great trees and at last almost lost amid wild creepers as it aspired in curves like those of a snail's shell to the lofty summit, with its coronet of churches and chapels now ethereal with the golden light of the young morning. With an eagle glance which seemed to perceive in that radiance an authentic sign from the Virgin of Guadalupe, whom he had adored from childhood, he exclaimed: "If yonder thou art, Mother of mine, unto thee I bear a sinner. He is my brother. Make me the road hard, dangerous. Put

[21] Priests.

me obstacles; all that may be necessary to make merit for my presentation before thee with Tiburcio—that is his name."

He wiped the sweat from his forehead with one finger, and continued in a tone of exaltation which thrilled the others.

"I will carry him to thee on my knees, over all those steps, unto thine altar! This act of devotion, I offer it to thee for the health of my sinner brother, that thou wilt permit him to move the body again, if thou thinkest he merits it."

And, having signed himself, he dropped to his knees and with much difficulty, Dolores assisting, hoisted Tiburcio to his shoulders with feet hanging down in front and hands clasping his brother's brow. Juan de Dios held his body upright, balancing carefully, as he felt his way upward, one knee after another, slowly—always slowly. Dolores followed, marveling at his sanctity. It being the rainy season, there was no great throng of pilgrims, but the few who were ascending to the shrine—some women carrying wax candles decorated with gold paper, others with plates of sprouting wheat of a delicate pallor from having been grown in the dark, and a few *Inditos* with bamboo cages containing fighting-cocks to be blessed in church that they might have fortune in battle—these remarked the superior zeal of Juan de Dios, and regarded him respectfully as a holy person, one whom it was fortunate to have seen. The same spirit was manifested by the sellers of blessed articles on the landings of the stair. While he rested, Juan de Dios caused Dolores to buy the largest and most beautiful candle obtainable, and thereafter she carried it, unlighted, in front of them. Also, for refreshment and edification of them all, they bought blessed fruit, blessed *tortillas* fried in chile sauce, and *tortillas* of the Virgin, which are made sweet and very small and dyed in different colors.

As he climbed, Juan de Dios prayed, and the more he suffered the more he thanked God. His white cotton trousers gave but the scantiest protection to his knees, and that not for long, yet he did not look for smooth places, and Tiburcio groaned more than he. Once he slipped on a rolling pebble, and after that he mounted every step with the same knee, lifting the hurt one after it. The time came when even his strength of *aguador* wore out, and he clawed the stone balustrade to raise himself and stopped on each step, his breath hissing between his locked teeth from which the lips were stiffly peeled; and still his eyes pleaded for martyrdom. Dolores at every opportunity would wipe Tiburcio's face where the thorns had scratched it.

When Juan de Dios reached the top he signed to Dolores to light the candle, and he held it at arm's-length as he continued his march into the ancient church of the hill, his knees leaving prints of red on the white marble pavement. Into the depth of the church, straight to the blazing shrine he went, and Dolores saw his face working frightfully as he unlocked his teeth to proclaim that he had kept his word; but no sound came from his throat, and he suddenly fell forward in a swoon, spilling Tiburcio, who executed a series of instinctive movements, too quick for eye to follow, which landed him on his feet, supple and free from pain; and he and Dolores threw themselves on their knees beside the unconscious one at the shrine, to recite a multitude of "*gracias*" for the miracle.

Dolores fully expected to become the little wife of Juan de Dios. He had come from the confessional when he said to them: "I now comprehend that I do not serve for this world. The love of woman confounds me too much. God will free me from committing more barbarities. I will remain in this saintly place, for which it seemeth to me I was ordained before my mother bore me. Thou, Dolores, and thou, Tiburcio, serve for this earth. Go, and may the good God accompany you always. Take this bag of money, that it may help you to marry and live justly as good Christians. The other bag I have given to the good padre, who will manage it so that I shall have enough prayers and masses said for the guidance of my steps while I live."

Much more he said to them in the same peaceful strain, and laid an obligation upon them to make pilgrimage every year for the feast of the Virgin of Guadalupe in remembrance of the miracle she had performed for Tiburcio.

They left him, and he continued to be an *aguador*, carrying water from the sacred well to the top of the sacred hill with which to refresh pilgrims, especially the sick and crippled, after the ascent. He himself was crippled, never recovering from a stiffness of one knee, which remained bent. And in this manner Juan de Dios became veritably John of God.

[November 1913]

The Emotions of María Concepción

María Concepción, having a favor to ask of her *papá* that morning, listened at the door of his dressing-room, which adjoined her own, and tried to augur an auspicious mood from the accent of the abstruse little cough with which he punctuated every delicate task. She heard his measured pacing to and fro, his opening and shutting of drawers, and the clash of dainty cup and saucer as he sipped his black coffee. Her delicate nose identified the aroma generated by *papá's* hair under the cordial embraces of a curling-iron, and the lilac perfume of the cosmetic with which those rampant waves and the heavy mustache and imperial[1] were licked into lustrous immobility. At last—welcome sound!—a cough of finality, and Senator Montes de Oca marched forth, serene in spotless, frock-coated, patent-leathered perfection.

Not yet, however, would his daughter present herself before him. First he must make his morning *reflexiones*,[2] a solemnity which involved his pacing for five minutes the circuit of the gallery, with head bent, and hands clasped behind his back, sometimes pausing to glance over the flower-decked railing into the patio, or to order his *mozo*[3] to remove some linnet or canary whose pipings interfered with his cerebral operations. According to domestic tradition, the senator, during that daily perambulation, exercised his intellect to a degree beyond the capacity of less formidable mortals to comprehend. Watching him furtively from the shelter of her room, María Concepción applied an extra coat of

[1] A small part of the beard left growing beneath the lower lip.

[2] Reflections.

[3] Servant.

powder to her already well-whitened features, and dexterously encircled her large eyes with artificial shadows, those *ojeras*[4] which promote luster and spirituality. She found time, too, to rehearse a languid comportment, and she gave some consideration to the project of sinking at her *papá's* feet in a graceful swoon, a maneuver sometimes effective as a stimulant to the granting of special indulgences.

Intense in all things, she had an intense desire to attend a brilliant affair at the Plaza de Toros[5] on the following Sunday. All society would be there, and El Mañoso[6] was to kill—El Mañoso, the youngest and greatest swordsman of Spain, who was now to make his first bow to the cream of Mexican fashion. María Concepción had never been present at a bull-fight. Before her arrival at an age for such fiestas her mother had died, and for five years the house of Montes de Oca had dragged through the successive stages of ceremonious mourning prescribed by Mexican etiquette. The senator had testified his grief *á lo gran señor,*[7] causing the finest chamber in his house to be converted into an exquisite private chapel, duly consecrated, where masses were celebrated daily in memory of the beloved. Upon his daughter, during those springtime years of hers, he had imposed the most rigid austerities. If ever a young gallant found opportunity to make "eyes of deer" at her, though he might possess all the virtues of St. Thomas, the indignant senator would suddenly discover in him all the hypocrisies of Judas. María Concepción often declared with tears to her adored twin-brother, Enrique, that if it were not for her expansions of soul with him, and with the heroines of innumerable surreptitious novels, she would have perished in the bud. Soon she would be eighteen. That very morning she had discovered a wrinkle, a very little one, it was true, and possibly no deeper than the powder; but it had made her weep. *¡Qué fatalidad!*[8]

Decisive as a signal-gun was the cough with which *El Senador* Don Enrique Montes de Oca y Quintana Ruiz announced to all the world that he had concluded his *reflexiones*. The household sprang into audible activity. The great doors of the coach-house rolled

[4] Rings around one's eyes.
[5] Bullring.
[6] The clever, the crafty one (nickname).
[7] In grand style.
[8] What a catastrophe!

open, and the senator's coupé swung into the patio. Now was the ordained moment for the bestowal of his benediction upon his daughter.

Even as the thought came to him, she approached—pale as a gardenia, her humid, dark eyes fixed upon him in a faint smile of reverence, submission, and affection. At what cost of vigilance and self-discipline she had studied to obliterate herself until the instant of need, and then to sparkle from oblivion with a smile, her *papá* never reflected, not deeming it any concern of his to discover the technique by which women compass the proprieties of their sex. But it did occur to him that she was growing every day more like her lamented mother, and that observation brought him an access of paternal tenderness as she kissed his hand.

She had brought a flower for his coat, a single violet selected from the mass which Refugio, the coachman's daughter, had placed on her dressing-table.

"But thy *papá* is too old for these fiestas," he protested indulgently as she sought to put it in his buttonhole. "Have more formality, Conchita!"

"It is so little and so pale," she pleaded— "so pale, dear *Papá*, that I think it must have grown in the moonlight."

Touched on his poetic side, he unbent so far as to permit himself to be decorated. But then—then, before she could frame the tactful phrases which were to lead up to the theme of the bull-fight, he made an announcement which swept that festival from her thoughts, and canceled every check that her imagination had ever drawn upon the bank of destiny. With an air of conferring an honor far beyond her aspirations, he said:

"Daughter of my soul, thou hast been this morning the subject of my reflections, with the consequence that God has illumined me to guide thee to happiness by making thee the companion and consolation of my remaining years on earth."

Her eyes and breathless mouth rounded in a trinity of O's. Pleased that his words had produced a palpable impression, and proud of the discretion with which he had attacked that delicate task, the making of an old maid, he coughed rhetorically and continued:

"Thou wilt rejoice that I have made thy future secure by liberating thee from the anxieties of youth and, above all, from the banalities of coquetry. Study to make thyself worthy of the consecration to which thou art elected. Invoke the sanctified spirit of thy mama, who doubtless is in heaven commending us to God. Preserve thy health, taking with diligence thine emulsion of oil of liver of codfish, that thou mayest be a comfort and not a care to thy desolate *papá*, who in a short time will have fulfilled half a century of this life, and who requires thy gentle ministrations to alleviate the dolorous path which he must follow to the tomb."

These words, pronounced in a deep and vibrating tone, affected María Concepción so piteously that, without one thought of artifice, she sank sobbing to the floor and embraced the paternal knees, entreating the senator to abandon such gloomy thoughts and to believe that she, his child, thanked Heaven for the privilege of dedicating her life to her beloved *papacito.*[9] Touched at this proof of a becoming feminine spirit, he raised her to her feet, and rewarded her with an affectionate embrace. His heart expanded, and it occurred to him that he was feeling uncommonly young and lively; nevertheless he thought it proper to utter a few pensive reflections on mortality.

When he had given her his benediction and departed for the palace María Concepción ran to change her dress. She had a habit of changing her dress under the stimulus of every new emotion, whether derived from life or from a novel. *Papá's* ministering angel! Never had she experienced an emotion so difficult to fit with the psychological frock. She must design a costume, something very spiritual, with a Sarah Bernhardt[10] collar. In the meantime she would put on her habit of the Daughters of Mary, which she had worn at the College of the Sacred Heart—black silk, with a silk cord about the waist, the only touch of color being the broad ribbon of blue sackcloth by which the blessed medal of the order was suspended from the devotee's neck.

Feeling particularly angelic in that demure but bewitching costume, María Concepción sought the chapel of her mama, and earnestly invoked the Virgin to purify her heart and to make her as worthy as possible of her tender and distinguished mission. And

[9] Daddy.

[10] French actress (1844-1923).

she felt herself uplifted as on wings. Returning to her own apartments and consulting the mirrors, she was impressed by the unearthly, soft splendor of her eyes, turned upward under their sweeping lashes in this new rapture of devotion. The contemplation of her own delicate beauty moved her to tears of appreciation. *Papá* should see that he had not been mistaken in her, that she did indeed rejoice at his having set her free from—what were his words? The "anxieties of youth," yes, yes, and the "banalities of coquetry." Coquetry, with those eyes of hers! What sacrilege!

She was startled by a whistle, shrill and peremptory. It was her brother's summons to his *mozo*, and a moment later she heart Enrique's eager voice arousing the Indian from his siesta with voluble instructions for the care of his English mare, heated after a long trot through the forest roads of fashionable Chapultepec.[11] María Concepción's first impulse was to run into some ambush; then, when he had searched for her in vain, to dart out upon him, kitten-like, with a bombardment of kisses and questions—questions about his ride, and the people he had seen, and the gossip at the club, and all the agreeable variety of things constantly going on in that portion of the world exterior to the walls of the mansion of Montes de Oca. But Enrique must learn that her playing days were over.

Hearing him approach, calling her, she sank on her knees at her *prie-dieu*,[12] and hastily swept her habit into graceful folds. The outline of her classic head and delicate features was etched against the shadows as with a pencil of phosphorus.[13] So ethereal was the picture that Enrique halted in the doorway, and did not speak until his sister had signed herself with reverence and risen sedately to greet him. Then, his vivacity returning, he demanded:

"Conchita, what news? Hast thou spoken to *papá* about Sunday? Will he engage a box?[14] Shall we see El Mañoso kill, Conchita of my life?"

With a grave and beautiful gesture she thereupon proceeded to make known to him the momentous role she had been appointed to play upon the stage of life. She chose her words kindly, anxious that he should not consider her puffed up in spirit or imagine that

[11] Park in Mexico City.
[12] Kneeling desk for prayer.
[13] Luminous element.
[14] I.e., a box seat, an exclusive compartment from which to witness the bullfight.

she loved him less because she could no longer share his frivolous preoccupations. On the contrary, she assured him, she would always piously remember that he and she had been born in the same hour, and that only through the trifling accident of sex was he, Enrique, ineligible for the post of *papá's* ministering angel.

Enrique was silent for some moments. Then, to her amazement and indignation, he laughed.

"By Santa Inez, little sister," he exclaimed, "I am glad thou art happy over thy celibacy. Every one to his taste, as the donkey-driver said after a dinner of hay. But this is not such news to me as thou thinkest, for I always believed that *papá* would find it convenient to cause thee to remain to dress the saints."[15]

What feeling was this that dilated the fine nostrils of María Concepción, and chilled the sacrificial ardor of her heart?

"But to bad weather a good face," Enrique continued. "Old age will come soon enough without our running to meet it, little sister of my soul."

She smiled with her lips, but her eyes fled sidewise, searching among the shadows about the floor.

"All the world will be there," Enrique went on in a fume of boyish enthusiasm, "the De la Vega, the Castro, the Gorricochéa. Americans are paying fabulous prices for *entradas*,[16] doubtless because El Mañoso killed before Spanish royalty, and received such rare recognition from Alfonso's angel-faced English queen. See, I have this photograph."

"The King's?"

"Bah! Who cares for a king's portrait? No, no, the great swordsman's. See his eyes, pale and distended like a cat's, as no doubt they look when he poises to deliver the fatal thrust which halts the ensanguined bull in its querulous assault and abases its proud neck beneath his conquering foot!"

María Concepción studied the face of the famous matador—a young face, as smooth as a priest's or an American's, but alight with the passion and innocent boldness of Spain. The pale, printed eyes seemed to penetrate her own. She shut hers with a frown. Enrique was saying:

[15] Literal translation of *quedarse para vestir los santos:* to remain an old maid.
[16] Tickets for admission.

"*Papá* may talk as he will about the vulgarity of Spain's great amusement, as if the Montes de Oca were of pure Indian blood; but even the proudest of unmixed Mexicans cannot be indifferent to such fame as El Mañoso has earned with his sword."

María Concepción opened her eyes and looked again at the picture. She seemed to have lived a long time since she had seen it first, and she felt astonished that it had not changed. *¡Qué simpático!*[17] Would Enrique never stop talking?

"Are we to drop out of the world just because *papá* chooses to make a reputation as a serious man? It would serve nothing for *me* to speak to him; he would only come out with, 'Today is Thursday,' and present me with a sermon and his benediction at the end of it. But thou, Conchita, thou hast little ways of thy own with *papá*, whom thou hast trained so cleverly to have anxieties about thy health. Come, show thy invention! A timely *ataque*,[18] eh? A few fainting-fits, a day or two of hysteria—what dost thou say, my little bird?"

"I say," she exclaimed in a ringing voice, "and I swear, Enrique, that we go! We will not continue to be zero at the left[19] for *papá*. As surely as my name is María Concepción, we will see El Mañoso kill!"

Enrique clapped his hands; but in that very instant he received a stinging box on the ear. *¡Cáspita!*[20] What did she mean? They faced each other like two angry game-chickens, exactly alike in feature, except for the crisp rigor of Enrique's chiseling, his tawnier color, and his thread of a mustache. She stormed at him. Why had he come to torment her with fiestas and with photographs at a time when she was experiencing a beautiful emotion over *papá*? How could she be a ministering angel without the emotion belonging to that role? Sustained by the appropriate emotion she could contest with pitiless tigers, yes, or with bulls; but unless so sustained, she could not live. Moreover, how dared he intimate that her *ataques* were a delusion and her fainting-fits a mockery? To all of which Enrique, of the burning ear, hissed tragically:

"¡Hipócrita! ¡Hipócrita! ¡Hipócrita!"[21]

[17] What a charming man!

[18] Attack.

[19] Literal translation of *ser un cero a la izquierda:* to be a nobody.

[20] Damn it!

[21] Hypocrite!

And then she had an *ataque* which was anything but a delusion. It left her bathed in tears of remorse, declaring that she was good for nothing and would kill herself, since her beloved Enrique would never forgive her. Enrique forgave her, and there were kisses. But that was not sufficient. She must make atonement for the blow by procuring him some greatly desired good. Apart from getting a box at the bull-fight, which was already settled in her mind, what was his dearest present desire? *¡Ay! ¡ay!* a thing beyond her power to obtain, he assured her, a gift of jealously sought after as a trophy and decoration—nothing less than one of the blood-stained *banderillas*[22] from El Mañoso's bull.

María Concepción lowered her eyes.

The black silk habit was laid away, for María Concepción had once more changed her dress. The greatest emotion of life had come to her. She loved. How she loved! *¡Ay, Dios! ¡Qué amor!*[23] Most faintly and inadequately was the condition of her heart symbolized by her newest, loveliest, and worldliest afternoon gown, a Paris model in tea-rose *peau-de-soie*,[24] as coherent as a veneer to her fifteen-inch waist, abetted by an agitating leghorn bonnet,[25] with hand-painted streamers coaxed into an amorous bow against one cheek.

Yes, she loved El Mañoso, whom she had not yet seen. But very soon she would see him. That was her present business in the landau,[26] by Enrique's side, an hour or two after her first view of the portrait which had altered the aspect of life to her. Yet *she* had not proposed this drive. No, she had merely engineered it, and so delicately that Enrique imagined that he had tempted her out upon an escapade. He thought, poor innocent, that it was he who had instigated a certain simulated *ataque* so alarming to all the servants and the "keeper of the keys" that his hurried ordering of the carriage to give the sufferer some air seemed a perfectly proper proceeding. But instead of seeking the Alameda[27] or the Paseo,[28]

[22] Decorated darts thrust into a bull's neck or shoulders during a bullfight.
[23] Oh God! What love!
[24] Smooth finely-ribbed satiny fabric of silk or rayon.
[25] Hat of fine plaited straw.
[26] Four-wheeled, enclosed carriage with a removable front cover and a back cover that can be raised or lowered.
[27] Tree-lined avenue, boulevard.
[28] A public walk or avenue.

the Montes de Oca carriage was threading the narrow business streets of the Centro, Enrique's design being to pass a certain café much frequented by bull-fighters for a glimpse—just a glimpse, he pleaded—of El Mañoso. And María Concepción played to perfection her role of fastidious reluctance, insisting on the top of the landau being closed, and keeping Enrique in a ferment of eager persuasion lest she should insist at any moment on turning back.

El Mañoso was sunning himself with other *toreros*[29] outside the Café of the Cardinal Virtues. A conspicuous group, with hats very wide and flat, jackets a little short of the waist-line, attitudes affected and graceful, faces carefully shaven and powdered, they viewed the moving spectacle with the eager frankness of children, and caused no little blushing and quick-stepping by the outspoken compliments they launched in their clipped Andalusian[30] speech at every pretty woman that met their appraising eyes. Only El Mañoso failed to avail himself of this immemorial privilege of their gild, perhaps dreaming of some bouncing Sevillana who could have tossed these mincing nymphs over her shoulder, or perhaps bewildered and disheartened by the insincerity of this alien capital, with its ostentatious polish and furtive barbarism, its swarthy complexions and elaborate hand-shakings.

"That is he!" Enrique hissed in his sister's ear.

He! As if she were not already baptizing the object of her *gran pasión*[31] with liquid *ojitos*—those "little eyes" which confess while affecting to conceal, which invite, inflame, provoke, pacify, scorn, rebuke, and plead, all in a few instants' fall and deflection under marbled lids, perhaps to conclude in a sweet stare of unseeing indifference.

"There, the one that moved," Enrique continued out of the corner of his mouth, "the one with blue eyes, looking this way. *¡Pst! ¡Disimula!*"[32]

And, in a sudden reaction of propriety, quickened by fear of his father's wrath, should this adventure reach the paternal ears, he spoke sharply to the Indian coachman, who had pulled up his horses, partly delayed by the traffic and partly engrossed in contemplation of the bull-fighters.

[29] Bullfighters.
[30] From Andalusia, the southernmost region of Spain.
[31] Great passion.
[32] Hide!

El Mañoso had indeed moved. Detaching himself from his companions, he made his way toward that vehicle with the silver plaque, so distinguished, freighted with that beautiful youth and maid, the latter of whom had honored him, El Mañoso, with *ojitos* more intoxicating than any of which he had hitherto been the target, and he the idol of Spain! Enrique trembled; María Concepción was calm.

Sweeping off his hat with the flourish of a troubadour, El Mañoso addressed to the Mexican *señorita* a suite of Andalusian compliments, opening with a blessing on the mother that had given her birth, continuing with praises for various parts of her person, coupling each with the name of some charming saint, and soaring prophetically to sentiments of distinguished consideration toward the numerous children of whom she would doubtless become the mother.

Enrique, blind with embarrassment and haughty rage, made a motion to strike at the respectful and breathless swordsman with his cane; but the carriage resumed its course with a suddenness which swayed him backward, almost dislodging his hat, to which he was compelled to give instant attention. Throughout the remainder of the drive he was extremely agitated, begging his sister's forgiveness for having exposed her to such an affront from a low-born *coleta* (epithet allusive to the queue in which all *toreros* proudly braid their hair), but advancing ingenious reasons why she should not permit this annoyance to revolt her against Sunday's fiesta. María Concepción fanned herself slowly and said nothing. She had seen him! *¡Simpatiquísimo!*[33] His eyes, of an intense and fiery blue—how they recalled the eyes she had adored in a certain picture of St. Michael, the archangel of the flaming sword! His voice, in that energetic patois, with its scorning of troublesome consonants, its softening of *madre* into *ma're*, and *Dios* into *Dio'*, surely she had heard it in dreams, subdued to the tender whisper, *"¡Concepcio', mi amo'!"*[34] Her eyelids fluttered, and she wondered whether El Mañoso had seen and retrieved the tightly folded morsel of paper that had shot from her fan as she opened it just before the starting of the carriage. Heaven sends it that brothers are the blindest of mortals. It was nothing, a mere entreaty, such as he

[33] The most charming man ever!

[34] Concepción, *mi amor* [my love].

doubtless received by the score, for one of the coveted *banderillas*. That was all; and yet—

That night she saw him, under the stars, wrapped in his Spanish cape, looking up at the windows of the house. What madness! He was standing beneath her father's balcony. And she—what madness!—she almost tossed him a camellia. Not yet, thou gallant youth! Soon enough thou shalt learn that María Concepción Montes de Oca y Quintana Ruiz knows how to love, that for thee she will reject every earthly allurement, including even the role of ministering angel to the most beloved and distinguished of *papás*.

A romantic elopement by the light of those Southern stars? No. Not for her that safety-valve of the Northern land, so serviceable to democratic equality in bestowing rich fathers-in-law upon young chauffeurs of comeliness and wit; not for her, or for any *señorita* of her race, her class, her unacquaintance with the barest conception of female liberty. She loved without a hope of ever touching her lover's hand; and the thought of contact with his lips would have troubled her with a sense of passion desecrated—passion all powerful, but also all delicate, immaterial, and remote compared with that which the North too confidently assumes to read in the smoldering eyes of the South.

María Concepción was suffering. Once more she changed her dress, this time for a vestal robe of white. It symbolized the virgin death to which she now resigned herself. In Mexico to die of love is something more than a dream of poets. Consumed by love—*consumida de amor*—the phrase has all the sobriety and authority of a coroner's verdict, and few families are so poor in romance, as to treasure no experience or tradition of the mortal reality it expresses. Thus to be consumed, María Concepción looked forward with an ardor similar to that of an evangelist on the eve of martyrdom. Her story would be an example to lovers. She thought of Héloïse, Boccaccio's Isabella, and other much-loving ladies of history and legend, and her throat swelled at the daring dream that she, who had but peeped out upon life from the doors of her father's house, might prove worthy of promotion into their noble company. But her own world, the fastidious world of fashion, what would it say when the little daughter of Montes de Oca died for love of an *espada?*[35] The scandal of it! *¡Cuánta murmuración!*[36] She shuddered with delight. Before dying, she would manifest her consuming flame to him who had kindled it, and, if necessary, to all the world. And she would be a witness of his triumph and glory in the arena. Which reminded her that she had yet to work her will with *papá*.

For three days—Thursday, Friday, and Saturday—the house of Montes de Oca suffered much alarm over the health of María Concepción. "*¡La pobre niña!*"[37] the servants spoke of her in hushed tones, while tears ran down their dark faces. Never had she been the victim of *ataques* so frequent and so prostrating. Her pretty, round body seemed to lose its form and become *raquítico*[38] before one's eyes. The family doctor looked as wise as he could, and applied leeches (his art was of the old school, as befitting old families) the sanguinary extortions of which the sufferer endured with a sweet fortitude that excited Enrique to gratitude and the senator to tears. Aside, the good physician made it plain to the anxious father that the malady baffled his skill. He would strongly advise the immediate gratification of any caprice that his honored patient might manifest, and in particular he would stake his professional reputation on the excellent results to be expected from any diversion sufficiently animated to arouse her out of herself. In saying which, the excellent man believed that he was expressing his own ideas, whereas they were the ideas María Concepción, instilled into his mind by suggestive processes too insidious for detection.

On Saturday afternoon Enrique, at his father's command, hastened to secure the last box available for the great occasion at the Plaza de Toros, and the senator was beguiled into believing that he was acting on his own initiative.

She chose to be exacting in her caprices, this little girl who was going to die. She did not spare her *papá's* foibles, one of which was an abhorrence of anything conspicuous about a woman, but insisted on appearing at the bull-fight *á la española*,[39] her head and shoulders draped in a delicate *mantilla*[40] arranged over a very high

[35] Sword, swordsman.
[36] How much gossip there would be!
[37] The poor girl!
[38] Feeble.
[39] In the Spanish style.
[40] Lace scarf worn by Spanish women over their hair and shoulders.

comb. It was white, like the rest of her costume, and beneath it her eyes seemed of startling darkness and size, while her little face looked like mother-of-pearl. The only *mantilla* on the side of the arena called "the shade"—there were plenty on the side called "the sun," where the common people sat—it caused much *murmuración*[41] and pointing of opera-glasses; and the sensitive senator perspired freely. María Concepción reflected that he would forgive her all when the end came.

That measured clamor, swelling until it drowned the strains of Bizet's[42] music, what was it? Rising from "the sun," that agitated coast of sweeping color, all a tossing confusion of fans, parasols, headdresses, scarfs, and faces, it extorted from the self-conscious occupants of "the shade" a more than indulgent echo. "*¡Otro toro! ¡Otro toro!*" María Concepción felt it tighten her throat and send the blood jumping to her temples. Of the six bulls dignified with a share in the entertainment, one had played his part and made his exit, dragged by four gaily decked mules, and deaf to the funeral march played jocosely in his honor; and now, this monotonous chorus, timed with a beating of multitudinous feet, "*¡Otro toro! ¡Otro toro!*" Imperious as a cry for bread, rhythmic as drums of war, persistent, good-humored, ferocious, that sonorous cadence proclaimed the popular exigency for "Another bull!" The chant did not vary until it lost itself in a joyous storm of acclamation for the junior *espada* of the occasion, and its supreme attraction, El Mañoso, "The Full-of-Tricks," the favored of royalty, the master-swordsman of his time.

Even the appearance of her love, princely in blue silk, overlaid with a complexity of gold embroidery, fringes, and galloons,[43] his supple legs delicately sheathed in white stockings, could not add to the emotion that possessed María Concepción. Her heart was fluttering as if preparing to escape between her lips. She scarcely breathed. So strongly was life fermenting in her that she felt as if any further excitation would expel it suddenly, leaving only a tired little body. As the time for that had not yet arrived, she concentrated the whole force of her will to prevent the tension from increasing; and by this means she brought herself to a trance-like

[41] Gossip.

[42] Georges Bizet, French composer (1838-1875), best known for the opera *Carmen.*

[43] Narrow, close-woven braids of gold, silver, silk, cotton, etc. used to trim garments.

condition, in which sights and sounds were extremely diminished, as if she were perceiving them from a great distance. El Mañoso became the graceful leader of some inexplicable fairy gambol: the *capeadores*,[44] waving their capes, were scarlet butterflies; the bull was no more than a shiny beetle, blundering and desultory, fair game for the mockery of those exquisite sprites. As for the hubbub of the crowd—the warnings, suggestions, criticisms, taunts, acclamations, upbraidings, and commands with which it assumed to direct every step of the conflict—it swept by her ears unheeded, as a gusty wind. Scarcely more attentive was she to Enrique's running fire of explanation. His gratification over the ferocity and cunning of the bull seemed to her inadequately grounded. His comments on the accuracy and iron muscle of a *picador*,[45] in holding the plunging bull from his horse with the short point of his lance planted against the beast's shoulder, seemed overdrawn praise for such child's play; and even when the second picador went down with his gored mount, necessitating hasty tactics on the part of El Mañoso and the fluttering *capeadores* to divert from him the menace of the dripping horns, it was no more to her than a fantastic frolic over a fallen chessman. She had almost a sense of detachment in a certain esthetic enjoyment of the young matador's harmony of movement, his joyous activity, and his masterly manner of directing every detail of the performance according to the exacting rules of bullfighting, at the same time losing no opportunity to delight the crowd with some daring and insolently graceful exploit.

Without comprehension she witnessed the mortal peril of one of the *banderilleros*, those fleet-footed artists, second in popularity to the matador himself, who succeeded the *picadores* in the arena, and whose business it is to implant each his pair of beribboned darts on each side of the ridge of the victim's neck. Twice the trick had been played without fault; but the decorated monster had gained in cunning. At first he feigned a reluctance to charge his challenger—it is only while man and beast are running toward each other that the feat may be performed—then he tried to take him unaware by darting forward with short and speedy stride. The youth ran likewise, arms uplifted, and hurled his banderillas, but whirled aside an instant too late. He was rolled in the dust like a

[44] Amateur or novice bullfighters.

[45] Mounted man with a lance who goads the bull in a bullfight.

rubber ball, and lay bleeding, while the cool gallantry of El Mañoso once more averted death from a fallen comrade. There were hisses for the unlucky one as he was carried off to the infirmary; a *torero* has no more right to get himself hurt than a tenor to sing a false note.

However, the offense was wiped out by a brilliant ensemble in which every performer vied with every other in piquing and bewildering the common enemy, even to vaulting over his back with a pole, at the climax of which, all with one accord scaled nimbly from his view, leaving him to thunder against the palisade, and turn, bellowing through his foam, to attack the impartial sunshine.

A flourish from the judge's trumpet, the signal for death! A stir, a long sigh. The ladies ceased fanning themselves and leaned forward. All save María Concepción! A great pride kept her very indifferent and queenlike. El Mañoso's love must be above anxiety. With a laugh that rang silvery in that moment of suspense, she rallied Enrique on the tensity with which he started at one of the doors in the palisade. It opened for an instant, that stout door, and closed decisively behind El Mañoso. With the confidence of a knight and the elastic step of a ballet-dancer, he presented himself before the box of the president, who had risen to his feet. In a few words, with a gallant gesture, he dedicated himself to the deed he was about to perform. The president bowed. "The sun" acclaimed, expecting that the great *espada* would now favor it with his countenance for the purpose of designating the lucky beauty to whom he elected to pledge his victim, now snuffing the dust and peering at him with red eyes.

But the hero had higher aspirations. Still with his back to "the sun," he wheeled before the box of Senator Montes de Oca, and in ringing tones proffered the fruit of his valor to the lovely and virtuous daughter of that astounded dignitary. María Concepción smiled dreamily, unaware of the startled silence, and of the *murmuración* which followed it. Ages in the past, it seemed to her, this same thing had happened just thus. She raised her bouquet to throw it at the feet of her champion; but her arm was seized in a paralyzing grip. It was the senator, with face of bronze, only his congested eyes, the cording of his forehead, and the bruising power of his grasp, betraying what was passing within him. El Mañoso, bewildered, turned away without the customary "favor" from the object of his homage—turned to face a reversal of mob sentiment, which he perceived as definitely as an odor even before the populace buzzed at him like a hive of exasperated bees. Misguided man! Intoxicated by *ojitos* extraordinary, love instantaneous, dreams presumptuous, he had scandalized "the shade" and slapped the face of "the sun."

And himself betrayed to public mockery, his love scorned, his proud blood of *torero* made to boil by the slighting of the fruit of his sword! His sword—he shook it free of the enwrapping red cloth, hung flagwise on a little staff for which he had discarded his cape, and poised it in his trembling hand. A stinging taunt from "the sun" pierced him like a bullet; then another, followed by a shout of laughter; at the height of which the bull, which had sidled toward him inquisitively, gave a flirt of its tail, and ran at him from behind.

His nerves of *torero* caught, through all the clamor, the vibration of the hoofs, and unaided by a glance, goaded him to an amazing leap, which swung him just clear of that galloping death: it brushed him as it passed. In the yell that greeted his escape relief was almost submerged in censure. Sobered, bottling his rage in his heart, he addressed himself to his work of *espada*. He followed the bull, provoked it, played with it, coaxed and eluded its horns in a hundred capricious feints and maneuvers. He had changed, this El Mañoso. He had lost his belief in justice, his kinship with the people, his gaiety, his dreams—all but his skill, which was diabolical. Never had the Plaza de Toros witnessed such *atormentamiento*.[46]

María Concepción was among the stars. Her spirit soared in revolt, magnificent and comprehensive, against circumstances, society, destiny, against *papá* himself. Unfortunately, her body could neither soar nor revolt, as it was still held tightly in its seat by *papá's* grasp upon her arm, his one desperate idea being to simulate unconsciousness of the appalling disgrace which had overtaken the house of Montes de Oca. But *papá* could not pinion her soul. It was as free at that moment as it would be on the triumphant day when her body should have no more life in it. Already she felt upon her the delicious languor of death—possibly the good doctor's leeches had something to do with that—and while her swimming eyes followed each movement of El Mañoso,

[46] Torture.

her imagination swiftly pictured the course of her closing days on earth. *Papá* would undoubtedly condemn her to return to her beloved College of the Sacred Heart, there to be edified by the good sisters, under durance, and with appropriate penances, until such time as the *escándolo*[47] she had caused in the world might be partly forgotten, and herself graced with sufficient *sobriedad*[48] to restrain her from a repetition of behavior fit only, in *papá's* judgment, for tourists *de los Estados Unidos*.[49] And quite unexpectedly, probably in a week or ten days, she would breathe her last. El Mañoso would hear that news, of course. She hoped that he would live on; but would her spirit have power to dissuade him from following the example of all the love-crossed matadors of romance, who in tragic immolation had presented their breasts to the devastating horns of bulls?

But, see, he kneels, El Mañoso, before her eyes! The bull charges! *¡Qué horror!*[50] She prepared in that instant to expire. But no! The monster's head struck the unresisting cloth. There arose a shout from the crowd, its resentment long since swallowed up in noisy delight. El Mañoso showed his teeth in a caustic smile. He had beaten that two-faced mob to his feet! Royally he had entertained it, far beyond its expectations or deserts, and now it clamored respectfully for the supreme act in the ritual of the bull-ring. So be it! But first he would give those pigs a lesson in manners.

María Concepción heard his voice, addressed to "the sun," to all the world. She heard the stream of Sevillan[51] scurrility, bitterly personal and shockingly frank, with which he lashed the populace who had turned against him, and then turned again. *This* her hero, this bandier of abuse with the unclean mob! Icy cold all over, she saw his sinister laugh as he tempted his victim to embark upon the charge of death. And at the moment of moments, when the bull's agitated heart at last received the sword, and four thousand human mouths gasped as one—then, in the spasm of supreme effort that transfigured his countenance as he celebrated the sacrament of his order, she divined the soul of a high priest of the abattoir. Die of love, she? Rather let her die of shame!

[47] Scandal.

[48] Sobriety.

[49] From the United States.

[50] How horrible!

[51] From Seville.

His triumphal march around the arena, with effeminate swagger and conceited smile, acknowledging the gifts showered upon him—cigars, money, trinkets, and what-not, to be gathered up for him by his attendants; hats and caps to be tossed back to their owners; a ceremonious bag of gold from the president—she saw it all. She looked at her *papá*. He had grown old. Her *papacito*, her handsome little *papá* of the many foibles! She saw him as an ill-used child, to whom she should have been a mother—she, far older now than he. Instead of which, what thing had she done! A trickle of discreet laughter in "the shade" made her heart leap. What if *papá* should be compelled to challenge someone, to fight a duel for the honor which *she* had exposed to mockery? With anguish she implored the Virgin to avert that peril by causing the journals and the gossips at the Jockey Club[52] to be polite and reticent about this affair! Without turning her head, she felt people's eyes playing on her skin like points of fire. She tried to rise, to escape from that abominable place and go home, where she could at least change her dress. But *papá* was exchanging diplomatic bows and smiles with neighboring friends, and pinching her to follow his example. *Papá's* pinches were of a severity to stimulate the most despairful to a renewed interest in life. Four more bulls remained to be despatched, two by the senior matador, and two by that insufferable junior. And hark! "The sun" was beginning again: "*¡Otro toro! ¡Otro toro!*"

[January 1914]

[52] Meeting place for the elite in Mexico City, a "center of Porfirian wealth and elegance" (Camin and Meyer 60).

The Education of Popo

Governor Fernando Arriola and his amiable *señora* were confronted with a critical problem in hospitality: it was nothing less than the entertaining of American ladies, who by all means must be given the most favorable impressions of Mexican civilization.

Hence some unusual preparations. On the backs of men and beasts were arriving magnificent quantities, requisitioned from afar, of American canned soups, fish, meats, sweets, *hors d'oeuvres*, and nondescripts; ready-to-serve cereals, ready-to-drink cocktails, a great variety of pickles, and much other cheer of American manufacture. Even an assortment of can-openers had not been forgotten. Above all, an imperial had gone out for ice, and precious consignments of that exotic commodity were now being delivered in various stages of dissolution, to be installed with solicitude in cool places, and kept refreshed with a continual agitation of fans in the hands of superfluous servants. By such amiable extremities it was designed to insure the ladies Cherry against all danger of going hungry or thirsty for lack of conformable aliment or sufficiently frigid liquids.

The wife and daughter of that admirable *Señor* Montague Cherry of the United States, who was manipulating the extension of certain important concessions in the State of which Don Fernando was governor, and with whose operations his Excellency found his own private interests to be pleasantly involved, their visit was well-timed in a social way, for they would be present on the occasion of a great ball to be given by the governor. For other entertainment of the Arriola family would provide as God might permit. Leonor, the only unmarried daughter, was practicing several new selections on the harp, her mama sagaciously conceiving that an abundance of music might ease the strain of conversation in the event of the visitors having no Spanish. And now Próspero, the only son, aged fourteen, generally known as Popo, blossomed suddenly as the man of the hour; for, thanks to divine Providence, he had been studying English, and could say prettily, although slowly, "What o'clock it is?" and "Please you this," and "Please you that," and doubtless much more if he were put to it.

Separately and in council the rest of the family impressed upon Popo that the honor of the house of Arriola, not to mention that of his native land, reposed in his hands, and he was conjured to comport himself as a true-born *caballero*.[1] With a heavy sense of responsibility upon him, he bought some very high collars, burned much midnight oil over his English "method," and became suddenly censorious of his stockinged legs, which, accompanying him everywhere, decoyed his down-sweeping eyes and defied concealment or palliation. After anxious consideration, he put the case to his mama.

"Thou amiable companion of all my anguishes," he said tenderly, "thou knowest my anxiety to comport myself with credit in the view of the honored Meesees Cherry. Much English I have already, with immobile delivery the most authentic and distinguished. So far I feel myself modestly secure. But these legs, Mama—these legs of my nightmares—"

"*¡Chist, chist!*[2] Thou hadst ever a symmetrical leg, Popo mine," expostulated Doña Elvira, whose soul of a young matron dreaded her boy's final plunge into manhood.

"But consider, little Mama," he cried, "that very soon I shall have fifteen years. Since the last day of my saint I have shaved the face scrupulously on alternate mornings; but that no longer suffices, for my maturing beard now asks for the razor every day, laughing to scorn these legs, which continue to lack the investment of dignity. Mother of my soul, for the honor of our family in the eyes of the foreign ladies, I supplicate thy consent that I should be of long pantaloons!"

[1] Gentleman.
[2] Ssh! Hush!

Touched on the side of her obligations as an international hostess, Doña Elvira pondered deeply, and at length confessed with a sigh:

"It is unfortunately true, thou repose of my fatigues, that in long pantaloons thou wouldst represent more."

And it followed, as a crowning graciousness toward Mrs. Montague Cherry and her daughter, that Popo was promoted to trousers.

When the visitors arrived, he essayed gallantly to dedicate himself to the service of the elder lady, in accordance with Mexican theories of propriety, but found his well-meaning efforts frustrated by the younger one, who, seeing no other young man thereabout, proceeded methodically to attach the governor's handsome little son to herself.

Popo found it almost impossible to believe that they were mother and daughter. By some magic peculiar to the highly original country of the *Yanquis*,[3] their relation appeared to be that of an indifferent sisterliness, with a balance of authority in favor of the younger. That revolutionary arrangement would have scandalized Popo had he not perceived from the first that Alicia Cherry was entitled to extraordinary consideration. Never before had he seen a living woman with hair like daffodils, eyes like violets, and a complexion of coral and porcelain. It seemed to him that some precious image of the Virgin had been changed into a creature of sweet flesh and capricious impulses, animate with a fearless urbanity far beyond the dreams of the dark-eyed, demure, and now despised damsels of his own race. His delicious bewilderment was completed when Miss Cherry, after staring him in the face with a frank and inviting smile, turned to her mother, and drawled laconically:

"He just simply talks with those eyes!"

There was a moon on the night of the day that the Cherrys arrived. There was also music, the bi-weekly *serenata*[4] in the plaza fronting the governor's residence. The band swept sweetly into its opening number at the moment when Don Fernando, with Mrs. Cherry on his arm, stepped out upon his long balcony, and all the town began to move down there among the palms. Miss Cherry,

[3] Yankees, natives of the United States.

[4] Serenade.

who followed with Popo, exclaimed at the romantic strangeness of the scene, and you may be sure that a stir and buzzing passed through the crowd as it gazed up at the glittering coiffure and snowy shoulders of that angelic *señorita* from the United States.

Popo got her seated advantageously, and leaned with somewhat exaggerated gallantry over her chair, answering her vivacious questions, and feeling as one translated to another and far superior planet. He explained as well as he could the social conventions of the *serenata* as unfolded before their eyes in a concerted coil of languid movement—how the ladies, when the music begins, rise and promenade slowly around the kiosk of the band, and how the gentlemen form an outer wheel revolving in the reverse direction, with constant interplay of salutations, compliments, seekings, avoidings, coquetries, intrigues, and a thousand other manifestations of the mysterious forces of attraction and repulsion.

Miss Cherry conceived a strong desire to go down and become merged in that moving coil. No, she would not dream of dragging Doña Elvira or Leonor or mama from the dignified repose of the balcony; but she did beg the privilege, however unprecedented, of promenading with a young gentleman at her side, and showing the inhabitants how such things were managed in America—beg pardon, the United States.

So they walked, together under the palms, Alicia Cherry and Próspero Arriola, and although the youth's hat was in the air most of the time in acknowledgment of salutes, he did not really recognize those familiar and astonished faces, for his head was up somewhere near the moon, while his legs, in the proud shelter of their first trousers, were pleasantly afflicted with pins and needles as he moved on tiptoe beside the blonde *Americana*, a page beside a princess.

Miss Cherry was captivated by the native courtliness of his manners. She thought of a certain junior brother of her own, to whom the business of "tipping his hat," as he called it, to a lady occasioned such extreme anguish of mind that he would resort to the most laborious maneuvers to avoid occasions when the performance of that rite would be expected of him. As for Próspero, he had held tips of her fingers lightly as they had descended the marble steps of his father's house, and then with a charming little bow had offered her his arm, which she with laughing independence had declined. And now she perused with sidelong glances the infantile curve of his chin, the April fluctuations of his lips, the occasional quiver of his thick lashes, and decided that he was an amazingly cute little cavalier.

With a deep breath she expelled everything disagreeable from her mind, and gave up her spirit to the enjoyment of finding herself for a little while among a warmer, wilder people, with gallant gestures and languorous smiles. And the aromatic air, the tantalizing music, the watchful fire that glanced from under the *sombreros* of the *peons* squatting in colorful lines between the benches—all the ardor and mystery of that unknown life caused a sudden fluttering in her breast, and almost unconsciously she took her escort's arm, pressing it impulsively to her side. His dark eyes flashed to hers, and for the first time failed to flutter and droop at the encounter; this time it was her own that lost courage and hastily veiled themselves.

"That waltz," she stammered, "isn't it delicious?"

He told her the name of the composer, and begged her to promise him the privilege of dancing that waltz with her at the ball, in two weeks' time. As she gave the promise, she perceived with amusement, and not without delight, that he trembled exceedingly.

Mrs. Cherry was a little rebellious when she and Alicia had retired to their rooms that night.

"Yes, I suppose it's all very beautiful and romantic," she responded fretfully to her daughter's panegyrics, "but I'm bound to confess that I could do with a little less moonlight for the sake of a few words of intelligible speech."

"One always feels that way at first in a foreign country," said Alicia, soothingly, "and it certainly is splendid incentive to learn the language. You ought to adopt my plan, which is to study Spanish very hard every moment we're here."

"If you continue studying the language," her mother retorted, "as industriously as you have been doing to-night, my dear, you will soon be speaking it like a native."

Alicia was impervious to irony. Critically inspecting her own pink-and-gold effulgence in the mirror, she went on:

"Of course this is also a splendid opportunity for Próspero to learn some real English, which will please the family very much, as they've decided to send him to an American college. I do hope it won't spoil him. Isn't he a perfect darling?"

"I don't know, not having been given a chance to exchange three words with— Sh-h! Did you hear a noise?"

It had sounded like a sigh, followed by a stealthy shuffle. Alicia went to the door, which had been left ajar, and looked out upon the moonlit gallery just in time to catch a glimpse of a fleeting figure, as Próspero raced for his English dictionary, to look up the strange word "darling."

"The little rascal!" she murmured to herself. "What a baby, after all!" But to her mother she only said, as she closed the door, "It was nothing, dear; just one of those biblical-looking servants covering a parrot's cage."

"Even the parrots here speak nothing but Spanish," Mrs. Cherry pursued fretfully. "Of course I am glad to sacrifice my own comfort to any extent to help your dear father in his schemes, although I do think the syndicate might make some graceful little acknowledgment of my social services; but I'm sure that papa never dreamed of your monopolizing the only member of this household to whom it is possible to communicate the most primitive idea without screaming one's head off. I am too old to learn to gesticulate, and I refuse to dislodge all my hairpins in the attempt. And as for your studies in Spanish," she continued warmly, as Alicia laughed, "I'd like to know how you reconcile that pretext with the fact that I distinctly heard you and that infant Lord Chesterfield[5] chattering away together in French."

"French does come in handy at times," Alicia purred, "and if you were not so shy about your accent, Mama dear, you could have a really good time with Doña Elvira. I must ask her to encourage you."

"Don't do anything of the kind!" Mrs. Cherry exclaimed. "You know perfectly well that my French is not fit for foreign ears. And I do think, Alicia, that you might try to make things as easy as possible for me, after my giving way to you in everything, even introducing you here under false pretenses, so to speak."

"It isn't a case of false pretenses, Mama. I've decided to resume my maiden name, and there was no necessity to enter into long explanations to these dear people, who, living as they do in a

[5] Title of Philip Domer Stanhope (1694-1773), English earl and diplomat known for his "honeyed words" (James Boswell).

Catholic-country, naturally know nothing about the blessings of divorce."

"So much the better for them!" retorted Mrs. Cherry. "However much of a blessing divorce may be, I've noticed that since you got your decree your face has not had one atom of real enjoyment in it until to-night."

"Until to-night!" Alicia echoed with a stoical smile. "And to-night, because you see a spark of reviving interest in my face, you try to extinguish it with reproaches!"

"No, no, my darling. Forgive me, I'm a little tired and nervous. And I can't help being anxious about you. It's a very trying position for a woman to be in at your age. It's trying for your mother, too. I could box that wretched Edward's ears."

"Not very hard, I'm thinking. You wanted me to forgive him."

"No, my dear, only to take him back on probation. We can punish men for their favorite sins much more effectually by not giving them their freedom."

"I couldn't be guilty of that meanness, and I shall never regret having shown some dignity. And I think that closes the subject, doesn't it, dearest?" Alicia yawned.

"Poor Edward!" her mother persisted. "How he would have enjoyed this picturesque atmosphere with you!"

Alicia calmly creamed her face.

Próspero spent a great part of the night over his English dictionary. Again and again he conned the Spanish equivalents listed against that word "darling." A significant word, it seemed, heart-agitating, sky-transporting. He had not dreamed that the harsh, baffling English language could contain in seven letters a treasure so rare. *Predilecto, querido, favorito, amado*[6]—which translation should he accept as defining his relation to Mees Cherry, avowed by her own lips? The patient compiler of that useful book could never have foreseen the ecstasy it would one day bring to a Mexican boy's heart.

He was living in a realm of enchantment. To think that already, on the very day of their meeting, he and his blonde Venus should have arrived at intimacies far transcending any that are possible in Mexico except between the wedded or the wicked! In stark free-

[6] Synonyms: preferred; loved, darling; favorite; dear, beloved, sweetheart.

dom, miraculously unchaperoned, they had talked together, walked together, boldly linked their very arms! In his ribs he still treasured the warmth of her; in his fingers throbbed the memory that for one electric instant their hands had fluttered, dove-like, each to each. Small enough, those tender contacts; yet by such is the life force unchained: Popo found himself looking into a seething volcano, which was his own manhood. That discovery, conflicting as it did with the religious quality of his love, disturbed him mightily. Sublimely he invoked all his spiritual strength to subdue the volcano. And his travail was richly rewarded. The volcano became transformed magically into a fount of pellucid purity in which, bathing his exhausted soul, young Popo became a saint.

In that interesting but arduous capacity he labored for many days, during which Miss Cherry created no further occasion for their being alone together, but seemed to throw him in the way of her mama, a trial which he endured with fiery fortitude. He was living the spiritual life with rigorous intensity, a victim of the eternal mandate that those fountains of purity into which idealism has power to transform the most troublesome of volcanoes should be of a temperature little short of the boiling-point.

His dark eyes kept his divinity faithfully informed of his anguish and his worship, and her blue ones discreetly accepted the offering. Once or twice their hands met lightly, and it seemed that the shock might have given birth to flaming worlds. When alone with her mama, Alicia showed signs of an irritable ardor which Mrs. Cherry, with secret complacency, set down to regrets for the too hastily renounced blessings of matrimony.

"Poor old Ned!" the mother sighed one night. "Your father has seen him, and tells me that he looks dreadful."

On the morning of the night of the ball the entire party, to escape from the majordomo[7] and his gang of hammering decorators, motored into the country on a visit to Popo's grandmother, whose house sheltered three priests and a score of orphan girls, and was noted for its florid magnificence of the Maximilian period.[8]

[7] Head servant of a wealthy household.

[8] Maximilian, Archduke of Austria, was declared the emperor of Mexico by France's Napoleon III in 1863. He was executed by Mexican troops in 1867.

Popo hoped that some mention might be made in Alicia's hearing of his grandmother's oft-expressed intention to bequeath the place to him, and he was much gratified when the saintly old lady, who wore a mustache *á la española*,[9] brought up the subject, and dilated upon it at some length, telling Popo that he must continue to make the house blessed by the presence of the three padres, but that she would make provision for the orphans to be taken elsewhere, out of his way, a precaution she mentioned to an accompaniment of winks and innuendoes which greatly amused all the company, including the padres, only Alicia and Popo showing signs of distress.

After dinner, which occurred early in the afternoon, Popo maneuvered Alicia apart from the others in the garden. His eyes telegraphed a desperate plea, to which hers consented, and he took her by the hand, and they ran through a green archway into a terraced Italian garden peopled with marble nymphs and fauns, from which they escaped by a little side gate into an avenue of orange-blossoms. Presently they were laboring over rougher ground, where their feet crushed the fat stems of lilies, and then they turned and descended a roughly cut pat winding down the scarred, dripping face of a cliff into the green depth of a little *cañón*,[10] at the upper end of which a cascade resembling a scarf flung over a wall sang a song of eternity, and baptized the tall tree-ferns that climbed in disorderly rivalry for its kisses.

Alicia breathed deeply the cool, moss-scented air. The trembling boy, suddenly appalled at the bounty of life in presenting him with his sovereign concatenation of the hour, the place, and the woman, could only stammer irrelevantly, as he switched at the leaves with his cane:

"There is a cave in there behind the waterfall. One looks through the moving water as through a thick window, but one gets wet. Sometimes I come here alone, all alone, without going to the house, and *mamagrande*[11] never knows. The road we came by passes just below, crossing this little stream, where thou didst remark the tall bamboos before we saw the porter's lodge. The mud wall is low, and I tie my horse in the bamboo thicket."

[9] In the Spanish style.

[10] Canyon. *Cañoncito*: little canyon.

[11] Grandmother.

"Why do you come here?" she asked, her eyes tracing the Indian character in the clear line of his profile and the dusky undertone of his cheek.

"It is my caprice to meditate here. From my childhood I have loved the *cañoncito* in a peculiar way. Thou wilt laugh at me—no? Well, I have always felt a presence here, unseen, a very quiet spirit that seemed to speak to me of—*¿quién sabe?*[12] I never knew—never until now."

His voice thrilled, and his eyes lifted themselves to hers, as if for permission, before he continued in ringing exaltation:

"Now that thou hast come, now that thou appearest here in all thy lovely splendor, now I know that the spirit I once felt and loved in secret was a prophecy of thee. Yes, Alicia mine, for thee this place has waited long—for thee, thou adored image of all beauty, queen of my heart, object of my prayers, whose purity has sanctified my life."

Alicia, a confirmed matinée girl, wished that all her woman friends might have seen her at that moment (she had on a sweet frock and a perfectly darling hat), and that they might have heard the speech that had just been addressed to her by the leading man. He was a thorough juvenile, to be sure, but he had lovely, adoring eyes and delightfully passionate tones in his voice; and, anyhow, it was simply delicious to be made love to in a foreign language.

She was extremely pleased, too, to note that her own heart was going pitapat in a fashion quite uncomfortable and sweet and girly. She wouldn't have missed that sensation for a good deal. What a comfort to a bruised heart to be loved like this! He was calling her his saint. If that Edward could only hear him! Perhaps, after all, she *was* a saint. Yes, she felt that she certainly was, or could be if she tried. Now he was repeating some verses that he had made to her in Spanish. Such musical words! One had to come to the hot countries to discover what emotion was; and as for love-making! How the child had suffered!

As he bowed his bared head before her she laid her hands, as in benediction, where a bronze light glanced upon the glossy, black waves of his hair; and that touch, so tender, felled Popo to the earth, where he groveled with tears and broken words and kisses for her little shoes, damp from the spongy soil. And she suddenly dropped

[12] Who knows?

her posings and her parasol, and forgot her complexion and her whalebones,[13] and huddled down beside him in the bracken, hushing his sobs and wiping his face, with sweet epithets and sweeter assurances, finding a strange, wild comfort in mothering him recklessly, straight from the soul. At the height of which really promising situation she was startled by a familiar falsetto hail from her mama as the rest of the party descended into the *cañoncito*, whither it had been surmised that Popo had conducted Miss Cherry.

After flinging an artless yodel in response to the maternal signal, and while composing Popo and herself into lifelike attitudes suggestive of a mild absorption in the beauties of nature, she whispered in his ear:

"The next time you come here you shall have two horses to tie in the bamboos."

"*¡Ay Dios!* All blessings on thee! But when?" he pleaded. "Tell me when!"

"Well, to-morrow," she replied after quick thought; "as you would say, my dear, *mañana*. Yes, I'll manage it. I'm dying for a horseback ride, and I've had such a lovely time today."

To be the only blonde at a Mexican ball is to be reconciled for a few hours to the fate of being a woman. Alicia, her full-blown figure habited in the palest of pink, which seemed of the living texture of her skin, with a generous measure of diamonds winking in effective constellations upon her golden head and dazzling bosom, absorbed through every pore the enravished admiration of the beholders, and beneficently poured it forth again in magnetic waves of the happiness with which triumph enhances beauty. Popo almost swooned with rapture at this apotheosis of the being who, a few hours earlier, had actually hugged him in the arms now revealed as those of a goddess. And to-morrow! With swimming brain he repeated over and over, as if to convince himself of the incredible, "*¡Mañana!*"

Almost as acute as the emotions of Popo, in a different way, were those of a foreign gentleman who had just been presented to the governor by the newly arrived Mr. Montague Cherry. So palpably moved was the stranger at the sight of Alicia that Mrs.

[13] Plates from the upper jaw of some whales, used to corset women's dresses.

Cherry laid a soothing hand on his arm and whispered a conspirator's caution. Presently he and Alicia stood face to face. Had they been Mexican, there would have ensued an emotional and edifying scene. But all that Alicia said, after one sharp inspiration of surprise, was, with an equivocal half-smile:

"Why, Edward! Of all people!"

And the gentleman addressed as Edward, finding his voice with difficulty, blurted out hoarsely:

"How are you, Alicia?"

At which Alicia turned smilingly to compliment Doña Elvira on the decorations.

Mr. Edward P. Winterbottom was one of those fortunate persons who seem to prefigure the ideal toward which their race is striving. A thousand conscientious draftsmen, with that national ideal in their subconsciousness, were always hard at work portraying his particular type in various romantic capacities, as those of foot-ball hero, triumphant engineer, "well-known clubman," and pleased patron of the latest collar, cigarette, sauce, or mineral water. Hence he would give you the impression of having seen him before somewhere under very admirable auspices. Extremely good-looking, with long legs, a magnificent chin, and an expression of concentrated manhood, he had every claim to be classed as "wholesome," cherishing a set of opinions suitable to his excellent station in life, a proper reverence for the female of the species, and an adequate working assortment of simple emotions easily predicable by a reasonably clever woman. Of the weaknesses common to humanity he had fewer than the majority, and in the prostration of remorse and desire in which he now presented himself to Alicia he seemed to offer timber capable of being made over into a prince of lifelong protectors.

Alicia had come to feel that she needed a protector, chiefly from herself. Presently, without committing herself, however, she favored him with a waltz. As they started off, she saw the agonized face of Popo, who had been trying to reach her. She threw him a smile, which he lamentably failed to return. Not until then did she identify the music as that of the waltz she had promised him on the night of that first *serenata*. After it was over she good-naturedly missed a dance or two in search of him, meaning to make amends; but he was nowhere to be found.

With many apologies, Doña Elvira mentioned to Alicia, when she appeared the following morning, that the household was somewhat perturbed over the disappearance of Próspero. No one could remember having seen him since early in the progress of the ball. He had not slept in his bed, and his favorite horse was missing from the stable. Don Fernando had set the police in motion. Moreover, *la mamagrande*, informed by telephone, was causing masses to be said for the safety of her favorite. God would undoubtedly protect him, and meanwhile the honored *señorita* and her mama would be so very gracious as to attribute any apparent neglect of the canons of hospitality to the anxieties of an unduly affectionate mother.

Alicia opened her mouth to reply to that tremulous speech, but finding no voice, turned and bolted to her room, trying to shut out a vision of a slender boy lying self-slain among the ferns where he had received caresses and whispers of love from a goddess of light fancy and lighter faith. She had no doubt that he was there in his *cañoncito*. But perhaps he yet lived, waiting for her! She would go at once. Old Ned should escort her as far as the bamboos, to be within call in case of the worst.

Old Ned was so grateful for the privilege of riding into the blossoming country with his Alicia that she rewarded him with a full narration of the Popo episode; and he received the confidence with discreet respect, swallowing any qualms of jealousy, and extolling her for the high-minded sense of responsibility which now possessed her to the point of tears.

"It's all your fault, anyway," she declared as they walked their horses up a long hill.

He accepted the blame with alacrity as a breath of the dear connubial days.

"One thing I've demonstrated," she continued fretfully, "and that is that the summer flirtation of our happy land simply cannot be acclimated south of the Rio Grande.[14] These people lack the necessary imperturbability of mind, which may be one good reason why they're not permitted to hold hands before the marriage ceremony. To complicate matters, it seems that I'm the first blonde with the slightest claim to respectability that ever invaded this part of Mexico, and although the inhabitants have a deluded idea that

[14] River forming the natural border between Texas and Mexico.

blue eyes are intensely spiritual, they get exactly the same Adam-and-Eve palpitations from them that we do from the lustrous black orbs of the languishing tropics."

"Did you—ah—did you get as far as—um—kissing?" Mr. Winterbottom inquired, with an admirable air of detachment.

"Not quite, Edward; that was where the rest of the folks came tagging along. But I promise you this: if I find that Popo alive, I'm going to kiss him for all I'm worth. The unfortunate child is entitled to nothing less."

"But wouldn't that—hum—add fuel to the flame?" he asked anxiously.

"It would give him back his self-respect," she declared. "It isn't healthy for a high-spirited boy to feel like a worm."

Mr. Winterbottom, while waiting among the bamboos in company with three sociable horses–Popo's was in possession when they arrived—smoked one very long cigar and chewed another into pulpy remains. Alicia not having yodeled, he understood that he had found the boy alive, and he tried to derive comfort from that reflection. He had promised to preserve patience and silence, and such was his anxiety to propitiate Alicia that he managed to subjugate his native energy, although the process involved the kicking up of a good deal of soil. She reflected, when she noted on her return his carefully cheerful expression, that a long course of such discipline would go far toward regenerating him as a man and a husband.

"Well, how is our little patient today?" he inquired with gentle jocosity as he held the stirrup for her.

"I believe he'll pull through now," Alicia responded gravely, "I've sent him up to his grandmother's to be fed, and he's going to telephone his mother right away."

"That's bully," Mr. Winterbottom pronounced heartily; and for some moments, as they gained the road, nothing more was said. Alicia seemed thoughtful. Mr. Winterbottom was the first to speak.

"Poor little beggar must have been hungry," he hazarded.

"He had eaten a few bananas, but as they're not recognized as food here, they only increased his humiliation. You know, banana-trees are just grown to shade the coffee-plants, which are delicate."

Mr. Winterbottom signified a proper interest in that phase of coffee culture, and Alicia took advantage of a level stretch of road to put her horse to the gallop. When he regained her side, half a mile farther on, he was agitated.

"Alicia, would you mind enlightening me on one point?" he asked. "Did you—give him back his self-respect?"

"Perhaps I'd better tell you all that happened, Edward."

"By Jove! I wish you would!" he cried earnestly.

"Well, Popo wasn't a bit surprised to see me. In face, he was expecting me."

"Indeed? Hadn't lost his assurance, then."

"He had simply worked out my probable actions, just as I had worked out his. Of course he looked like a wild thing, hair on end, eyes like a panther, regular young bandit. Well, I rag-timed up in my best tra-la-la style, but he halted me with a splendid gesture, and started a speech. You know what a command of language foreigners have, even the babies. He never fumbled for a word, and all his nouns had verbs waiting, and the climaxes just rolled over one another like waves. It was beautiful."

"But what was it about?"

"Me, of course: my iniquity, the treacherous falseness residing as ashes in the Dead Sea fruit of my beauty, with a lurid picture of the ruin I had made of his belief in woman, his capacity for happiness, and all that. And he wound up with a burst of denunciation in which he called me by a name which ought not to be applied to any lady in any language."

"Alicia!"

"Oh, I deserved it, Edward, and I told him so. I didn't care how badly he thought of me if I could only give him back his faith in love. It's such a wonderful thing to get *that* back! So I sang pretty small about myself; and when I revealed my exact status as an ex-wife in process of being courted by her divorced husband, his eyes nearly dropped out of his head. You see, they don't play 'Tag! You're it!' with marriage down here. That boy actually began to hand me out a line of missionary talk. He thinks I ought to remarry you, Ned."

"He must have splendid instincts, after all. So of course you didn't kiss him?"

"Wait a minute. After mentioning that I was eleven years older than he, and that my hair had been an elegant mouse-drab before I started touching it up—"

"Not at all. I liked its color—a very pretty shade of—"

"After that, I told him that he could thank his stars for the education I had given him, in view of the fact that he's going to be sent to college in the U.S.A., and I gave him a few first-rate pointers on the college widow breed. And finally, Ned, I put it to him that I was anxious to do the square thing, and if he considered himself entitled to a few kisses while you were waiting, he could help himself."

"And he?" Mr. Winterbottom inquired with a pinched look.

"He looked so cute that I could have hugged him. But he nobly declined."

"That young fellow," said Mr. Winterbottom, taking off his hat and wiping his brow, "is worthy of being an American."

"Why, that was his Indian revenge, the little monkey! But he was tempted, Ned."

"Of course he was. If you'd only tempt *me*! O Alicia, you're a saint!"

"That's what Popo called me yesterday, and it was neither more nor less true than what he called me today. I suppose we're all mixtures of one kind and another. And I've discovered, Ned, that it's the healthiest kind of fun to be perfectly frank with—with an old pal. Let's try it that way next time, shall we, dear?"

She offered her lips for the second time that day, and—

[March 1914]

The Birth of the God of War

When I had been attentive and obliging, my grandmother would tell me stories of our pristine ancestors. She had many *cuentos*[1] by heart, which she told in flowery and rhythmic prose that she never varied by a word; and those epic narrations, often repeated, engraved a network of permanent channels in the memory-stuff of one small child. Indeed, the tales of *mamagrande*[2] were so precious to me that I would pray for afternoons of shade, which were the propitious ones, and I almost hated the sun, because when it baked our patio my grandmother would not occupy her favorite hammock, nor I my perch near by, on the margin of the blue-tiled fountain. And I invented a plan by which I could earn a reward.

Her cigarettes, which were very special, came from the coast once a month, packed in a cane box. Tapering at one end and large at the other, in wrappings of corn-husk, they were fastened together in cone-shaped bundles of twenty-five, and tied at apex and base with cornhusk ribbon. Now, I knew that *mamagrande* disliked to untie knots (she had often called me to unknot the waxed thread of her embroidering), so I would privately overhaul her stock of cigarettes, making five very tight knots at each end of each cone; and then at the golden hour I would watch from behind the flowerpots on the upper gallery for her tall figure in spreading black silk, with her fan in her hand and her little gold cigarette-pincers hanging at her waist. When she appeared, I would wait breathlessly for the business of her getting settled in her hammock, and suddenly calling me in a sweet, troubled voice to release a cone of cigarettes;

[1] Stories.

[2] Grandmother.

whereupon I would run down to her and untie those bad little knots with such honeyed affability that she would proceed to recompense me from her store of Aztec mythology.

It was not mythology to me; no, indeed. I knew that *mamagrande* was marvelously old—almost as old as the world, perhaps—and although she denied, doubtless from excessive modesty, having enjoyed the personal acquaintance of any gods or heroes, I had a dim feeling that her intimate knowledge of the facts connected with such unusual events as, for instance, the birth of Huitzilopochtli,[3] was in its origin more or less neighborly and reminiscent.

Huitzilopochtli was the god of war. More honored anciently in sacrificial blood than any other deity ever set up by man, I loved him once for his mother's sake, for his gallant and wonder-stirring birth, and for the eagle light in the black eyes of my grandmother as she pronounced his name.

It is not so difficult to pronounce as might be thought. "Weet-zee-lo-potchtlee," spoken quickly and clearly with the accent on the "potch," will come somewhere near it, though it lack the relishing curl of my grandmother's square-cut lips. And the god's sweet mother Coatlicue may safely be called "Kwaht-lee-quay," with the accent on the "lee." But I had better begin at the beginning, as my grandmother always did, after lighting her first cigarette, and while adjusting the gold pincers in a hand like a dried leaf.

"The forests have their mysteries, which are sung in their own language by the waters, the breezes, the birds."

Thus *mamagrande* would begin in a hushed voice, with a wave of the hand that would make the blue smoke of her cigarette flicker in the air like a line of handwriting.

"Nature weeps and laughs, sings and cries, and man listens to that weeping and that laughter without knowing the cause. When the branch of the tree inclines itself under the weight of the wind, it speaks, it sings, or it cries. When the water of the forest runs murmuring, it tells a story; and its voice may be accordingly either a whisper or a harsh accent.

[3] Chief deity and god of war of the Aztecs. "He is said to have guided the Aztecs during their migration from Aztlan. . . He was also god of the sun, and it was believed that he was born each morning from the womb of Coatlicue, goddess of the earth" (*Columbia Encyclopedia,* 1993 ed.).

"Listen to the legend of the forest; listen to it as sung by the birds, the breezes, the waters! The hunters have arrived. The forest is full of the thunder of their cries, and the mountain repeats from echo to echo those shouts which threaten peace and happiness. Our ancestors, the Aztecs, loved the hunt because it was the counterpart of war.

"Camatzin has given the signal to begin. His dart traverses the air and, trembling, buries itself in the heart of the stag, which falls without life. Only the great hunter Camatzin can wound in this manner; only from his bow of ebony can spring the arrows that carry certain death. At the running of the first blood the fury of the hunters is kindled. All at one time draw their bows, and a thousand arrows traverse the air, covering as a cloud of passage the brilliant face of the sun. The slaughter has begun, the fight between the irrational and man, between force and cunning."

Alas! The sonorous imagery of those well-remembered phrases loses much in my attempt to render them in sober English. Hasten we, then, to the encounter between Camatzin and the lioness, which, with its cub, the hunter has pursued to its lair.

"She raises the depressed head, she opens the mandibles, armed with white and sharp teeth. Her red tongue cleans hastily the black snout. She contracts her members of iron, and prepares to launch herself upon him who approaches.

"Camatzin is valiant. He trembles not before death, but he understands the danger of the fight with the ruler of the forest. Woe to him if he misses his aim!

"The gaze of the lioness finds that of Camatzin. Two clouds meet; they clash, and give forth a ray which strikes death. The dart sings from the bow, and nails itself in the body of the cub. Roars this for the last time—"

"Ruge éste por la vez postrera," as it rolled out in my grandmother's voice, the *éste* signifying that ill-fated cub, for which I always wept. I render the construction literally because it seems to carry more of the perfume that came with those phrases as I heard them by the blue-tiled fountain.

"Roars this for the last time, and the mother roars with sorrow and anger. She sniffs at the blood that issues from the body of her young. She crouches, and so launches herself outside of the cave.

"Shines the solar ray in her red pupils! Moves *suavemente*[4] her tail, which strikes her sides! Walks her gaze all around her!"

How expressive, in the mouth of *mamagrande*, was that desperate reconnoiter, and how plainly I could see the beast's yellow gaze "walking" from object to object!

"She straightens her members, as if to assure herself that they will not relax. She crouches with all her weight on her rear feet, and throws herself at Camatzin. He, without retreating, aims his bow, and the wild beast falls with its loins to earth, wounded in the right eye.

"Roars she, and the forest trembles to her roaring. She recovers, she rises, and so rapid is her movement that Camatzin cannot aim in time. The arrow falls without point at the foot of the rock. The bow is useless, brave Camatzin; take the *macana!*[5] He lifts his great saber of wood edged with sharp flint, and the lion receives a well-aimed blow in the center of the forehead. Now the attack is body against body! Falls the *macana*, but already the beast has driven its potent claw in the muscular arm of Camatzin. He wishes to show his force, which has made him respected by all; but the beast continually tears his flesh, and he grows weaker."

But in mercy to the reader I'll leave the end of that ferocious conflict to the imagination, and turn to the fortunes of the beloved and blessed Coatlicue.

"Now, Camatzin had a wife," my grandmother would continue softly, after I had supplied her with a fresh cigarette, "of noble lineage, like himself. She was called the loving wife, the saintly woman, by the hearth and in the temple; and her name was Coatlicue.[6]

"Coatlicue sees the night arrive and turn darker and darker. The owl sings; the husband delays longer than usual. The wind moans in the forest, and the branches bend as in prayer. When the hunters return at last, their arrival startles Coatlicue, as they had not announced their coming with the usual cries of victory. On their shoulders they bring the spoils of the day—the torn body of Camatzin! Coatlicue embraces the corpse of Camatzin, and her

[4] Smoothly.

[5] Ironwood club used by some indigenous peoples.

[6] The mother of Huitzilopochtli. "Goddess of love and of sin, with the power to create and devour life" (Rebolledo 51). This goddess has been a central figure in Chicana literature and revisionist literary theory.

children gaze with tear-blurred eyes at the relic that death has sent them."

After a moving description of that first night of bereavement—a description in which the mystic voices of nature sounded their significant notes, my grandmother would proceed to recite in measured rhetoric the spiritual stages by which Coatlicue found consolation in religion. For the Aztecs, apart from and above their hero demigods, to one of whom this saintly widow was destined to give birth, worshipped an invisible Ruler of the Universe.

"Daily, when the afternoon falls, Coatlicue burns incense in the temple to the god of her ancestors, at the feet of whose image her beloved Camatzin had deposited a thousand times the laurels of his victories in the hunt and in war. Religion is the consolation unique in these afflictions. When cries the soul, only one balsam exists to cure its wound. Pray, souls that cry, if you wish that your pains be diminished!

"Arrived the autumn, and the afternoons became painted with rich reds, the nights tepid and clear. The first night of full moon bathed in its pale light the temple and Coatlicue, who prayed there. That night she felt a certain pleasure in her weeping. It was no longer that which tears the heart in order to come forth; no, it was the sweet balsam that cures a wound. When her children saw her coming in, they felt themselves happy, because for the first time they saw her smile."

My grandmother would dwell significantly on that smile, which seemed to mark a vague annunciation in the legend of miraculous birth, to be followed in the morning by a miracle of conception narrated with a naïve brevity which always took my breath away.

"Then came the *aurora,*[7] and it was the first day that the heavens had beautiful color and light since the first day of orphanage. Ran Coatlicue to the temple, and censed the idol and cleaned the floor carefully, according to her custom. The sun was ascending when a white cloud concealed the radiant face of the king of the heavens.

"Lifts Coatlicue her eyes, and fixes them in space. With all the colors of the rainbow appears one brilliant little cloud that, tearing itself from heaven, reaches the temple: it was a ball of plumes; not

[7] Dawn.

more brilliant have the birds of the earth. It rolled over the altar, and fell to the floor. Coatlicue, with respectful gesture, took the plumes and guarded them in the bosom of her white robe. She censed the idol anew, prayed, and started for home. Before descending the last step of the temple she looked in her bosom for the plumes, but they had vanished!"

Such was the conception of the Mexican god of war, and it brought strife into the home of Coatlicue. All ignorant of the miracle that had been wrought, the children of Camatzin presumed to be scandalized at the ineffable happiness that had descended upon their mother, and to conspire against her life. Her own daughter was the malignant ringleader, taunting her two brothers with cowardice, and invoking vengeance in the name of the dead father's honor. And she, with her younger brother, sealed a pact of blood. Their mother felt a change in their regard, and trembled with fear before them, and marveled greatly at the remembrance of the celestial token that had disappeared in her bosom. Meditating on her unworthiness, she deemed it impossible that she should have been chosen by the divinity to engender a god, and she went to the temple to pray for light.

In sharp whispers, with narrowed eyes, my grandmother would go on to describe how the two conspirators followed their mother furtively into the gloom of the temple. Armed with a knife, the son fell upon her as she prayed. A terrible cry filled the space.

"Son of mine, stop thy hand! Wait! Give heed!"

"Adulteress!"

She feared not death, but wished to pray for the assassin, whose fate, she knew, would be more dreadful than his crime. But now sounded a new voice, a stentorian voice which made the temple quake:

"Mother, fear not! I will save thee!"

How it thrilled, the voice of *mamagrande*, as she repeated the first words of the god! And how it thrilled the little heart of the never-wearied listener! And then:

"The hills repeat the echo of those words. All space shines with a beautiful light, which bathes directly the face of Coatlicue. The assassin remains immobile, and the sister mute with terror, as from the bosom of Coatlicue springs forth a being gigantic, strange. His head is covered with the plumage of hummingbirds; in his right hand he carries the destructive *macana,* on his left arm the shining shield. Irate the face, fierce the frown. With one blow of the *macana*, on his left arm the shining shield. Irate the face, fierce the frown. With one blow of the *macana* he strikes his brother lifeless, and with another his sister, the instigator of the crime. Thus was born the potent Huitzilopochtli, protector-genius of the Aztecs."

And Coatlicue, the gentle Coatlicue of my childish love? Throned in clouds of miraculously beautiful coloring, she was forthwith transported to heaven. Once I voiced the infantile view that the fate of Coatlicue was much more charming than that of the Virgin Mary, who had remained on this sad earth as the wife of a carpenter; but *mamagrande* was so distressed, and signed my forehead and her own so often, and made me repeat so many credos, and disquieted me so with a vision of a feathered Apache coming to carry me off to the mountains, that I was brought to a speedy realization of my sin, and never repeated it. Ordinarily *mamagrande* would conclude pacifically:

"Such, attentive little daughter mine, is the legend narrated to the Aztec priests by the forests, the waters, and the birds. And on Sunday, when *papacito*[8] carries thee to the cathedral, fix it in thy mind that the porch, foundation, and courtyard of that saintly edifice remain from the great temple built by our warrior ancestors for the worship of the god Huitzilopochtli. Edifice immense and majestic, it extended to what today is called the Street of the Silversmiths, and that of the Old Bishop's House, and on the north embraced the streets of the Incarnation, Santa Teresa, and Monte Alegre. I am a little fatigued, *chiquita.*[9] Rock thy little old one to sleep."

[May 1914]

[8] Your daddy.
[9] My dear little girl.

Doña Rita's Rivals

With her packet of love-letters in her hand, Alegría returned to the roof—Alegría Peralta, the band-master's daughter, who had committed the error of loving above her. She should have known better than to imagine that she would ever be received into a family of hat, she who was of shawl.

Such distinctions are not to be ignored, for Mexico is the land of resignation. The females of a family of shawl—*de tápalo*—do not aspire to decorate their heads with millinery, for the excellent reason that God has not assigned them to the caste *de sombrero*. Their consolation is that they may look down upon those *de rebozo*. No maid or matron of shawl would demean her respectable shoulders with the *rebozo*—it is woven long and narrow, and is capable of being draped in a variety of graceful and significant ways—but, contrariwise, young ladies of hat, authentic *señoritas*, to whom the mere contact of a shawl would impart "flesh of chicken," delight to dignify the national investment by wearing it coquettishly at country feasts. Persons of *rebozo*—one never speaks of "families" so far down the social scale—are the women of petty tradespeople, servants, artisans. They, in their turn, have consolation.

As for the family of Jesús María Ixtlan, who had taught Alegría Peralta to love him, it was even more than of hat, as Doña Rita Azpe de Ixtlan had just reminded the young woman, in the course of the long and convincing speech whereby she had prevailed upon her to surrender her lover's letters and her own hopes—more than of hat, for by warrant of antiquity of inveterate usage it was of carriage.

Doña Rita, the mother of Jesús María, was waiting for Alegría on the roof of the populous "house of neighborhood" in which Peralta, the band-master, made his home. The girl had escorted her elegant visitor to the roof because it was quieter there than in the Peralta *vivienda*[1] in the second patio, and was mercifully secluded. She foreboded humiliation from this unannounced and clandestine visit. Now that she had been brought to believe the incredible—that Jesús María had bent like grass beneath the wind of tradition, and that all was over—she bore herself remarkably well. Doña Rita was pleased to see her approach with a light step, holding her head proudly, although the blood had gone from her cheeks, leaving them the color of burned milk. She was a tall girl, slim and square-shouldered, not considered handsome. Her eyebrows were too thick, her mouth was too large, and her temples and jaws were veiled with a fine, bluish down, shading into the line of her hair. However, her nose was delicately aquiline, and her eyes were of the type most admired in Mexico—very long and oblique, shadowed with heavy lashes; the irises were the color of cognac. There was a legend among the neighbors that she was talented; it was certain that she had a peculiar habit of pressing her hands to her temples.

She made that identical gesture now as she resigned her packet of letters and looked out over the flat roofs of the city, and something in the curve of her throat recalled to Doña Rita the memory of a young stag she had once seen at the edge of a forest. She felt sorry for the girl and made her a particularly gracious speech, praising her for her excellent sense, giving her a multitude of good wishes, and promising to commend her in her prayers. Then, leaving her on the roof, she slowly descended the stone steps, delighted with the reward of her intrepidity. She to have ventured alone and on foot into a neighborhood of shawl, and so to have saved her darling son! And the day, how well chosen! A baptism was being celebrated in the interior patio; the air thrilled with a tinkling of laughter and mandolins, and the rest of the house was deserted. She passed the porter's room and the charcoal-seller's without being seen. How God was on her side! It was true that she had lied to the girl, but with a motive how noble! And even although Jesús María had not delegated her to do this thing, on the contrary had not known of her discovery of his love, she felt

[1] Self-contained unit or floor within a house or larger building.

assured that she could easily have brought him to the proper frame of mind if she had deemed it politic to take him into her confidence before dealing with his inamorata. Now, with the help of God and a little diplomacy, she could manage him admirably. How fortunate than an anonymous letter should have warned her of that folly in time for her to interfere!

When she reached the street, some men were lifting a woman from the pavement. Doña Rita was turning away, supposing it a case of drunkenness, when she heard one say, "It is Alegría Peralta." She almost cried out: "It cannot be! Alegría Peralta is on the roof!" but her throat suddenly dried. The dress looked familiar. They were carrying her into the porter's room. Doña Rita wished to follow, to find out whether she was hurt much, to proffer aid, and above all to ask her how she had happened to fall; but caution impelled her to walk away from that neighborhood as fast as she could. She entered the first church on her way, and prayed for a long time. Then she began to read the letters her son had written to that girl.

They made her tremble. She had lived until that hour to learn that a young woman of shawl might be capable of moving an Ixtlan to woo her with all the delicacy of his caste, and a little more; to learn that her studious, docile Jesús María was a poet. All her maternity, all the sex in her, vibrated to the passion of his phrases. Dried flowers slipped into her agitated hands, and perished there; and their particles drifted away in the gloom like ghosts of dead kisses. She wept. Why, why had she never divined and absorbed her son's heart, she who had adored him? She read on through later letters, born of ripened sympathies of heart and mind, and then through letters which told her that Jesús María was infected with that most dangerous of distempers, patriotism. Her child to be playing fearlessly with scorpions masquerading under specious titles—*reforma electoral,*[2] *cumplimiento de garantías constitucionales,*[3] *civilización para los peones,*[4] *¡Méjico para los Mejicanos!*[5] He, son of a general immortalized equestrianly in bronze, student at the military college, sole surviving hope of a line the perspective of which vanished among the lords and priests of an extinct civilization—he,

[2] Electoral reform.
[3] Fulfillment of constitutional guarantees.
[4] Civilization for the laborers.
[5] Mexico for the Mexicans!

Jesús María Ixtlan y Azpe, to be imperiling his future by concerning himself about the base fortunes of *los enredados!*

Last, although far from least in the table of social precedence, consolation of the unregarded persons of *rebozo* (*los enredados* are literally "the wrapped-ups"). They do not live in cities, these, but a few straggle in from neighboring pueblos with great baskets of country produce, which they sing in the patios in haunting, minor cadences. They are pleasing to the artist eye, and are full of sorrows. Strong, supple, ingratiating, skillful at fashioning curious and exquisite treasures out of nothing, they are natural minstrels and persifleurs,[6] prone to humor, irony, hypocrisy, and the melancholy that complains as a requiem in their very dances. Easily moved to tears, sensitive in love, swift and treacherous in quarrel, with plastic gestures, and eyes as lovely as those of Jersey cattle, they are ignorant of all save the saints, who do not help them. Sometimes they are slaves in all but name, and sometimes they are bandits—one chooses one's trade—but for the most part they live in peaceable squalor, with song and suffering and weaving of flowers, replenishing the earth. The social superstructure, with its mines, plantations, and railroads, its treasure-house cathedrals, and its admired palace of government, rests on their backs—for they are the people, prolific of labor and taxes—but otherwise they do not count, unless it be with God. He who would uplift them must brave the doom that may overtake a man in the secrecy behind prison walls.

Doña Rita delicately tore the incautious letters into small pieces, and those into smaller, and pulled off her gloves to tear more effectually, until her little thumbnails had reduced all those pages of love to a heap of powdery flakes; and still her fingers burrowed there destructively, as she searched her brain for a policy that might attach to herself the wandering heart of her son.

Jesús María kissed his mother's hand, and was about to put on his cloak and hat when Doña Rita, who had made her toilet with the care of a coquette, asked him to play to her. As he hesitated for an excuse, she gaily took him by the arm, and led him into the *sala*,[7] where, with such sprightly volubility as to disarm reluctance,

[6] Persons who indulge in light banter or raillery.

[7] Drawing room.

she took his violin from its case, placed it graciously in his hands, and fluttered into a chair in a bewitching attitude of attention, with her profile toward him (her profile had always been admired). Unconsciously she was employing with him the arts by which she had striven, alas! without success, to keep his father, the general, at her side. She felt a great necessity of preventing him from seeing that girl tonight. Her rival! What if the accident she had met with should result in her becoming an incurable cripple? *¡Misericordia de Dios!*[8] That might mean that Jesús María would become chivalrously entangled with her for life. Would God permit a faithful mother's intervention to end in a fiasco so diabolic?

Her son had executed an ornamental piece without making many mistakes, and was putting away his violin. She stopped him. Pale beneath her powder, she begged him not to leave her. She urged a hundred reasons of loneliness and affection, employed a hundred graces of appeal and persuasion. She grew magically younger. Tonight she would be his sister, and they should have a fiesta, just they two. More music, and games of the ping-pong, yes, and even a waltz to the music of that barbarous *fonógrafo*[9] from the United States. A late supper, too, and a bottle of champagne. The servants marveled greatly at that fiesta, and Jesús María went to bed a trifle intoxicated. It was very late, but not until, listening in the corridor, she heard her son begin to snore, did Doña Rita feel assured of her victory.

Next morning, after her son had left the house, she read in *El Imparcial* an account of how a young woman named Alegría Peralta had fallen, or else thrown herself, from the roof of the house in which she lived with her family; and how she had lingered several hours in great suffering, but without speaking, until she had sunk into a stupor destined to be continuous until death, which had released her before midnight. Doña Rita wept over this little tragedy of the ordinary, which had slanted so perilously into the orbit of her own existence. Her tears brought relief, and a sense of peace with herself. She was glad for the poor girl's sake that she no longer suffered. But her soul? If a suicide, she had died in mortal sin. *¡Qué audacia é impiedad!*[10] Nevertheless, Doña Rita would

[8] Lord, have mercy!
[9] Phonograph.
[10] What audacity and impiety!

have offered a prayer for her soul had she not felt that all her prayers were needed for her son.

He did not return home that night. She divined where he was, in the home of that family of shawl, mingling his tears with theirs. No doubt he would reproach himself for having failed to go to his love on that particular night of her great need of him, and unconsciously he might have a feeling of coldness toward the fond mother who had detained him. Never should he be reminded of the incident by seeing her again in the character she had assumed that night! No; on the contrary, her spirits must be very low, still lower than his own, so that he would be beguiled into ministering to her, and so perforce forget his bereavement, and reconcentrate his affections in a rightful channel. But upon what pretext could she achieve the desired lowness? On reflection, she decided in favor of sudden illness.

Doña Rita became ill with such energy that the old *nana*, her lifelong attendant, got her immediately into bed, with incantations to all the saints in paradise. And now the atmosphere of the establishment became redolent of camphor, ammonia, mustard, vinegar, arnica, and other proper evidences of infirmity, including various odorous simples known to the *nana*, and prepared by her, under strong encouragement from the afflicted one, in the form of steaming embrocations, fomentations, footbaths, and cataplasms. Doña Rita, between her moans, caused a lamp to be filled with blessed oil, and to be burned significantly before a picture of the Virgin of the Remedies; and she ordered a pot of tea, in Mexico a desperate remedy, to be set boiling at her bedside, her intention being to swallow a quantity of it before the very eyes of her son.

But three days and nights passed, and he did not return. On the morning of the fourth day, when the entire household was tarantula-bitten from the nervousness brought about by the invalid, and when she herself felt ready "to finish with all," the *nana* suddenly appeared at her bedside with fear in her brown face. In response to Doña Rita's look of inquiry, she ejaculated cautiously:

"Don Chucho!" (Chucho is the diminutive of Jesús.)

Doña Rita gasped:

"He has arrived?"

"God has heard our prayers, *niña*."[11]

[11] My dear (literally, little girl).

"Praised by the Holy Name! Quick, *nana*, my face-powder, the compress on my brow! The curtains, the tea—why move you not?"

"*El niño*[12] Chucho, notwithstanding his arrival, continues to detain himself in the street, meditating there in a *coche*[13] of red flag."

"What scandal!" (A red flag distinguishes the second of the three classes of licensed carriages.) "But why does he detain himself so? What passes with him?"

"Can it be, *niña*," the old Indita whispered, tremulously signing herself, "that our little *niño* is bewitched?"

"*¡Imbecilidades!*"[14]

Doña Rita sprang out of bed, "better than new," so the bewildered *nana* afterward asseverated, and rushed to the balcony; but all she could see below was a particularly shabby *cochero*[15] vulgarly counting his money on the roof of a particularly shabby carriage. Vehemently she turned to the *nana*.

"Answer me now with yes and no, and without additional barbarities! What passes with my son?"

"As you ordain, *niña* of my soul, I will relate that which the *portero*[16] has told me. He is a good man, and has done what God commands; but Don Chucho, whom I have watched over from the breast, seems to act with a mind not his own, resisting to be removed from the *coche* of red flag, and answering with strange voices. As for me, I am an ignorant old one, full of sins and without merit; but I know many charms against the different classes of magic, and if the *niña* wishes—"

Doña Rita was dressing. Something told her that her valetudinary days were over, and she was not deceived. Jesús María was to be the invalid now. He had returned home drunk, not drunk in the competent Northern fashion, but *borracho*[17] in the poignant, morbific mode of Indian blood newly inoculated with alcohol in its ungentler tropic disguises. This condition, with its coefficient of devastating grief, brought havoc to a body of delicate mold and innocent habit. For the first time since his babyhood Doña Rita had

[12] The boy.
[13] Carriage.
[14] Nonsense!
[15] Coachman.
[16] Doorman.
[17] Drunk.

her son all to herself. He was very ill for many weeks, during which time she joyously wore out her strength in loving and jealous service, dethroning the indignant *nana*, and sleeping fitfully, when she slept at all, on a stretcher beside his bed. Even in his babyhood she had never possessed him so richly. He was helplessly dependent on herself alone, thus appeasing for a time the supreme soul-and-life hunger of the implicit mother toward the man-child, and drenching her being in a wild sweetness such as she had never known. His convalescence arrived as a dear autumn to crown that dearest of summer-times. Laughably weak, he adored her first from his pillow and then from his chair, in which on bright days he would be rolled out on the corridor overlooking the patio, where he could see the peacocks dip their trailing feathers in the fountain.

One thing Doña Rita felt to be lacking to her happiness, but not for long. By arts of which she was a natural proficient, she soon extorted from him that which many women value above all other trophies of triumphant sex—the plenary confession of an adult male. She listened to the tragic tale of Alegría, as far as her son knew it, with an admirable air of startled sympathy and many piteous exclamations, edging closer to him, and taking his hands in order to drop a veritable tear upon it. It did not occur to her to reciprocate with a confession on her own account; on the contrary, she beguiled him into believing that if he had only confided in her from the beginning, she would have had an open mind to discover in the remarkable young woman, although of shawl, all the excellences of intellect and personality that he now eloquently dilated upon. Jesús María wept at the thought of how different everything might have been if he had not been so blind to the grandeur of his mother's soul, and he composed an exalted poem in which the spirit of Alegría was pictured kneeling at Doña Rita's feet upon the entrance of that lady at the portal of heaven. Doña Rita had him make her a delicate manuscript of the poem on vellum, and she hung it at the head of her bed beside an antique rosary.

Having thus converted her dead rival into a powerful ally, she turned a cautious front toward her living rival, whose formidable name was Patria, and soon she was giving hospitable ear to her son's dreams for the regeneration of his unhappy country. At first she chose a vein of sympathy somewhat lighter than before, and varied by occasional sprightly darts to a semi-skeptical point of view, as by pointing out the indolent and pious resignation of the dear Inditos, and wondering naïvely whether education, property rights, and an audible voice in government might not spoil their Arcadian virtues and dispel their truly delightful picturesqueness. But even from his mother's lips Jesús María could not endure to hear the cant with which ramparted feudalism masks its crimes, and so she brought herself speedily to the point of declaring passionately for every reform in the program of the Young Scientifics,[18] the secret group of which her son was a member. At some such moment, as his eyes dwelt upon her inspired and ever-manifest profile, he received the stimulus for another poem, "Mi Camarada," in which Doña Rita was visioned as the Mexican Joan of Arc. In secret the good lady prayed for an indefinite postponement of her début in that martial role, and gave particular care to her complexion.

The first time Jesús María ventured out alone he was gone for two days, and returned in a worse condition than before, stammering piteously of Alegría. Before long the servants recognized kindly and fatalistically that *el niñito*[19] was a lost one, *¡se fué á todos los diablos, pobrecito!*[20] His mother, contemplating the wreck of her labor of love, divined the hand of that girl of shawl stretched forth from perdition to clutch him to herself, and solemnly she cursed her. Still she would find heart's-ease in the intervals of acute distemper during which the poor profligate became once more her *bebecito,*[21] *tierno retoño de su cuerpo*—tender sprig of her body.

In due time Jesús María was expelled from the military college. His father's name had less potency in the capital than in Puebla. The estate left by the general had consisted chiefly of debts, law-suits, and magnificent, but dubious, claims against the Government. Mother and son had come to the capital with the retainers, the peacocks, and the cumbersome carriage, tokens of the Ixtlan quality, partly for the all-important business of Jesús María's being trained for a career of arms, his mother's choice for him, and

[18] A group of men appointed by Diaz to create a plan for Mexico's modernization.
[19] The dear boy.
[20] He went straight to the devil, poor thing!
[21] Little baby.

partly to enable his mama to smile the powers of the national treasury into paying the general's claims. But powers change, and treasuries grow empty, and generals' widows pass the age at which smiles are cogent. As times grew harder, even her widow's pension ceased to be forthcoming except in rare installments. She had bought the house in which they lived, decayed and in a forgotten quarter, but of a grandeur, albeit cracked and faded, suitable to the peacocks and the carriage. Now she offered it for mortgage or even sale; but the land lay prostrate in the asphyxia of a money famine, and there was none to heed her. She sold the horses, one after the other, at the price of goats, and cast the cook and the coachman adrift with tears and a benediction. The indispensable *portero* did what odd services he could for neighbors, and was grateful for a handful of beans and a little lard. The *nana*, who was growing blind, performed all else that was needful, and descended to the coach-house every day to polish the general's carriage, and perhaps in her simplicity to pray to it. Revered fetish of caste, grown more august in dimly cloistered desuetude, no stranger would have bought it even had Doña Rita dared to conceive the awful thought of parting with it.

Jesús María obtained a clerkship in the post-office, and by a miracle of self-mastery kept it for five months. After that he descended precipitously, goaded by shame of his own weakness, broken in spirit by expulsion from the Young Scientifics, a serious and Spartan band, and haunted always by a wild regret, now tinged with superstitious fantasy, that he had not gone to Alegría in the hours of her mute passing. A day came when he lay with shrunken limbs, flushed face, and cracked lips, talking to his dead love as if she were in that room. His happy, hurried speech to her went on for hours; its sources seemed inexhaustible; though the doctor thought that very soon he would fall into sudden silence, never again to speak to the dead or the living.

On her way to fetch a priest, Doña Rita took a wrong turning—her eyes, too, were failing, washed out with tears—and presently she found herself at the end of a blind street; and afterward, in making toward the church, she struck into a very narrow street, in which harsh Spanish voices resounded. As she passed one house, a casement window was opened, and she saw through the grille a face which appeared to be that of Alegría Peralta. It was impossible, of course. Blaming her eyes and trembling from the shock, Doña Rita hurried on; but before she had passed three houses she turned back. The girl was still looking out of the window. Her likeness to the dead was extraordinary, but her expression was less pleasing; she looked sullen. When Doña Rita spoke to her, she pushed the window shut.

Next morning Jesús María sank into a stupor. All thought that the end was at hand; but Doña Rita, to her *nana's* amazement, went out very swiftly. Easily confused, she had to inquire her way to the narrow street, the name of which she had noted—Calle del Niño Perdido. People looked at her strangely as they directed her to it. As she entered that Street of the Lost Child, she saw the young woman of her search coming out of a hair-dresser's shop. Again Doña Rita spoke to her. The girl was startled at the reappearance of that wild-looking *señora* of hat, who seemed to pursue her, and she turned pale; and Doña Rita saw that her cheeks, where the paint ceased, were the color of burned milk. She said:

"Will you please come with me?"

"Where, *Señora*?" whispered the girl, shrinking.

"To my house. It is not far, and perhaps I shall not detain you too long."

"Dispense me, *Señora*.[22] I have not the liberty to go with you. By favor permit me to pass."

"I understand why you speak so. I can see what you are, and I wish to God it were otherwise. But it has no remedy. You have the face—the face that once bewitched him—my son, who is dying."

"Do I know your son, *Señora*?" the girl inquired in a low, troubled voice.

"No, but you are the counterpart of one that was dearer to him than his life. She fell from a roof. I can prove the truth of what I tell you; a broken-hearted mother does not lie. I am the widow of General Ixtlan. We are from Puebla. God will reward you for coming, and perhaps pardon your sins. Or, if you want money, I will give you some, although not very much. If you wish to arrange anything at that house or to change your shoes, I will wait for you."

"No," said the girl, "the people of that house would not let me go with you."

"You will follow me, then. What is your name?"

[22] A literal translation of the Spanish *dispénseme,* forgive me, excuse me.

"I am called La Palma.[23]"

"Your name of Christian woman, not of sinner."

The girl hesitated, then said:

"I was Piedad."

"Piedad! It is sad when one must be ashamed of a name so blessed. But remember, if the *señor,* my son, opens the eyes and sees you, and calls you Alegría, then you must be Alegría."

"Yes, *Señora*; I will be Alegría."

When they reached the house the doctor was there, striving perfunctorily to goad the slackening life with stimulants. Slowly Jesús María opened his eyes. The false Alegría was looking at him. He smiled, and called her to him with broken words, and pressed her hand to his face for a little while, and then asked her to lie down beside him. That was far from being within the scope of Doña Rita's program; but the doctor, with a peremptoriness which could be excused only on the ground of professional enthusiasm, commanded that the strange young woman be permitted to obey. So Piedad lay down on the bed, and Jesús María whispered to her, and kissed her many times; but presently he got very tired, and gave a little sigh, and fell suddenly asleep, with his cheek against hers. The doctor cautioned her with a gesture not on any account to stir, and she held herself as still as the dead. Chancing to meet the fixed gaze of Doña Rita, she closed her eyes. After a while there passed a trembling over the dark sweep of her lashes, and a tear pushed out and rolled to the roots of her hair on the side away from the sleeping man. Another followed, while her throat worked silently, and then many more, flooding all her face. Doña Rita leaned over the bed, and with her handkerchief carefully stanched the drops that were wetting her son's cheek and mouth; but still the girl wept on, as if the springs of her life would run dry.

Soon after Piedad had started for the Street of the Lost Child that evening, after refusing to accept any payment for the service she had rendered, she heard swift footsteps behind her and a voice calling her name. It was Doña Rita, come to beg her to return with her, for Jesús María was weeping for the girl with sobs which shook his body. Now, Piedad was a unit in a system under official regulation, and she had a number, like a cab, in the archives of the

[23] The Palm, sign of virginity and victory.

Departamento de Sanidad Pública,[24] and she knew not what her civic obligations might be in this particular emergency; so she quietly abandoned all her possessions, which were at the house in the Street of the Lost Child, and adopted the Ixtlan home as a sanctuary for as long as it would shelter her.

What anguish of spirit it cost Doña Rita to breathe the same air with this creature, sometimes of necessity even to touch her, and, worse than all, to see her caressed as a bride by Jesús María, cannot be described. However, it was impossible to shut the eyes to the truth that the girl was his medicine; that hour by hour her being enticed his from the edge of the grave. God sometimes ordains unworthy instruments to work His will in their blindness, and with that thought the mother strengthened herself to tolerate the obnoxious presence as long as might seem needful for the recovery of her son.

In those days Jesús María did not know his mother, and as her watchful figure in a corner seemed to trouble him with vague apprehensions, the doctor counseled her to efface herself for a little while. She obeyed with bitterness in her heart, and Jesús María absorbed peace from his hours, oftentimes quite silent, with her whom he called Alegría.

One morning, however, he looked at her with such new, perturbed eyes that she trembled and ran to call Doña Rita. And now he recognized his mother and also the *nana*, and both wept for joy. Doña Rita, her heart in a divine tumult at the thought that her son would once more be her own, caused Piedad to remain away from his room. He was very gentle, and his eyes acknowledged his love as of old; but there seemed to be something on his mind of which he feared to speak, and he would pause often to listen, looking doubtfully at the door, until he grew very hot and flushed, with a partial return of delirium. Thereupon Piedad was called in to stroke his brow with her fingers until he slept.

A day or two later he said suddenly to the girl in his mother's presence:

"I know you are not Alegría. I wish you to tell me, by favor, who you are."

She replied:

"I am Piedad."

[24] Department of Public Health.

He meditated for some time and seemed to sleep; but suddenly he said in a stronger voice:

"Piedad—little Piedad! What a great little daughter thou hast grown, Piedacita! Thou didst not promise to be so like her then. How long ago was it?"

"A year and a half."

Here Doña Rita mastered her consternation, and interposed with an affectionate fluttering; but he only smiled at her, and turned again to the other.

"How didst thou find me, little one?"

"I did not find you, Don Chucho," replied the girl, who was in tears and had not perceived Doña Rita's warning signal. "The *señora* your mother saw me first as I looked out at a window in the Street of the Lost Child, and God sent her again to seek me and bring me to your bedside, not knowing who I was, but only for the blessing of my likeness to my sweet sister, whose name I am unworthy to speak."

He did not answer her then, but seemed to commune with himself or with the unseen; and toward the fall of the afternoon he said without preface, as if she had only just spoken:

"I will answer for Alegría that, whatever thou hast done or suffered, thou art not unworthy to speak her name freely for comfort of thee and me, little sister."

"Now that you know the truth, Don Chucho," she said very simply, half looking in fear at Doña Rita, "shall I not go?"

He smiled at her and said:

"Thou knowest not this mother of mine, Piedacita."

With a feeble motion he beckoned to Doña Rita, who was as still as an image in a shrine; and she came, and the girl kneeled, and he placed his mother's hand on her head, saying:

"She is now thy mother, too. Consider how she found thee, as Pharaoh's daughter found the Jewish babe."

The girl cried softly, and so did he until he was stopped by a new thought.

"But, *Madrecita*—little mother of my soul—thou hadst never seen Alegría. How, then—"

Without waiting for him to frame the question, she looked on high and answered in an unruffled voice:

"Oh, my son, canst thou not see in that the hand of God working for thy salvation? It is true that thou hadst described to me most minutely the features of thine Alegría, but that was not enough; it needed God to guide my lost steps into that street, and to illuminate mine eyes that I might know the face when I should see it in the window. And by that miracle, my son, God calls upon thee to believe."

"I believe one thing," said Jesús María, with a smile, "and that is that thou art a saint among women."

A saint among women—Doña Rita would have worn that distinction with complacency had it not implied an indefinitely continued tolerance of that girl both of shawl and of sin, her latest and greatest rival, whom by some ironic involution Doña Rita's own acts had caused to be installed in her son's very chamber. Brooding on this, she fell into a habit of jealous solitude, nursing her secrets, her deceptions, and her grievances, all of which corroded her heart. Day by day she saw the furrows marching upon her face and encamping about her eyes and mouth; and she could not bear to look upon the face of Piedad, which now shone with the cloudless enchantment of childhood.

Once she ventured to convey a warning to her son, to the effect that girls like Piedad had a natural inclination toward that life, from which nothing could detach them for long; but the look he gave her, and the words he spoke in celebration of his little sister's purity of soul, were hard for that mother to hear. Purity of soul! Her religion, it was true, countenanced the doctrine that women had souls; but her intelligence forbade her to attach the slightest value to a man's judgment of such recondite accessories in the case of her sex. As for purity, she knew of only one standard which could be recognized without gross injustice to every woman of irreproachable life, else where the reward for conquering temptation? Her wrongs growing greater as she examined them, she reflected that every effort she had ever made to attach to herself an enduring love had ended in failure. If she had listened to much of the intercourse between Jesús María and Piedad, she might have obtained a glimmering of the truth that great love is great simplicity, with a stripping of all veils; but even at a distance the poor lady could not endure to hear the endless, eager pulsing of their voices.

Until one day she was startled by a third voice—that of the violin—and then she crept to listen unseen. Jesús María was playing the Indian airs that he loved best. Then he sang a *danza*[25] of his own composing, dreamy and pensive, as a *danza* must be, but wedded to verses of his own which throbbed with love of the mother-soil and a latent wistfulness for liberty over all its length and breadth. The girl's murmured wonder came from a heart much moved, and Jesús María wept as he told her how he had once dreamed of working for the regeneration of Mexico, but how he had failed in the test of manhood, and was now a broken creature whose dreams lay all behind him. But Piedad refused gaily to listen to that, and they began to discuss plans; and presently he was all on fire with a new scheme of patriotic service.

Los enredados, those children of time, how could their slumber of resignation be pricked into wakefulness more surely than through their music? Why might not he, the rejected, pull the rags of his life about him and set out to fertilize the soil of freedom with his songs? More songs such as he had just sung her—songs of revolution so disguised as to deceive the authorities, and so decorated as to beguile the Inditos' implicit discernment of poesy and wit; songs that would pass from mouth to mouth, from pueblo to pueblo, from valley to valley, from table-land to the hot country, from the sands to the volcanoes, from the crumbling temples of the Mayas to the windy plains of the northern frontier; songs that he himself would sing and play and teach to old and young, wandering far and wide with staff and fiddle, like a minstrel of old, daring the jealous forces of feudalism and foreign capital, and spiritually armed for any fate, slowly, sweetly, and surely firing the heart of a people for great enterprises!

The girl laughed and cried at that picture of roaming under the roof of heaven, and her voice thrilled with understanding. But, alas! Doña Rita's interpretation of what he had heard was that the intruder, her rival, was inciting Jesús María to abandon his mother. She divined that if he ever did set out on that adventure, Piedad would inevitably accompany him. By and by her mind became fixed in the belief that the two were waiting and hoping for her to die. She no longer spoke to Piedad, and all her words to her son

[25] Dance.

were steeped in acid. One of her studied habits was to refer to Piedad, as if inadvertently, as "La Palma," and then to correct herself hastily, with a thin, significant laugh. The two suffered much from the thought that her health was failing, as indeed it was, and Jesús María excelled himself in filial consideration, but to no purpose. She became minutely secretive in her ways, often whispered with the *nana*, and, telling herself that she feared poison, refrained ostentatiously from tasting anything offered her by Piedad or her son.

She blamed herself for having introduced the pollution of which she now despaired of ever ridding the house of Ixtlan, and she wished passionately that her son had died before her arrival at his bedside with that daughter of Judas. Tortured by the present, appalled at the future, her mind took refuge in the past. One day she was missed in the house. It was thought that she had gone to church and had remained long in prayer. Toward evening Jesús María, leaning on the arm of Piedad—he was very weak—set out on an anxious search of the churches, the parks, the streets, and appealed at last to the police. As darkness came, the two returned home, only to find that there was no news. But now the *nana*, after long meditation and muttering, took a candle and went slowly down among the shadows in the patio, and fumbled at a great door; and soon she uttered a long, mournful cry, which froze their hearts and fetched them to her quickly.

Doña Rita was seated in the carriage, her hands folded in her lap, her head against the faded upholstery, her face serene in the inviolable aristocracy of death.

[September 1914]

The Vine-Leaf

It is a saying in the capital of Mexico that Dr. Malsufrido carries more family secrets under his hat than any archbishop, which applies, of course, to family secrets of the rich. The poor have no family secrets, or none that Dr. Malsufrido would trouble to carry under his hat.

The doctor's hat is, appropriately enough, uncommonly capacious, rising very high, and sinking so low that it seems to be supported by his ears and eyebrows, and it has a furry look, as if it had been brushed the wrong way, which is perhaps what happens to it if it is ever brushed at all. When the doctor takes it off, the family secrets do not fly out like a flock of parrots, but remain nicely bottled up beneath a dome of old and highly polished ivory, which, with its unbroken fringe of dyed black hair, has the effect of a tonsure; and then Dr. Malsufrido looks like one of the early saints. I've forgotten which one.

So edifying is his personality that, when he marches into a sick-room, the forces of disease and infirmity march out of it, and do not dare to return until he has taken his leave. In fact, it is well known that none of his patients has ever had the bad manners to die in his presence.

If you will believe him, he is almost ninety years old, and everybody knows that he has been dosing good Mexicans for half a century. He is forgiven for being a Spaniard on account of a legend that he physicked royalty in his time, and that a certain princess—but that has nothing to do with this story.

It is sure he has a courtly way with him that captivates his female patients, of whom he speaks as his *penitentes*,[1] insisting on confession as a prerequisite of diagnosis, and declaring that the physician who undertakes to cure a woman's body without reference to her soul is a more abominable kill-healthy than the famous *Dr. Sangrado*,[2] who taught medicine to *Gil Blas*.[3]

"Describe me the symptoms of your conscience, *Señora*," he will say. "Fix yourself that I shall forget one tenth of what you tell me."

"But what of the other nine tenths, Doctor?" the troubled lady will exclaim.

"The other nine tenths I shall take care not to believe," Dr. Malsufrido will reply, with a roar of laughter. And sometimes he will add:

"Do not confess your neighbor's sins; the doctor will have enough with your own."

When an inexperienced one fears to become a *penitente* lest that terrible old doctor betray her confidence, he reassures her as to his discretion, and at the same time takes her mind off her anxieties by telling her the story of his first patient.

"Figure you my prudence, *Señora*," he begins, "that, although she was my patient, I did not so much as see her face."

And then, having enjoyed the startled curiosity of his hearer, he continues:

"On that day of two crosses when I first undertook the mending of mortals, she arrived to me beneath a veil as impenetrable as that of a nun, saying:

"'To you I come, *Señor* Doctor, because no one knows you.'

"'Who would care for fame, *Señorita*,' said I, 'when obscurity bring such excellent fortune?'

"And the lady, in a voice which trembled slightly, returned:

"'If your knife is as apt as your tongue, and your discretion equal to both, I shall not regret my choice of a surgeon.'

"With suitable gravity I reassured her, and inquired how I might be privileged to serve her. She replied:

[1] Repentant sinners.

[2] A doctor whose sole remedies were bleeding and drinking of hot water; an ignorant pretender to medical knowledge.

[3] Hero of *Histoire de Gil Blas de Santillane*, a picaresque narrative by Alain René Lesage, French novelist and playwright (1668-1747).

"'By ridding me of a blemish, if you are skillful enough to leave no trace on the skin.'

"'Of that I will judge, with the help of God, when the *señorita* shall have removed her veil.'

"'No, no; you shall not see my face. Praise the saints the blemish is not there!'

"'Wherever it be,' said I, resolutely, 'my science tells me that it must be seen before it can be well removed.'

"The lady answered with great simplicity that she had no anxiety on that account, but that, as she had neither duenna nor servant with her, I must help her. I had no objection, for a surgeon must needs be something of a lady's maid. I judged from the quality of her garments that she was of an excellent family, and I was ashamed of my clumsy fingers; but she was as patient as marble, caring only to keep her face closely covered. When at last I saw the blemish she had complained of, I was astonished, and said:

"'But it seems to me a blessed stigma, *Señorita*, this delicate, wine-red vine-leaf, staining a surface as pure as the petal of any magnolia. With permission, I should say that the god Bacchus[4] himself painted it here in the arch of this chaste back, where only the eyes of Cupid[5] could find it; for it is safely below the line of the most fashionable gown.'

"But she replied:

"'I have my reasons. Fix yourself that I am superstitious.'

"I tried to reason with her on that, but she lost her patience, and cried:

"'For favor, good surgeon, your knife!'

"Even in those days I had much sensibility, *Señora*, and I swear that my heart received more pain from the knife than did she. Neither the cutting nor the stitching brought a murmur from her. Only some strong ulterior thought could have armed a delicate woman with such valor. I beat my brains to construe the case, but without success. A caprice took me to refuse the fee she offered me.

"'No, *Señorita*,' I said, 'I have not seen your face, and if I were to take your money, it might pass that I should not see the face of

[4] Greek and Roman god of wine.

[5] Roman god of love, son of Mercury and Venus.

a second patient, which would be a great misfortune. You are my first, and I am as superstitious as you.'

"I would have added that I had fallen in love with her, but I feared to appear ridiculous, having seen no more than her back.

"'You would place me under an obligation,' she said. I felt that her eyes studied me attentively through her veil. 'Very well, I can trust you the better for that. *Adiós, Señor* Surgeon.'

"She came once more to have me remove the stitches, as I had told her, and again her face was concealed, and again I refused payment; but I think she knew that the secret of the vine-leaf was buried in my heart."

"But that secret, what was it, Doctor? Did you ever see the mysterious lady again?"

"*¡Chist!*[6] Little by little one arrives to the *rancho, Señora.* Five years passed, and many patients arrived to me, but, although all showed me their faces, I loved none of them better than the first one. Partly through family influence, partly through well-chosen friendships, and perhaps a little through that diligence in the art of Hippocrates[7] for which in my old age I am favored by the most charming of Mexicans, I had prospered, and was no longer unknown.

"At a meeting of a learned society I became known to a certain *marqués*[8] who had been a great traveler in his younger days. We had a discussion on a point of anthropology, and he invited me to his house, to see the curiosities he had collected in various countries. Most of them recalled scenes of horror, for he had a morbid fancy.

"Having taken from my hand the sword with which he had seen five Chinese pirates sliced into small pieces, he led me toward a little door, saying:

"'Now you shall see the most mysterious and beautiful of my mementos, one which recalls a singular event in our own peaceful Madrid.'

"We entered a room lighted by a skylight, and containing little but an easel on which rested a large canvas. The *marqués* led me where the most auspicious light fell upon it. It was a nude, beautifully painted. The model stood poised divinely, with her back to the

[6] Ssh! Hush!

[7] That is, the practice of medicine. The ancient Greek physician Hippocrates formulated the "Hippocratic Oath," a long-venerated code of professional medical conduct and ethics.

[8] Marquis.

beholder, twisting flowers in her hair before a mirror. And there, in the arch of that chaste back, staining a surface as pure as the petal of any magnolia, what did my eyes see? Can you possibly imagine, *Señora*?"

"*¡Válgame Dios!*"[9] The vine-leaf, Doctor!"

"What penetration of yours, *Señora!* It was veritably the vine-leaf, wine-red, as it had appeared to me before my knife barbarously extirpated it from the living flesh; but in the picture it seemed unduly conspicuous, as if Bacchus had been angry when he kissed. You may imagine how the sight startled me. But those who know Dr. Malsufrido need no assurance that even in those early days he never permitted himself one imprudent word. No, *Señora*; I only remarked, after praising the picture in proper terms:

"'What an interesting moon is that upon the divine creature's back!'

"'Does it not resemble a young vine-leaf in early spring?' said the *marqués*, who contemplated the picture with the ardor of a connoisseur. I agreed politely, saying:

"'Now that you suggest it, *Marqués*, it has some of the form and color of a tender vine-leaf. But I could dispense me a better vine-leaf, with many bunches of grapes, to satisfy the curiosity I have to see such a well-formed lady's face. What a misfortune that it does not appear in that mirror, as the artist doubtless intended! The picture was never finished, then?'

"'I have reason to believe that it was finished,' he replied, 'but that the face painted in the mirror was obliterated. Observe that its surface is an opaque and disordered smudge of many pigments, showing no brush-work, but only marks of a rude rubbing that in some places has overlapped the justly painted frame of the mirror.'

"'This promises an excellent mystery,' I commented lightly. 'Was it the artist or his model who was dissatisfied with the likeness, *Marqués*?'

"'I suspect that the likeness was more probably too good than not good enough,' returned the *marqués*. 'Unfortunately, poor Andrade is not here to tell us.'

"'Andrade! The picture was his work?'

"'The last his hand touched. Do you remember when he was found murdered in his studio?'

[9] Bless my soul!

"'With a knife sticking between his shoulders. I remember it very well.'

"The *marqués* continued:

"'I had asked him to let me have this picture. He was then working on that rich but subdued background. The figure was finished, but there was no vine-leaf, and the mirror was empty of all but a groundwork of paint, with a mere luminous suggestion of a face.

"'Andrade, however, refused to name me a price, and tried to put me off with excuses. His friends were jesting about the unknown model, whom no one had managed to see, and all suspected that he designed to keep the picture for himself. That made me the more determined to possess it. I wished to make it a betrothal gift to the beautiful *Señorita* Lisarda Monte Alegre, who had then accepted the offer of my hand, and who is now the *marquesa*.[10] When I have a desire, Doctor, it bites me, and I make it bite others. That poor Andrade, I gave him no peace.

"'He fell into one of his solitary fits, shutting himself in his studio, and seeing no one; but that did not prevent me from knocking at his door whenever I had nothing else to do. Well, one morning the door was open.'

"'Yes, yes!' I exclaimed. 'I remember now, *Marqués*, that it was you who found the body.'

"'You have said it. He was lying in front of this picture, having dragged himself across the studio. After assuring myself that he was beyond help, and while awaiting the police, I made certain observations. The first thing to strike my attention was this vine-leaf. The paint was fresh, whereas the rest of the figure was comparatively dry. Moreover, its color had not been mixed with Andrade's usual skill. Observe you, Doctor, that the blemish is not of the texture of the skin, or bathed in its admirable atmosphere. It presents itself as an excrescence. And why? Because that color had been mixed and applied with feverish haste by the hand of a dying man, whose one thought was to denounce his assassin—she who undoubtedly bore such a mark on her body, and who had left him for dead, after carefully obliterating the portrait of herself which he had painted in the mirror.'

[10] Marquise (feminine).

"'*¡Ay Dios!* But the police, *Marqués*—they never reported these details so significant?'

"'Our admirable police are not connoisseurs of the painter's art, my friend. Moreover, I had taken the precaution to remove from the dead man's fingers the empurpled brush with which he had traced that accusing symbol.'

"'You wished to be the accomplice of an unknown assassin?'

"'Inevitably, *Señor*, rather than deliver that lovely body to the hands of the public executioner.'

"The *marqués* raised his lorgnette and gazed at the picture. And I—I was recovering from my agitation, *Señora*. I said:

"'It seems to me, *Marqués*, that if I were a woman and loved you, I should be jealous of that picture.'

"He smiled and replied:

"'It is true that the *marquesa* affects some jealousy on that account, and will not look at the picture. However, she is one who errs on the side of modesty, and prefers more austere objects of contemplation. She is excessively religious.'

"'I have been called superstitious,' pronounced a voice behind me.

"It was a voice that I had heard before. I turned, *Señora*, and I ask you to try to conceive whose face I now beheld."

"*Válgame la Virgen*,[11] Dr. Malsufrido, was it not the face of the good *marquesa*, and did she not happen to have been also your first patient?"

"Again such penetration, *Señora*, confounds me. It was she. The *marqués* did me the honor to present me to her.

"'I have heard of your talents, *Señor* Surgeon,' she said.

"'And I of your beauty, *marquesa*,' I hastened to reply; 'but that tale was not well told.' And I added, 'If you are superstitious, I will be, too.'

"With one look from her beautiful and devout eyes she thanked me for that prudence which to this day, *Señora*, is at the service of my *penitentes*, little daughters of my affections and my prayers; and then she sighed and said:

"'Can you blame me for not loving this questionable lady of the vine-leaf, of whom my husband is such a gallant accomplice?'

[11] Bless me, Mother of God!

"'Not for a moment,' I replied, 'for I am persuaded, *marquesa*, that a lady of rare qualities may have power to bewitch an unfortunate man without showing him the light of her face.'"

[December 1914]

The Sorcerer and General Bisco

Carmelita awoke very suddenly, and found herself gazing wide-eyed at a lacework of sky which glimmered, as pale as the inside of a shell, through a dark pattern of leaves and boughs and looping creepers. How wonderful to awake in a place she had never seen before! It had lightened into ghostly visibility, and appeared not at all as she had imagined it in the night, when hurtful branches had stretched as a tangle of unseen arms forbidding further progress. Now it was a dim chapel, carpeted and hospitable, solemn and faintly scented.

She expected at any moment to hear the noise of hoofs and crashing underbrush and the sonorous heraldings of Don Baltazar's[1] long-eared hounds. The crow of a cock startled her, so clear was the sound. Although she and Aquiles[2] had seemed to run vast distances in the darkness, the life of the *hacienda*[3] was still within hearing. At the most they had a few hours of life. But what hours! She filled her lungs with the breath of the imperturbable forest, and felt herself a new Carmelita, sister to the wind and the mountains, the clouds by day and the stars by night.

Now the forest was filled with little voices. From a thousand nests and roosts had begun a drowsy gossiping of the dawn, punctuated now and then with a rasping announcement from Heaven knew what half-awakened tree-dweller. High among the branches a whiskered face peered at Carmelita, and a slender monkey vaulted out of view with a complaining whistle. From all quarters came

[1] Balthasar, King of Babylon.

[2] Achilles.

[3] A large estate or plantation.

scandalized questions and comments. The sky was changing to pink. There was a furtive purr of wings, a discreet rustle of leaves. Suddenly a bold light gilded the tops of the trees. Some creature shrieked. All the choir burst into a businesslike clamor. Aquiles opened his eyes and smiled into the face of Carmelita.

They breakfasted in the fashion of the monkeys, selecting epicureanly from a hundred varieties of fruits and nuts, and competing with the hummingbirds for the swollen honey-balls of the red myrtle-bloom; and they kissed the stains of berries from each other's mouths and chased butterflies. When they were tired they lay with upturned eyes, exploring depth beyond depth of the blue until all sense of the earthly threatened to glide out of their lives. Returning from that excursion, they talked of things agreeable to lovers, such as death, liberty, eternity, and purity of soul, with side-lights on the bounteous friendliness of nature and the regrettable absence of coffee. Also, after the manner of their kind, they gossiped of Aucassin and Nicolette, of Paul and Virginia, and more particularly of Paolo and Francesca; and they vaingloriously acclaimed themselves the equals of those deathless ones, who, they decided, would welcome them fraternally when they, Aquiles and Carmelita, would journey presently to the mystic kingdom where the embraces of love never end.

"If this were ancient Greece instead of Tamaulipas,"[4] boasted the youth, "our death this morning would give birth to immortal legends. From this rock that shades us a crystal fountain would spring, and these myrtles would become a grove sacred to lovers, in whose gentle prayers would mingle forever the names of Carmelita and her Aquiles."

Carmelita smiled, sighed, and murmured:

"Only one night and morning! What a short life is ours!"

"My kisses were on thy lips before thou wast born," Aquiles declaimed.

"We must die in the same moment," she said. "Oh, if I should see thee suffer, I should die without a wound!"

Her tears fell upon his brown hand, which she pressed to her bosom.

"If we only had horses!" Aquiles muttered between his teeth.

[4] State in northeastern Mexico, on the Gulf of Mexico.

"They would not serve to carry us beyond the reach of his arm."

"If we could find a boat along the coast, or reach the seaport disguised—"

"Disguised in leaves?" she smiled, smoothing away his frown with her fingers. "Let me look at thee, Aquiles. Our time is so short, I cannot look at thee enough. This crisp line of thy hair, I have not kissed it yet. *¡Cielo!*[5] Two little moons on thy temple that I had not seen! Thou must not hide such enchantments from me, *picarito!*[6] This curly ear, too, asks for kisses. It seems that my poor ears have not pleased thee. *¡Úy! ¡Úy!*[7] Thy kisses will deafen me. Give me thy face; I breathe it as I would a geranium bush. Does not this morning of magic repay us for all that we have suffered? Tell me thy whole life, and I will tell thee mine. I was born last night, I live an eternity with thee, and I die today. But, no; born I was when I first saw thee. Was it years ago or only days? But I was not aware of the life that had come to me until last night, when I went to thee and took thy hand and ran with thee into the darkness."

"How I adore thee for thy valor!"

"It was the valor of fear, my beloved."

"What was thy fear?"

"I read his mind toward thee. Thou didst not see his face. He had surprised a look between us, the sudden look we passed yesterday, as if our eyes were drawn out of us."

"And our soul with them."

"I would have warned thee to escape from the *hacienda*, but I knew thou wouldst not leave me there."

"Never would I have left thee!"

"How blessed, that look! Without it we should have continued to sigh for each other, and I should have died without knowing that God had made thee and me from the same piece of heaven. Now death will come to us with laughing. Dost thou repent—yes?"

His answer was an embrace, in the ecstasy of which both felt supremely ready to yield their last breath. But, lo! in that very instant a craving for life stirred in them, bidding them snatch

[5] My darling! My dear!
[6] You little rascal!
[7] Oh! Oh!

greedily at minute after minute of survival together in the assured comradeship of the flesh. With one impulse they rose and pushed southward, keeping the road on their right and the sun on their left. Sometimes Aquiles had to cut a path with his knife, that friendly knife on which they depended in the last resort for immunity from capture.

The way was full of difficulties, but not of terrors. Even when a large serpent reared at them obliquely with a strategic hiss as it spurted into the rustling mystery of a marsh, Carmelita laughed with sympathy, and then laughed again at the transformation of her own once fearful and fastidious self. Scratched and sunburned, soaked to the knees in black swamp-ooze, her dress torn, her bosom laboring from the exertion of the march, she wove a wreath of narcissus for her loosened hair; and when Aquiles showed fatigue she enticed him on with snatches of song.

He looked at her with eyes reflecting the wonder of a miracle. That the mute and melancholy victim of his guardian's despotism should have been metamorphosed into this eager dryad! He did not suspect that he, too, had been transfigured until she pulled his head down to show him his new countenance shining in the mirror of a pool.

More prudent than she, he feared lest in her divine effervescence she should pour out her vitality suddenly, to the last drop; and at length he asserted his authority to call a halt. Her lips rebelled against the enforced rest, but her eyes suddenly consented, and she passed into silence.

He thought that she slept, although her lids were incompletely closed, leaving exposed two luminous crescents of bluish white, with now and then the trembling rims of brown irises. Troubled vaguely by the unrest of those lovely eyes, he closed them gently with his hand and held them covered so, but at moments felt them flutter faintly against his fingers and palm. Presently he became aware that her left arm, which crossed his shoulder, had become rigid. Fear knocked at his heart. He tried to wake her. Neither his voice nor his caresses seemed to reach the living spark of her. Only when he kissed her desperately on the mouth and eyes did she relax, stir, and open her eyes, saying:

"I am here. I came back, and felt thee trying to wake me. I heard thy voice and saw thy tears, but could not open my eyes."

"Thou hast given me fear," he faltered, "much fear."

"I know it, *pobrecito*.[8] If thou seest me so again, kiss me quickly on the eyelids, and I will return to thee from the ends of space."

"But thou, piece of my life, what passed with thee?"

"I was at the *hacienda*. I saw him."

"It was a dream," Aquiles stammered.

"He had received news, bad news, from a man who had arrived by horse at all speed from the North. The man was bleeding."

"It was a dream," Aquiles repeated confidently. "Think of it no more, my morning star."

He would have had her rest longer, but she could not. They continued their way through the wilderness. At intervals she would turn her head and listen toward the *hacienda*, with a questioning look. She no longer sang, and her feet were no longer swift and sure; sometimes she stumbled. Aquiles, troubled in his mind over the oddity of her sleep, tried to divert her with everything else under the sun. He carried her over the rough places, and willed strongly and secretly to reinforce her fainting ethereality with generous waves of his own tough constancy, thus spiritually pouring forth the reserve strength that he needed for the difficulties of the march.

As their way descended into impenetrable jungle and morass, he veered toward higher ground at the right, and that brought them to long laboring upward, under a brazen sun, through shifting sand laced with coarse, slippery grass. With the last of their strength, their mouths agape and their hearts hammering at their throats, they clambered to the border of a gracious little plateau. Aquiles, breathless with noises in his chest, lowered Carmelita to the earth and dropped on all fours beside her, every muscle benumbed.

His drumming ears registered a confused noise of approaching horsemen, but he could not stir or even think. Carmelita, too, heard those sounds, but did not turn her head. Fatigue had slain even the resolve for death before capture.

The earth trembled under many hoofs, and the peace was shattered by abrupt voices. The brain of Aquiles, fighting for lucidity to stand sentinel over the exhausted body, puzzled itself fitfully

[8] You poor little thing!

over the solidarity of the troop. The riders had dismounted. They were under a certain rude discipline. They called to one another in a dialect not often heard so far South. The brain of Aquiles was becoming clearer; of his body he had lost consciousness. Some low bushes, as he figured the case, lay between the horsemen and themselves.

Now came a reverberation of chopping, now a cracking and rendering, followed by metallic strokes and a singing of wire under machetes. Yes, he had observed the telegraph-wires crossing the plateau to avoid a detour of the road. Could these be El Bisco's[9] outlaws, arrived without warning miraculously near the seaport? But by all the laws of probability El Bisco's band should have been exterminated by a strong column of Federals that had gone north from the seaport for that particular purpose ten days before. It had not been heard from since, but—

A sudden shout. Aquiles was hauled rudely to his feet and maintained on them by a desultory series of thumps until his legs had recovered their stability. He snatched out his knife, but it was knocked from his hand. Carmelita was on her feet now, wildly trying to reach him, beating with her little hands the cotton-clad backs of those brown warriors. There was some cheerful talk of shooting Aquiles, but it died away with grumbling when the leader of the troop threatened to slay any man who attempted such an irregularity. All non-combatant prisoners were to be presented with consideration before General Bisco, in the name of God and the constitution.

General Bisco! Aquiles marveled at that grotesque dignification of El Bisco, "The Cross-Eyed." General Cross-Eyed! What was the world coming to? It had come to this. Having become the Hotspur[10] of a promising rebellion, with a victory-seasoned army some thousands strong to swear by his name, the sometime bandit had been dubbed general by an anxious revolutionary junta. A

[9] López's reading of the symbolic relationship between El Bisco and Don Baltazar Rascón is informative. She writes: "This story could be and probably was read as a metaphor for political struggles in Mexico. Bisco would represent Pancho Villa, the Mexican revolutionary who joined the rebels and fought vigorously for President Madero (and later against General Huerta and President Carranza)." Rascón, on the other hand, could represent either the dictator Porfirio Díaz, or the United States "with the figure of Bisco representing Mexico trying to unite a divided Central America" (López, note 28, 45).

[10] Nickname of Sir Henry Percy (died 1403), who plotted unsuccessfully to dethrone Henry IV.

special envoy of the junta had notified him of the honor, presenting him with an address and a highly ornamental sword of parade, and begging with tact to be informed of the illustrious victor's family name, that it might be blazoned in the pages of martial history and inscribed correctly in the archives of the revolution. El Bisco had searched his memory for some other appellative than The Cross-Eyed, and recalled that in early life he had been called Purificación.[11] The envoy had surmised that General Purificación would be a style of dignity and good omen. But suddenly El Bisco had rebelled. He had no objection to being a general—in fact, he had decided to promote himself to that rank, junta or no junta—but on no account would he show disrespect to the *distintivo*[12] under which he had made himself a terror to the rich and an idol to the poor. Since it was undoubtedly the will of God that he should remain cross-eyed in this world, let martial history emblazon him without hypocrisy as General Bisco. There had been no further argument.

Having annexed by enlistment two thirds of the column that had gone forth to exterminate him and demolished the remaining third, General Bisco had swept south, cutting the wires as he went, designing to place himself within striking distance of the seaport before the news of his victory and of his greatly augmented army should travel that far. As a base of attack upon the seaport he had selected the *hacienda* and *pueblo*[13] of Divina Merced,[14] over which Don Baltazar Rascón ruled as absolutely as any medieval baron. Before falling upon Divina Merced he had despatched a troop through a wild and disregarded little pass in the hills farther south to cut the wires between that point and the seaport. Into the hands of that troop the lovers had fallen.

As they neared the *hacienda* with their captors, a stifling smoke blew in their faces, troubling them with an odor of scorched flesh. In the garden, the orchard, the plantations, innumerable barbecues were in preparation. The invaders were in a mood for feasting, and Don Baltazar's cattle and sheep were fat. A line of outbuildings was ablaze, but no one paid the slightest attention to

[11] Purification.

[12] Distinction.

[13] Village.

[14] Divine Grace (ironic in this context).

it. Crops were trampled, fences were down, poultry and pigs were charging distractedly among the multitudinous legs of patriotism.

Of the blood spilled at the rebel occupation of Divina Merced almost all had been contributed by the beasts now smoking over the scattered camp-fires. Rascón's long-suffering *peons* would have made no attempt to resist El Bisco, savior of the poor, even if the absurdity of resistance had been less evident than it was. In the pueblo a church bell was pealing out an obstreperous welcome.

El Bisco sat magisterially in the great chair at Don Baltazar's library table. He would have been much more comfortable squatting on a mat, like most of his lieutenants; but he was determined to show his prisoner, the purse-round Rascón, that General Bisco could seat himself *como todo un señor*.[15] Don Baltazar, bound and under guard, studied El Bisco with crafty and piercing eyes.

He expected no mercy. The son of a Spanish usurer, he had set himself up in the style of a born *caballero del campo*,[16] and dared to oppress honest Mexicans as arrogantly as any patrician of indigenous descent. Nothing good was spoken of his life. Dark suspicions had been engendered by the death of his first wife, who had brought him property. It was known that by devious means he had become possessed of a large part of the inheritance of her young brother, Aquiles de la Vega, of whom the law had appointed him guardian. Indeed, at the time of the arrival of the rebel army the *peons* had been whispering over the disappearance of Don Aquiles since the previous night, and now that their tyrant had fallen, they were eager to accuse him of having murdered that most amiable young man. Doña Carmelita, too, the saintly Doña Carmelita, his second wife, young daughter of a family *muy distinguida*[17] which had been despoiled by Rascón and compelled to give him its cherished lamb in marriage, where was she? Search was being made for the bodies of those two in order that as many crimes as possible might be brought home to the oppressor before the eyes of the noble and just General Bisco.

The general was taking advantage of that search to delay action. In ordinary circumstances he would have given short shrift

[15] Just like a gentleman.
[16] Country gentleman.
[17] Very distinguished.

to such a shining mark for the bullets of patriotism, but Don Baltazar was said to be in league with the devil. Strange to say, he owed that reputation to the least unamiable side of his character, an amateur interest in physical science. General Bisco knew of the legend, but did not believe it. At the same time his skepticism was not altogether sure of itself. He feared nothing earthly, but he had no desire to meddle in the private affairs of the devil.

Avoiding the fixed gaze of his prisoner, he scowled moodily at a strange object on the table, a complicated structure of brass. He did not suspect that it was anything so blameless as a microscope. He smelled sorcery in it, black magic, occult mischief, Heaven knew what not. Nevertheless, he forced himself to look at it with an air of disdain.

Now came intelligence which proved that Rascón, whatever his previous crimes, had not murdered his wife and ward: They had been captured by the wire-cutting detachment. There was no further excuse for delay. The general was almost glad; he was a man of action, and reflection fatigued him. Now, for a throw of the dice between the devil and El Bisco. He seized the microscope and hurled it against the opposite wall.

No desolating consequence ensued. The general was wild with delight, while his followers murmured their admiration.

"Out!" he shouted—"out and tell what you have seen!" He turned to the guards of the prisoner. "Out, all of you, that my valiant army know once for all that General Bisco fears not the devil nor his instruments of sorcery!"

And when the room was cleared, he cursed the prisoner exuberantly, and cried:

"Call now your *compadre*[18] the devil to save you!"

Don Baltazar, whose legs were free, advanced to the opposite side of the table and said with an obsequious smile:

"Well I knew that your Exellency was too intelligent to believe the foolish superstitions of the *peons*. I and the devil do not carry each other. It is God above Who has permitted humble me to study the moon and stars and many mysteries of our earth. In this manner I have acquired the arts of looking into what will be *mañana* and beyond *mañana*, and of seeing what passes at a distance, and of reading the thoughts of men."

[18] Godfather.

"In a little moment you be telling me that you can read mine, I begin to think," inquired the general, ironically.

"With perfect ease," responded Rascón. "Your Excellency is thinking of the magazine pistol on the table near his hand, and considering that by shooting me while we are alone in this room he would receive almost as much credit from the ignorant as if he had slain the devil himself in single combat."

Verily the general's thought had been put into words; but the general was not the man to admit it.

"You lie!" he shouted, dropping his hand on the pistol. "If now I kill you, it is because all the patience that God has lent me is finished."

"I am prepared for death," said Don Baltazar, his voice steady, although his face was gray. "Is it the custom of your Excellency to grant the condemned a last request?"

"If it doesn't make too many fleas to kill," said the general, genially.

"It will make no delay. I wish only to hold something in my left hand as I die. You see the object before you."

He glanced at it where it lay on the table, a ball of crystal used as a paperweight. The general stared at it uneasily, then shook himself and sneered:

"Maybe it has magic to make my bullets soft like water, or sweet like caramels, eh?"

"Not that, your Excellency."

"Or maybe resuscitate your honor, like Lazarus, from the sepulcher?"

"That shall be as God wills," Rascón responded calmly.

The general started at his tone, shot a dubious look at him, then looked again at the crystal. With abrupt bravado he picked it up and examined it. Its surface baffled him; its depths were reticent, but luminously suggestive.

"I will pay for the privilege," said the prisoner in a deep tone. "I can reward your Excellency in coin more precious than gold. I can show him his own august future, as I have seen it myself."

Resolved to betray neither credulity nor fear, the general replied contemptuously:

"Show me of what you are capable, but move quickly."

"Your Excellency will see everything in the crystal ball if he will hold it up before his face in his left hand. So. A little higher and nearer the eyes—yet a little nearer. There. Be patient and look with concentration, thinking of nothing." His voice grew softer as he repeated, "Thinking of nothing—nothing." The general stretched out his right hand to the pistol, and quietly transferred it to his lap, but without taking his eyes from the crystal. Don Baltazar murmured:

"Patience! In a few moments your Excellency will see all that is to be revealed. First the crystal will grow cloudy. Then the eyes will grow heavy."

The muscles of the general's arms strained involuntarily against their bonds, and a dark flush crept up to the line of his scalp. While one of his eyes was fastened on the crystal, the other seemed to be mockingly studying Rascón's face. Seeing or unseeing, the scrutiny was difficult to bear. Soon it became apparent, however, that both eyes were growing heavy.

"Heavy eyes! Heavy eyes!" Don Baltazar intoned. "It is very difficult to hold them open."

The eyelids lifted with a flutter, then drooped a little lower than before.

"Difficult—almost impossible. Hold the crystal nearer. So. Now the hand cannot move from that position."

He hardly breathed. When he spoke again his voice sounded in his own ears like the dropping of water in a cavern.

"Close the eyes!"

El Bisco's eyes closed peacefully.

Rascón breathed heavily. The noises from outside, confused noises of a multitude near at hand, stormed in upon his consciousness, from which they had been banished by the suspense of his task.

"You will hear nothing," he said hurriedly—"nothing but the voice which addresses you. You cannot open the eyes. You do not wish to. You wish for nothing but to descent deeper and deeper into the beautiful cloud which embraces you. When the voice counts three, the legs and arms, the whole body, will become rigid, so that no power can move them, and you will go deeper, much deeper. One," he counted resolutely, "two, three."

A spasm passed over El Bisco's body as the muscles tightened. His left arm remained crooked upward, and the knuckles paled waxenly as the hand contracted like iron on the crystal ball. His face had cleared of suspicion, strife, and passion. It was ludicrously infantile.

"Your body feels very light," said Don Baltazar. "It seems to float."

He was drawing upon his own experiences to hasten the passing of his subject into the deeper stages of suggestibility. He had practiced the hypnotic art upon himself as well as upon others, and knew the first sensations of the liberated subliminal self—that self so accustomed to being dominated by its busy rival, the intellect, that when that tyrant has been lulled into oblivion it will espouse the tyranny of an alien voice from space.

"You are becoming unaware of your body. You have no longer a body. You are pure spirit, floating free. What happiness!"

El Bisco's features rumpled heavily into a docile smile.

"Now you shall behold as in a vision the glorious future of the illustrious General Bisco. When you awake, the vision will remain with you, but it will seem to you that you saw it in the crystal."

Loud footsteps on the gallery outside. The voice of Rascón froze in his throat. More footsteps, a scuffle, a fall, flight, pursuit, laughter below in the patio, an oath, and a song. The blood returned to Rascón's veins, as it seemed, from a distance.

When he had found his voice he went on to dictate such visions of battle, victory, plunder, political triumph, coarse pleasures, and popular adulation as might be expected to tickle the aspirations of such a man as he conceived El Bisco to be; and always in the background of the picture lurked the figure of Don Baltazar Rascón, faithful, beneficent, indispensable, a modest custodian of wisdom and conjurer of fortune. To all of which the muscles of El Bisco's face responded with a fluctuation of appropriate expressions.

"When you awake you will not know that you have slept. You will know only that your best friend is Don Baltazar Rascón. Cherish him as a dear brother. Protect his life as your own; indeed, more carefully, much more. Take not his money, nor divide his land among the ungrateful *peons*, but study to increase his wealth from the store of his enemies. Show them no mercy. Let your vengeance fall upon all who have offended him."

El Bisco's brow stamped itself obediently with an ugly frown. Save for that and his scarcely perceptible breathing, he might have been a piece of grotesque sculpture deposited carelessly in a Spanish leather chair. The voice from space quivered with stealthy triumph as Don Baltazar proceeded with his admonitions.

Aquiles and Carmelita retired into a corner of the patio. No one paid much attention to them, although they were well guarded in a desultory fashion. She brought him water from the fountain. In secret she tried to loosen his bonds, but the knots defied her little fingers. They thought of nothing but life now. The narrow world of the *hacienda* had been inundated with such astonishing waves of life, alien and irresistible, that they felt a buoyant promise of being swept away to freedom on some unknown and necessarily enchanting shore. They asked little of life, only to permit them to be together. And they were touched with the superstition of lovers that their love was pleasing to God, and that He would take good care of them. Had He not already sent the admirable General Bisco and his army to change the face of the world for them? And so in childlike faith they huddled together on the sun-warmed pavement, talking in low tones, and looking at each other with eyes asking for kisses.

They did not know what had become of Don Baltazar. He, the tyrant of the little world that had been, had been submerged somehow in that glorious inundation. Rebellion, revolution, whatever it meant to be or was, it was their friend; and before falling asleep, leaning against the wall and each other, they prayed for its prosperity.

Aquiles was awakened by a shake. The guards were commanding him to rise. Carmelita was not so easily aroused. Perceiving that she was again cataleptic, he kissed her on the eyelids. She said:

"There is danger."

"No, no," he whispered. "El Bisco, the good General Bisco, has sent for us."

She made no reply then, but as they were marched toward the library, after ascending to the gallery, she murmured:

"We are to see Don Baltazar. I do not understand clearly yet. Be resolute for all that God may permit to happen."

Don Baltazar was no longer bound. His bearing was a model of melancholy dignity, although Carmelita caught the flash of a savage sneer on his face as he looked upon Aquiles. He did not meet her gaze, but turned away with a gesture which seemed to imply that he was overcome with emotion too sorrowful for exhibition. The eclipse of his countenance seemed to disconcert the general.

"*Señor*," he ventured, "here you have the culpables."

"I resign them to be punished, at the hands of God and your Excellency," Rascón returned in a muffled voice.

The general scratched his head and seemed to commune with himself. Suddenly he sprang to his feet and thrust his face close to that of Aquiles, shouting:

"*Ingrato*,[19] dog that has bitten the hand of a generous master, I waste no time with you. You die—you die—"

"With formality," sounded the voice of Rascón.

"With formality, and not too quickly. My valiant soldiers from the far interior will have amusement. And this woman—this woman—"

"For the good of her soul," intoned Rascón.

"For the good of her soul, she sees you die. But she, for the good of her soul, she lives at the mercy of her lord, the good Don Baltazar Rascón, that he may teach her the virtue of repentance."

Carmelita placed herself before the general. Her eyes were very large, and she was strong in spirit.

"Ask the *peons* of Divina Merced," she cried, "In the name of the blessed Virgin of Guadalupe,[20] whether Don Aquiles deserves to die. Has General Bisco come to kill the innocent, who have comforted the poor and plotted to shield them from a cruel oppressor? Does the valiant general destroy those who have blessed him as their savior? We went into the forest, we two innocents, with no other thought than to die together; but our love was so holy that death rejected us, and the very serpents turned away from us in

[19] Ingrate.

[20] The patron saint of Mexico.

kindness and God smiled upon us and sent you, General Bisco, to bring us life."

"*Blasfemia!*"[21] ejaculated Rascón.

"*Blasfemia!*" echoed the general.

"It is not blasphemy," Carmelita declared. "General Bisco does not speak with his own voice. His voice was taken away from him when he looked in the crystal."

"What crystal or what pumpkins?" he blustered; but his eyes traveled furtively to the paper-weight.

"She mocks you, General!" warned Rascón.

"*Ea! Ea!* You mock me?" stammered the general.

"Not I; it is *he* who mocks you," she retorted. "It is *his* voice that you speak with."

"*Chist!*[22] How can that be?"

"While you looked into the crystal he made himself your master, as he is master of many others, as he was of me until I freed myself and learned to use his own arts to spy upon him—I, little and weak as you see me, with no power but love."

"Be silent, thou without shame!" stuttered Rascón. "You hear, General? She boasts of her infamy!"

But the general was musing, and he muttered:

"My master?"

He tried to look at Don Baltazar, but his eyes dropped to the floor.

"My friend," began Don Baltazar.

"I am your friend, eh?"

"My more than friend, brother, companion of my future, illustrious conqueror and savior of the constitution, in whose service God has commanded me to spend the remaining years of my life . . ."

"Wait a moment," stammered the general. "Fewer words and more explications. I am infirm with these mysteries. I have no longer my feelings of El Bisco. I feel myself a great hole here." He thumped himself on the stomach. "How can a man live without the feelings proper to him?"

"It is the guilty woman. She is possessed, and has tried to bewitch your Excellency."

[21] Blasphemy.
[22] Ssh! Hush!

"*Ay, Dios mio!*"[23] wailed the general. "It is true that I no longer walk with my own feet, but fall this way and that without understanding. What remedy is there?"

"Death for the woman! I revoke my mercy to her. Does your Excellency command immediate execution?"

"*Sí, sí, pronto!*"[24] And he shouted to his men, "Out with the prisoners!"

But Carmelita held up the large gold cross that hung at her neck and kissed it resoundingly, with a passion of truth, and cried:

"By this cross I saw him work the magic with you! My dream was a true dream, sent by God. You looked in the crystal, and he commanded you to close the eyes, and you obeyed him. And you saw all that he commanded you to see, and he stole away your will, your understanding, all your natural feelings."

"*Señor*, she bewitches me again!" whimpered the general. "I do not know myself. Are you my brother?"

"I am your Excellency's most devoted brother."

"I feel to you the same, Brother, and yet I do not. With my feelings of El Bisco I loved you less than a snake of rattle."

"Your Excellency's eyes have been opened to my modest merits."

"You are not my master, no?"

"God guard me from such presumption!"

"Why, then, do I condemn these two, when their faces are honest and please me, but your honor's face I have no longer power to look at?"

His eyes, which had tried in vain to lift themselves to Don Baltazar's face, were fixed upon the wall beyond him, and now they filled with tears.

"I am no longer El Bisco," he blubbered. "I am nothing. I am less than that tarantula there."

A tarantula! Fear and antipathy stung Don Baltazar into swift movement, and he wheeled to face the loathed invader of his library. At the turning of his back the general experienced a reaction of freedom. Instinct reinvaded him. In that moment he probably did not reason, certainly not in terms of supernormal psychology as expounded in many of the books on Don Baltazar's

[23] Oh, my God!
[24] Yes, yes, quickly!

shelves. He did not theorize on any method for liberating a personality from external control. He merely became a practical man with a magazine pistol.

His psychic experiences had not impaired his arm or his quickness on the trigger. Don Baltazar had no more than glimpsed the tarantula when there came a sputtering of fire and mad confusion, in the midst of which he toppled over a chair, and then slid to the floor, pierced with many bullets. The rending din seemed to last for ages, but a heavenly shock of silence came at last, and then a voice, loud, careless and confident, cried:

"*¡Dios!* I think I am El Bisco once more, yes?"

Then came the trembling voices of Aquiles and Carmelita as they groped toward each other through the smoke.

[April 1915]

Marriage by Miracle

Pancrazio, the cobbler, was the first of the humble neighbors of the Ramos Blancos to notice that *la niña*[1] Clarita had a pretender.[2] From across the *plazuela,*[3] where he had his stool and his strings of shoes festooning the wall beneath his gay canopy of tacked-together bull-fight programs, he had seen what was going on and prayed that, by the mercy of God, Doña Rosalia might not perceive the discreet signs with which her little one acknowledged the devoted presence of the strange young man in the shadow of the House of Colors.

It was the most exciting thing that had happened in the Little Square of Marvels for many a year, and the knowledge of it burned the mouth of Pancrazio until he had passed it on, over a jug of *pulque*,[4] to his *compadre*[5] the charcoal-seller, who whispered it to his *comadre*, the *tortillera,*[6] as she patted her little cakes flat in the palms of her hands, and she did not fail to pass it on to the water-carrier, who launched it to all the world at the public fountain.

And now all the *peladitos,* barefooted offspring of the unregarded Indian populace, washed their little brown faces and feet and assumed expressions of astonishing intelligence and zeal in the hope of being selected for such confidential service of love as might become needful. But soon all knew that Agapito, the *cargador*[7] at the corner, was the lucky one. The

[1] The girl.
[2] Suitor.
[3] Small square.
[4] A fermented drink.
[5] *Compadre, comadre:* neighbor (male, female).
[6] Tortilla vendor.
[7] Porter.

señor pretendiente[8] had been seen to speak to him, and doubtless had engaged him to deliver *billetitos amorosos*[9] to the retainers of the House of Colors; for when he appeared next day his white cotton trousers were newly washed, and a gaping hole in his *sombrero* was sewed up, and he showed the world a face of such length and importance that one might be sure that he would not recognize his own mother if she were to pass him at his post.

The House of Colors had its nickname from the blue and yellow tiles covering the whole of its façade in a gay design which passing centuries had blemished with cracks and gaps. It dominated the Little Square of Marvels as any palace has a perfect right to dominate any slum. Many such palaces in the City of Mexico have been reduced to shabby uses as well as to shabby company, but this one had been preserved from trade by its family of origin, which had decayed companionably with and within it.

Not entirely had it been defended from invasion, however, for Doña Rosalia de Ramos Blancos had found it necessary, in order that she and her two daughters should keep their bones clothed with flesh, to lease the better half of the immense dwelling to another family, fortunately almost as quiet, although not nearly as well-born, as themselves.

Small as was the rent paid by these tenants, it enabled the Ramos Blancos to maintain themselves in the station not only "of *señoras*," but also "of carriage." The difficulty of their being no longer able to afford the luxury of horses was overcome by the generosity of the godmother of the elder daughter—there is no limit to the responsibilities of a godmother in Mexico—who every Sunday patiently lent them her black mare and coachman, thus enabling them to drive to the twelve o'clock mass, which is the fashionable one, in their own carriage, conformably with the traditions of the Ramos Blancos.

Their true difficulties and sacrifices were buried in the almost deathlike secrecy of their inner life. Even their tenants across the patio or the *portero*[10] below would have been shocked beyond words could they have known that the elaborate daily dinner ostentatiously served by the *nana*, clattering along the gallery from

[8] Aspiring suitor.
[9] Little love letters.
[10] Doorman.

kitchen to dining-hall with course after course of covered dishes, was largely a symbolic rite by which the Ramos Blancos deceived their neighbors, and, I think, even their stomachs, so sincerely was it performed. The wealth of nourishment proclaimed in rotation by the old serving-woman according to her recollection or fancy—the wet soup, the dry soup, the fish, the omelet, the pigeons, the fried fruits, the *frijoles*, the cheese, ices, and pastry, all with their appropriate wines—resolved itself as a matter of reality into whatever God permitted that day, perhaps a substantial soup and a dish of beans, with warm *tortillas*.

They never complained, but made as many reverences over their meager fare as though it had been all that the family ritual professed it to be, their eyes shining at the thought of saving every *centavo* to appear before the world as well as possible. They always dressed for dinner, and would have done so even if there had been no dinner to dress for; and although their gowns had been made over and over and the laces mended and dyed, the sleeves and necks and the style of draping were always of the latest mode. And they chattered frivolously over their meals as if their life had been one round of social festivity.

It was customary for Ernestina, the elder daughter, who had a sonorous and flexible voice, to begin the gaiety by reciting some graceful *vers de société*, and this performance was always greeted by the other two with a clapping of thin little hands and reckless cries of "*¡Viva!*" and the like. One day, however, after she had rendered a popular favorite by Juan de Dios Peza entitled "Carrying on a Flirtation," Doña Rosalia refrained from applauding, and presently said in a constrained tone:

"Apropos of flirtations, I demand to know this instant which one of my daughters is scandalizing the neighborhood."

She looked at Ernestina, but it was not Ernestina who uttered a sound between a gasp and a squeal and stuffed her mouth full of fingertips. Ignoring that breach of deportment on the part of the palpitating Clarita, Doña Rosalia continued:

"I have noticed a youth playing the bear[11] under our balconies with more diligence than I permit—that is, without knowing what mother gave him birth."

[11] Literal translation of *hacer el oso*, to court. "He has played me the bear": He has courted me.

Still she looked with studied guile at poor Ernestina, who was twenty-five and hopelessly disfavored, with her nose of ridicule, her eyes like two fleas, and her bony figure, who looked, as her mother often lamented, as if St. Joseph had passed the plane over it. But now Clarita, who was eighteen and surprisingly plump, considering her diet, and who had long, gray eyes which always appeared half closed, spoke up in a trembling voice:

"Ernestina is not the culpable one, *Mamá*. It is to me he pretends."

Majestically, Doña Rosalia turned her eyes upon her temerarious daughter.

"To thee! Since when this liberty without my permission?"

"It makes now three months that he followed me from church, *Mamá*, and he has played me the bear with all regularity ever since."

Doña Rosalia drew in a hissing breath and threw up her eyes, exclaiming:

"What cynicism God has given this daughter of mine!"

"We know each other only of sight, Mother mine," the girl protested dutifully.

"But who is this sinner?" her mother demanded. "What signs does he give of what family he comes? Or does one take interest in a mortal without inquiring who he may be?"

"He appears well from far," Clarita stammered, casting down her eyes.

"So does the neighbor next door. Has he taken the liberty to write?"

"Yes, *Mamá*; but we have not yet passed the period of my refusing the letters," Clarita murmured wistfully, but with conscious discretion.

"By whom has he sent them?" her mother persisted.

"They have reached the house through Agapito, who has been well instructed. The first month he gave them to Chucho, the porter's child, the second month to Rótulo himself, and this month to the *nana*. Rest tranquil, *Mamá*, that all has been done with propriety and of elegant manner. The youth has rewarded the servants with dollars."

This last, which slipped out with a touch of involuntary pride, the girl immediately felt to be a wrong note. Doña Rosalia frowned.

"Who is speaking of dollars?" she cried harshly. "Is he of good family?"

"*¡Por Dios!*[12] Thou askest more questions than the catechism of Father Ripalda!" cried poor Clarita, and burst into tears.

Ernestina's pathetically plain face distorted itself in sympathy. She took the little one in her arms, and with a glance implored her mother to forbear. Indeed, that lady had learned all that the culprit was in a position to tell her.

Doña Rosalia knew her duty. Her first step was to revoke Clarita's "hour of balcony." For further precaution she nullified all the balconies except her own, causing the awnings to hang adroop at all hours and locking the French windows of access. It was true that by this means the innocent Ernestina also was deprived of her hour of balcony, but as she had never known what it was to have an admirer and never expected to have one, she made no complaint. Meanwhile the *portero*, under instruction, spread abroad the rumor that there was indisposition in the family.

These demonstrations, while they perturbed the youthful "bear," did not deceive him. Still less did they discourage him. Constancy in love reaches astonishing lengths in Mexico, and it is well that this is so, for in no other land is love itself viewed parentally with so much disfavor and vexed with so many obstacles and indignities.

It was a boast of Doña Rosalia that she could smell family distinction a mile away. Having duly inspected the pretender through her opera-glasses from behind her curtains, she announced confidently that he was of no family whatever. Of his being comely, honest-looking, and excellently dressed she made no mention, as those attributes did not enter into her point of view.

"If God intended my daughters for the life of marriage," she argued, "He would certainly make His blessed will known to me by sending a pretender with a name worthy of being added to that of Ramos Blancos."

[12] For God's sake!

Meanwhile love, after its manner, grew greater for the restrictions imposed upon it. By devious means the pretender's letters continued to arrive, and Clarita effected her graduation from the stage of refusing to receive them to that of reading them without replying, then to replying with formality, then to a thrilling exchange of photographs, and on to the tender formula of "thee" and "thou," and gloriously forward to vows of eternal fidelity telegraphed in every mood and tense from eyes to eyes through the dim vistas of an incense-swimming church.

Then the pretender's father took a hand. His limousine, a miracle of whispering speed and luxury, with French chauffeur and English footman in pale blue and gold, made as much stir in the Little Square of Marvels as the irruption of an archbishop or a first-class matador could have done. Señor Maldonado would have been better advised to have approached the seat of the Ramos Blancos more humbly. Although he was armed with perfectly proper and even weighty introductions, Doña Rosalia chose to subject him to a long wait in an antechamber before admitting him to an audience.

The elder Maldonado was a financier, famous and as rich as the Indies, but as to family a mere mushroom; indeed, it was said that his father had been a Spaniard and kept a *bodega.*[13] All that saved this fine fellow from a stinging rebuff was his beguiling amiability, enhanced by an outspoken sense of inferiority to the Ramos Blancos. Doña Rosalia felt that she was treating him with more than Christian forbearance in that, instead of openly scouting the idea of an alliance between their families, she merely affected to postpone the matter until such time as her elder daughter should have been married. Señor Maldonado, who had never seen the face of Ernestina, was profuse in his expressions of respectful gratitude.

Clarita had taken care to overhear that conversation, and now she ran to communicate its effect to her sister. Ernestina's eyes filled with tears, and her unfortunate nose grew pink when she learned that Clarita's happiness must wait upon her own marriage.

"Then for thee is no hope, *pobrecita!*"[14] she cried.

"Say not so, or I shall die!" whimpered Clarita. "If thou lovest me as I love thee, thou wilt get thee a husband of some sort and that quickly."

[13] Shop selling wine and food.

[14] Poor little thing.

"But where?" stammered Ernestina, looking about her wildly. "God knows, little sister, that for love of thee I would become the bride of any Christian man graced with a desire for me and the approval of *mamá*."

"Thou art an angel!" Clarita cried, embracing her. "Then all we lack is a man."

"A man is all we lack," Ernestina assented as encouragingly as she could. "God send us one somewhat short of vision, for this face of mine would frighten the devil himself."

"*¡Chist!*[15] Thou art *muy simpática*,[16] and thy face is not so bad in this light, with the awnings down. *Mamá* has always exaggerated the matter; but for charity do not wrinkle thy forehead so. We will both pray with great zeal, and burn many candles to Saint Anthony that he send thee a husband *pronto, prontito*."[17]

Ten rainy seasons washed the House of Colors, but Ernestina did not capture a husband. Neither did she grow beautiful.

In vain the prayers, in vain the candles, in vain the fortunes that the *señor pretendiente* continued to lavish on the chapel of St. Anthony.

"As constant as Don Luis" had become a proverb in the Little Square of Marvels, and if a child was eight years old, its mother would say, "My creature was born when Don Luis carried two years of suitor."

Speaking of children, the officious Agapito had begotten seven or eight, to all of which Don Luis had stood godfather, and otherwise the neighborhood was overrun with little brown Luises, distinguished variously as Luis the Long, Luis the Fool, or the Snuffling, the Intelligent, the Without Teeth, or what-not, all named in honor of "the *patrón* of the corner."

Through the generosity of Don Luis, Pancrazio now had a large white umbrella over his stool in place of the tacked-together bullfight programs; and by other little benefactions he had helped to rejuvenate the *plazuela* while he himself had been growing older.

[15] Ssh! Hush!
[16] Very nice.
[17] Quickly, very quickly.

Older and not a little stouter was that good *señor pretendiente*, and his hair was salt-sprinkled about the ears; for he was of middle life now—past thirty, no less. He and Clarita had come to believe that nothing less than a miracle could unite them until after the death of Doña Rosalia.

And Doña Rosalia was very well indeed. In the language of her friends, "Not a day had passed over her." Strangers often took her for a sister of her daughters. No doubt it did her good to have one of the richest bachelors of the capital languishing away his best years beneath the windows of the Ramos Blancos.

As for Clarita, she had become very thin, but some still considered her pretty; and although she had ceased to weep very much, she seemed as ardent as ever. So sure was Doña Rosalia of her filial piety that she made no further attempt to restrict the courtship, and it remained stationary, with never the touch of a hand at the genteel stage of balcony whisperings and passionate letters raised and lowered with a long white ribbon. That fishing process was the one excitement of Clarita's life, and she would make the most of it, with a leisurely and Delsartian* technic, exhibiting the grace of her arms, especially when there was a moon to silver them and make wild shadows.

One night Don Luis fumbled strangely over the business of attaching his letter to the dangling ribbon. His voice was so hoarse that at first he could not speak, but at the moment when the letter left his hands on its upward journey he managed to articulate:

"*¡Hay esperanza!*"[19]

When the letter, which was uncommonly bulky, had reached her hands he stammered:

"There is hope, my adored—hope for thy sister and for us. Read—read promptly!"

He flourished his cane as a general his sword. When she questioned him he hissed:

"All is within the envelope. Read, little daughter—read, meditate, and pray with thy gentle sister that God give her valor! *¡Adiós!*"

[18] Francois Delsarte (1811-71), French teacher of acting, formulated certain principles of aesthetics that he applied to the teaching of dramatic technique.
[19] There is hope!

And with an agitated gesture he went away, walking like a drunken man.

Clarita retired hastily within her chamber and tore open the envelope. It contained a long letter from Don Luis, accompanied by an attractive illustrated booklet. From one and the other she made out that a surgeon of beauty from the United States had set himself up in the City of Mexico and was anxious, for a consideration, to improve the faces of its inhabitants.

Certain miracles that this practitioner had wrought with faces in the United States were set forth frankly in the illustrations of his booklet. Clarita was particularly struck with two contrasting portraits of a lady, described as of the highest society in the City of New York, taken before and after the surgeon of beauty had exercised his art upon her. Certainly Ernestina at her very worst had never shown the world a countenance so multifariously blighted as that of this lady in her first picture; indeed, it was wonderful that she had possessed the valor to sit for a picture at all. In the second one, however, she had effloresced into such beguiling beauty that the members of her own family must have found it extremely difficult to recognize her.

Moreover, Don Luis declared in his letter, this admirable surgeon of beauty was already beginning to achieve brilliant results in the newly rich, Americanized society of the Mexican capital. Thanks to him, the pretty and coquettish Consuelo Quiroz, who was nicknamed "La Chata"[20] because of the slight flatness of her features, had come out with a Grecian nose of the most delicate modeling, while the widow Amalia de Alvear had lost all her wrinkles and acquired two captivating moles, one on the eyelid and one on the neck, which were making her the rage among the young men.

In fine, there was every reason to hope, the agitated Don Luis concluded, that a similar course of treatment for Ernestina would multiply a thousandfold her hitherto meager prospects of finding a husband.

It might be supposed that Ernestina would have welcomed the proposed plan, but although she had always been dissatisfied with her face in its original condition, she now argued that it had been given her by God, and that it would be the height of impiety to have it made over by a surgeon of beauty from the United States or any-

[20] The pug-nosed.

where else. Not until Clarita, in a tearstorm of passion, swore that a refusal would cause her, Clarita, to disgrace forever the name of Ramos Blancos by eloping with her adorer, did the terrified spinster consent, with many prayers, to be made beautiful.

One day Clarita whispered to her mother that Ernestina had promised God a retreat of six weeks. The sisters had just returned from church, and Ernestina was heavily veiled.

Doña Rosalia, in whom religion dominated every other consideration, with the possible exception of family, took early occasion to boast to all her friends of her elder daughter's piety. Ten times a day she would conjure Clarita to take example by her sister, and when she passed Ernestina's door she would make the sign of the cross, pausing with bowed head as if to receive some touch of sanctity from the inspired one within.

As it is a sin to speak to or even to look at a holy one in retreat, Ernestina had ample opportunity for seclusion and meditation. As she passed on her way to church, the neighbors, with eyes lowered, would furtively touch her dress or her long black veils, and deem themselves blessed thereby.

The truth was that Ernestina, by the grace of a generous loan from her godmother, had offered herself to the excruciating attentions of the surgeon of beauty, and was now undergoing the process of healing, her face clamped in an armor of bandages which her penitential array effectually concealed. But let it not be thought that she sustained her pious reputation in a spirit of unmitigated hypocrisy: on the contrary, she sought to atone for the deception by dint of devotions and austerities which gave an intense reality to her period of penance.

The day for her final visit to the surgeon of beauty came. The anxious Clarita went with her. Would that I could give a true conception of their emotions when, the bandages having been removed, they beheld the pale and symmetrical face, as smooth as an egg, which was now Ernestina's.

What little face of blessed one! *¡En nombre de todos los santos!*[21] Not only had every wrinkle and blemish disappeared, not only had a nose of ridicule become a nose of dignity, not only had the sagging redundancies of jaw and neck given place to the precise contours of youth, but the eyes, once like two fleas, now

[21] In the name of all the saints!

actually represented eyes, and the whole face, by some new trick in the angle of the brows, had acquired a look of noble spirituality which would be highly creditable to a virgin martyr.

In fact, the surgeon of beauty ventured to think that he had done a pretty good piece of work, and he was piqued when the sisters with one impulse fell upon their knees and poured out all their gratitude to God.

But presently Ernestina made a discovery which alloyed her enthusiasm. She could no longer smile. *¡Ay Dios! ¡Qué fatalidad!*[22] Something in the rearrangement of skin or muscles had brought it to pass that the faintest approach to a smile was met with an alarming tension, followed, unless the impulse was immediately checked, by sharp twinges of pain.

In answer to her outcries the surgeon of beauty assured her that an expression of English immobility was in the latest mode cultivated by the most fashionable *señoras*, and advised her to resist all impulse to smile, a very simple matter if she would only make up her mind never to feel amused. Clarita praised his sagacity, and offered comfort to her sister by reminding her that she had ever been given to tears rather than to laughter, and remarking that her condition would have proved far more embarrassing if she had found herself inhibited from weeping abundantly and in perfect comfort, as at that moment.

Not being very logically inclined, Ernestina found no comfort in these arguments, and although she had thanked God for her new face, she now blamed the surgeon of beauty for its limitations as an instrument of mirthful expression.

Fortunately her dissatisfaction was short-lived. Such a profound impression did her metamorphosis make upon her mother, and thereafter upon all the world, that she very quickly reconciled herself to a lifetime of smilelessness. For, emerging from her self-imposed retreat with a countenance so changed and so spiritualized, she became famous far and wide as a saint whose piety had been rewarded with a visible, unequivocal signet of divine favor.

In the light of the legend of the miracle, her holiness was manifest to all, and all paid gratifying tribute thereto. Fastidious young women friends who in times past had gracefully refrained from giving her the customary two kisses, one on each cheek, at greet-

[22] Oh, God! What a catastrophe!

ing and parting, now fervently pressed their pretty lips to her smooth and sanctified face, praying silently for forgiveness and benediction. Sick friends would leave their beds and drive to the House of Colors, designing under the pretext of a social call to sit near Ernestina and, if possible, to hold her blessed hand. Expectant mothers plotted or pleaded for her presence on interesting occasions, that her holy face might be the first on which the eyes of their babes should light. As for the common people, they frankly kneeled when she passed.

And Clarita? Her joy knew no bounds until one day when she learned that Ernestina had peremptorily declined to consider an offer of marriage from an eligible widower as pious and well born as he was wealthy. Pains of all the martyrs! From her balcony that night the love-sick virgin rained tears upon the upturned, anguished face of Don Luis.

The fact was that the world's conception of Ernestina's holiness had awakened an unmistakable echo in her own soul. No one believed in the miraculous character of her transfiguration more sincerely than she herself, and in this faith she was confirmed by her father confessor, who preached an eloquent sermon on the subject. The first offer of marriage was followed by many more, from widowers and bachelors of excellent pedigree and serious disposition, but from the rarefied heights on which she now dwelt a descent to the banality of marriage was out of the question.

However, the good creature was not so lost in heavenly contemplation as not to have kept a human corner in her heart for her little sister, and such was her influence upon Doña Rosalia that the constancy of Don Luis was at length rewarded as it deserved. His long years of playing the bear had not spoiled his disposition, and if you had known Clarita in the past and could see her now with her three lovely children, I believe you would consider her transfiguration just as wonderful as that of the saintly Ernestina.

[March 1916]

The Soul of Hilda Brunel

The portrait was almost finished. Two more sittings—well, perhaps three—and she would come to the studio no more. Standish painted away in silence, but somewhere underneath his blouse a little voice babbled impertinently: "No more! No more! She will come no more!"

From time to time he stopped to look at her, his eyes puckered into narrow peep-holes. And she knew that those eyes were engaged solely in their business of digging out color, with exactly the same kind of regard for her woman's face and body that they would have paid to a well-composed arrangement of flowers, fruit, or fish. For it was no mystery to her, that power of his to escape from the actual in pursuit of the ideal. The same power in her enabled her to send her voice—yes, and her very personality—soaring into the remote spaces of great opera-houses, modulated to every hue of terror, pity, passion, tenderness, or despair, while her inmost self remained in supreme command, unswayed by the hollow mountain of dim humanity beyond the orchestra no less than by the savor of garlic in the torrent of divine *bel canto*[1] pouring from the throat of the stout tenor at her side.

While Standish, his brush tripping fruitfully between palette and canvas, played with a delectable problem of warm shoulder glowing through a wave of gauze, the little voice under his blouse changed its cadence and began to question the woman on the model-throne.

[1] Operatic singing characterized by a full, rich, broad tone and legato phrasing.

"You, who seem to know everything," it said to her, "do you know what you have done to me? But you must know—you couldn't miss it. Why not let me know, then, by some of those signals that women have at their fingers' ends for the encouragement of serious fellows like me, that I needn't hesitate to declare myself? Or don't you care? Is it just a silly delusion of mine that you and I together could reach unguessed heights and depths of being, and that the fact of our meeting was fated to start an interesting reaction of some sort in the spiritual chemistry of the universe?"

Standish liked that phrase so much that he wished Hilda Brunel might have heard it. But she held her pose untroubled, and her intelligent eyes met his with their usual tranquillity. On Standish himself, the voice was reacting as a strong stimulant. His very brush seemed to respond to it, licking up the divinely ordained pigments in advance of his thought, blending them in a jiffy, and whipping them on the canvas in clean strokes that evoked astonishing clarity and truth. It was one of the golden moments when that great artist, the soul, pushes aside its laggard apprentice, the brain, and takes the job into its own hands. And now the little voice under the painter's blouse grew bolder, intoxicated by the freedom of silent confession.

"What sort of a woman are you?" it went on to Hilda Brunel. "Will you laugh at me if I show you my heart? No; I don't believe it. The world, while it does its best to spoil you, turns up its eyes behind your back and calls you heartless. Why, if you had divorced fifty husbands instead of one, if you had waded through seas of mud and picked up shoals of oyster-shells in search of a pearl to match the one in your breast—all that wouldn't matter a snap of the fingers to me, my dear! I would lead you to the high altar of my worship—yes, even if you were broken and soiled, your voice and beauty gone, your fame turned to ridicule—and there, by the Eternal, I would kneel to you proudly in the sight of the whole gaping pack, who never saw your soul and couldn't have understood its glories if they had!"

Standish was breathing hard, his heart aching with a keen mixture of pain and joy. With all his soul in his eyes, he flashed a wide-open look at Hilda Brunel. What was this? Her dark eyes were strangely fixed and shining. As he looked at them in wonder, they suddenly closed. Two tears pushed out and rolled down her cheeks. Standish put down his palette and brushes. Without opening her eyes, she gave him a little smile, and said:

"You mustn't be alarmed by a tear or two. They're a part of my stock in trade, you know."

The words pained him. He went near her, not knowing what to say. His impulse was to sit on the dais at her feet, but his courage failed him. She opened her eyes with an encouraging smile and shifted her feet to make room for him.

"Do you read my thoughts?" he asked, in amazement.

"If I do," she said, "they get so mixed with my own that I can't tell which is which."

His eyes questioned her desperately.

"Would you mind telling me why you were crying just now?"

"Will you tell me first," she bargained, "what you were thinking about at that moment?" He took a deep breath and considered the matter. "Meanwhile," she continued, with a smile, "may I look at my picture, please?"

He sprang to his feet, handed her from the dais, and led her to the best point from which to view the canvas that he had enriched with the best work of his life.

"Do you know what you have done?" she whispered, after looking at it for a long time. "You have painted me with a soul."

He was overcome.

"I wonder has anyone else ever seen it as I do," he stammered. "Let me tell you this: I love you! I love you in such a way that I'd welcome any trial, however terrible, to prove it!"

"But that was it—that was what made those tears come! I seemed to see your love in shapes of power and holiness, daring all things—humiliation—"

He seized her hands.

"You saw all that?"

"And I felt that you were giving me a soul."

"I—giving *you?*" His tone was a protest. He wished to tell her that she was the giver and he the receiver, but she, reading his thought, shook her head, saying:

"No; all I can give you is life. I'll give you that in good measure, my sweet master. But the soul—a woman has no soul until she loves. And I—do you know that I didn't want to have a soul, that I was afraid of it and fought against it? Ah, you have taken me into your hands! What will you do with me?"

His voice had no answer ready, but his lips found hers. She had promised him life, and he felt its sources quicken at the crushed sweetness of her mouth. It was Hilda who halted that magic before it could carry them quite beyond the realm of thought.

"Remember," she whispered breathlessly, as she struggled to free herself," "remember that we have found each other, for pain as well as for joy. There was never a love like this without pain."

"I am ready for pain," he said quietly. "That is nothing to me. And I'm ready for the hardest thing of all—to give pain to another."

"Yes; that is the hardest. Do you think she loves you?"

"She is not very affectionate. She isn't that kind of a woman at all. You've met her two or three times. What do you think?"

"I think she is fond of you," said Hilda frankly. "No woman could help being fond of you, because you are kind and unselfish."

"You don't know me," he protested, shaking his head ruefully. "I'm awfully thoughtless and troublesome. There are lots of ways in which I have disappointed poor Estelle's ideals." Hilda smiled, and stroked his cheek with her finger. "She's going to suffer, of course. I know how indignant she'll be. I wonder if we can make her understand that the thing that has happened to us is stronger than we are—that it is life raised to its highest power, supremely good and—"

Hilda uttered an exclamation and left his side to inspect an unframed picture that had caught her eye where it lay among other studio litter in the shadow under the balcony.

"Where is that place?" she asked him abruptly.

"Let me see. Oh—that's down on the Connecticut shore. Do you like the sketch? Wait a minute—let me dust it."

He took it from her hands and cleaned it off with a rag, then placed it in a good light. Hilda studied it intently, with a curious expression of concentration.

"But that's the place exactly!" she murmured, more to herself than to him. Her face and voice were still full of wonder.

"You've been there?" he inquired. "That would be strange."

She looked at him with a bewildered smile, and then at the picture again.

"If I could only tell you how strange the feeling is! I've seen it, just like that, on gray days when the sky and water melted into one, and, at other times, I've seen it in storms, with waves dashing here at the end of the point."

"Yes, yes; that's where they do dash," said Standish. "But when were you there?"

"If I only knew!" She shook her head anxiously. "There's just one thing that is different," she said. "That factory chimney in the distance across the marsh—that wasn't there."

"But it must have been, if this is really the place you've seen. That factory chimney has always been there—at least, as long as I can remember, and probably before you were born."

She looked at him strangely and said, in a low tone, "It's the same place."

A trifle startled at the importance she seemed to place upon it, he tried to answer in a matter-of-fact tone, although he had a curious feeling that the case was not a matter-of-fact one at all.

"Well, to make sure, we'll ask old John about it," he said.

"Old John? Is he from that shore?"

"Yes; I inherited him along with the farm. You can't see much of the farm in the sketch, but it runs down to the shore here. I used to call old John my wet-nurse, because he taught me to swim and sail a boat. He looks after my boats now in summer, and potters around the studio here in winter. My mother's family, the Buckles, have looked after him ever since a misfortune he had down there, before my time."

"A fire," said Hilda.

He looked at her quickly.

"What made you say that?"

"I don't know. I simply seemed to know that it was a fire."

In that instant, as he looked at her, a strange thing befell Walter Standish. He seemed to slip free from the limits of time and solidity and to launch into some fluid element in which all things perished and were born again by enchantment; and, in one stroke of illumination, he became aware that, at some point of eternity, just beyond the trembling border of conscious memory, he and Hilda Brunel had both existed on that Connecticut shore.

He spoke. He heard his own words as if they had been uttered by another.

"You're right about the factory chimney," the voice ran; "it was not there in those days."

They stared into each other's eyes. Standish heard the fumbling of a latch-key and the opening and shutting of the outer door as old John let himself into the anteroom. He had been to the bank to cash a check. After stowing away his hat and coat, he came shuffling into the studio with the money in his hand. He was a little old man with a closely trimmed, yellowish white beard. His eyes were pale blue, and the right one, which was smaller than its mate, was always winking, while the whole of that side of his face had a shrunken look. His right arm, also, was twisted and helpless. Always sparing of speech, he handed Standish the money without a word and was going out again, when Standish stopped him with a question.

"John, can you remember," he asked, "when Slosson's factory over on the creek was built?"

The old man considered carefully for some seconds, and then replied, in a dull, gentle voice:

"There was a bricklayer by the name of Ryan that fell from the top of that stack just when it was finishing. I was on the coroner's jury. That was in 'eighty-seven."

"A year before I was born," said Standish to Hilda.

"So you and I are the same age," she remarked, without surprise. "Evidently it was not in this life that we—"

She checked herself and watched old John as he shuffled off to his post in the anteroom. Then she turned to the picture.

"In this life, I've been there only in dreams," she said. "But they haven't been like ordinary dreams. They haven't had the dream-quality. I can't describe their quality, but I had the very same kind of feeling when you and I were introduced over the teacups at Mrs. Weatherby Jones's, a few Sundays ago."

"I, too," said Standish thoughtfully. "At least, I suppose it was the same sort of feeling. Something inside me seemed to call out: 'Hello! Here she is at last!'"

Hilda smiled, and put her hands on his shoulders.

"Do you know what I purpose doing?" she said. "But, of course, you don't. You've heard, though—haven't you?—about my being the daughter of a wise woman."

"I've read in the papers," he confessed cautiously, "that your mother was a highly gifted—er—"

"Fortune-teller—don't be afraid to say it. And I suppose I would have followed in her footsteps if I hadn't been caught young and packed off to Europe to have my voice made into something, and myself, too. But mamma was more than a fortune-teller. She knew secrets of being that are not known to many outside of the Orient. And I know a few myself, dear; and you shall learn all that I know, and we'll travel on together, learning more and more forever and ever—for there are no shores to the ocean of knowledge, and the greatest of pilots there is Love!"

Until that moment, he had not dreamed that a mortal face could glow with such a pure flame of aspiration as he now saw in hers. With the eye of intuition, he glimpsed, for one dazzling instant, unsuspected reaches in his art, vanishing toward the mystic abode of absolute beauty.

"Come," she said. "I want your help while I try to get below the surface of things as they seem to be."

A sudden misgiving seized upon Standish.

"With your temperament," he stammered, "so emotional, so impressionable, do you think it is wise to—"

She looked at him earnestly.

"If we are honest with fate, Walter," she said, "the truth cannot harm us."

"But can you be sure?"

"Today, I feel capable of anything!"

She looked around and selected an armchair of low and reposeful lines. With feverish energy, she dragged it into position with its back to the light, then sat in it, settled herself comfortably, and closed her eyes.

"This will do beautifully. Ah, I'm off already! Come and put your hand on my forehead. How cool it is! I feel that I'm really going to get results. Now listen: Don't get frightened and try to wake me up too soon. Remember that I shall be just on the other side of a thin partition, and that I can even pass back and forth, and talk to you most of the time. In face, if I stop talking too long, I want you to insist on my telling you what I'm experiencing. And tell me to remember to be sure not to forget anything when I come back to the present."

"But suppose"—his voice shook slightly—"suppose there should be any difficulty about your coming back?"

"I'll come back—to you." She spoke a trifle laboriously, as one speaks in a foreign language. "Please move the hand down lightly over my face—like that—then back again—down—rhythmically—a little faster. I'm back at Mrs. Weatherby Jones's tea. I'm shaking hands with you—Mr. Standish."

Across her unseeing face flitted a shadow of the smile with which she had greeted the introduction, reproduced in all its artificiality, and thereby contrasting strongly with the frank smiles she had learned to give him since. After that, she sighed and seemed to fall into an apathy. For half a minute, perhaps, he continued the passes in silence.

"What now?" he ventured. There was no reply. He repeated the question. She seemed to arouse herself.

"Paris—not worthwhile—passes a little quicker."

He increased the tempo. Tenderly and ardently he watched her face, feeling half awed by the thought of the journey on which her spirit was fleeting, although half ashamed of himself for harboring even a small measure of faith in such an experiment. Sometimes she stirred. Once or twice she frowned faintly. Again would come the shadow of a haughty smile or the ghost of a short laugh. Of what adventures were these the phantom signals? Standish burned with jealous curiosity, but not for worlds would he have questioned her.

Suddenly she startled him. Leaning forward, with an animated motion of the head, she began to sing Mimi's song from *La Bohême.* He ceased the passes, although he hardly expected her to sing more than a few bars. With perfect aplomb, however, she continued to fill the studio with soaring melody, her exquisite voice modulated to all the lights and shades of the sewing girl's lyric account of herself, her toil, her poverty, and her prayers. He knew the music by ear, and marveled at the accuracy with which she measured the pauses as though they were punctuated by the veritable surging of a great orchestra.

When the last note had rung out, the singer remained tense for a moment, her eyelids fluttering so that the whites showed in glimpses underneath. Gently he placed his hand over them. She relaxed and sank back in the chair.

"Covent Garden,"[2] she murmured. "The king and queen—Puccini[3] in another box."

He resumed the motion of his hand, and again the minutes sped faster than years. Once, after an unusually long interval of silence, it developed that a small Hilda Brunel was playing with other school-children in Stuyvesant Square, not far from her mother's home on Second Avenue, New York. She gave a beating with her fists to a hateful boy who had called her mamma a witch. She wept because a little girl who lived in the square and had a governess, and whom she adored for her daintiness, was not allowed to play with her. A minute or so later, she was sitting in a basket in her mother's flat, eating a cake. Her mother was at the window, crying. Why? Because Hilda's father had gone away.

"Why are you sitting in a basket?" Standish inquired.

"I can't walk yet."

He struggled against a growing impression of weirdness. Doubtless, Hilda's mother had told her at some time about the basket and the cake. He reminded himself of auto-suggestion and other handy labels that material science supplies for immaterial riddles. Meditating on these mysteries, he continued the passes without questioning her, until it occurred to him, with a little shock, that she had sunk into a deeper lethargy. Her face was expressionless, and her breathing hardly perceptible. He spoke to her twice, but she returned no answer. Remembering her instructions, he tried hard to overcome any feeling of alarm.

"Wherever you are," he said firmly, as his hand rose and fell lightly over her face, "you must not forget anything. Remember, when you come back, every single thing that has happened to you."

A moment later, he heard a gurgling sound. Her lips were moving. He stooped down with his ear toward her mouth.

"Jim!" she ejaculated, in a choking voice. "Jim!"

Standish had to steady his voice, so startled was he.

"Who are you?" he demanded.

"Emily," she replied impatiently. "I'm Emily Haff." Her face became a mask of fear and distress, and she groaned.

"Hilda, that's enough!" he cried. "Come back!"

[2] Area in London site of the Royal Opera.

[3] Giacomo Puccini (1858-1924), composer of *La Bohême*.

With a violent contortion of the body, she cried hoarsely, like an animal:

"The barn's on fire! Somebody has padlocked the door!"

Standish caught up her hands.

"Hilda Brunel!" he cried, in a shaking voice. "Hilda Brunel, come back to me!"

He kissed her on the eyes. Immediately they opened and stared at him.

"Oh, what a headache I have!" Hilda complained, with a smile.

For a few minutes, while he ministered to her, nothing was said about the experiment. Suddenly, she announced gaily:

"Things are coming back to me. Didn't I sing Mimi's song?"

"Yes; you sang it beautifully," he said. "It was very mysterious."

She smiled and fell into meditation. After a while, she said:

"I was a baby, a little bit of a baby, eating a cake with seeds on it. Poor mamma! How young she looked, and so sad!" For a long time after that, she was silent, and when she turned to Standish again, her face had changed.

"I remember the fire," she said quietly. "Yes; we did live on that shore, you and I. We couldn't be together, but we couldn't keep our eyes and thoughts off each other. I was Johnny Haff's wife, and you were another woman's husband. When I saw you go into the barn that time, I had just been making some doughnuts. That was in my house, not far from your barn. I took a dish of the doughnuts over to the barn to give them to you. I didn't care who saw me. It was the same to me whether I lived or died if I couldn't be near you. You asked me to call you 'Jim.' You kissed me, and asked me to run away with you. You told me you couldn't live without me."

Standish picked up his brushes and began to wipe them on a painty rag. His eyes were dim.

"I thought I heard something at the barn door," she continued, "but I didn't care. We were in the harness-room. A little bit later, we smelled the smoke. Tell me the whole story, dear," she said. "I know you know it."

"In my grandfather's time," he said slowly, "there was a barn burned, with two people in it. One of them was Johnny Haff's wife. The other was my uncle James. He was my mother's favorite brother. My mother wasn't there at the time, fortunately for her. She hadn't long been married. She has shown me pictures of uncle James. He—he looked like me."

"He *was* you!" Hilda whispered.

"I wonder. He was a bit wild—couldn't settle down at anything. He had recently returned home after an absence and brought a wife with him. They say that she was a quiet little thing, with nothing particular about her except that she always seemed to be watching him. But if she had noticed anything between him and Johnny Haff's wife, it doesn't seem that anybody else had."

"I take it," said Hilda, "that what is left of Johnny Haff is your old John?"

Standish nodded.

"Johnny Haff was a neighbor. He had a little place on the cove where he rented out boats and fishing-tackle, and he sailed his own oyster-sloop. I've heard this story from him. Nobody but uncle James's wife saw Johnny Haff's wife go to the barn, and not a soul saw uncle James's wife go there after her. There was a lantern with a box of matches beside it on a shelf near the door, and the supposition is that she took these matches before closing and padlocking the door. Nobody knows just how she set fire to the barn, but it burned like tinder in the strong southerly breeze that was blowing. She had taken the key out of the padlock. Old John believes that she returned all the way to the house with that key in her hand before she changed her mind."

"She changed her mind?" Hilda was almost voiceless.

"That's old John's idea—and that she started running back to the barn, meaning to let them out."

"She must have heard you," Hilda whispered. "You were shouting: 'Annie! Annie! Annie!'"

"That may have been it. But, in her hurry, she dropped the key. When Johnny Haff came running over from the cove, he saw her crawling about on her knees in the middle of the meadow lot, pulling up handfuls of grass. He went at the door with the first heavy object he could find—he doesn't remember what it was—and, after a while, he got it open. The flames rushed out, and at first he didn't see the bodies, but a moment later he did. He got pretty badly burned getting them out. He thinks they were asphyxiated before the flames reached them, because the faces were quite peaceful."

Standish and Hilda sat in silence for some time. Old John came in to ask if he might go to his lunch. Hilda observed him with frank and searching pity. He kept his winking eye away from the light.

"That's *one*," she said, when he had wandered off, "and the *other?*"

"Uncle James's wife? A child was born, but it didn't live. She did, however. She is quite harmless now, but has to be looked after, poor old soul! She's always stooping and searching—for that key."

Again Hilda's eyes seemed to take firm hold of a picture.

"Walter," she said suddenly, "do you believe in God?"

"I do now, since I have found you," he answered simply.

"And I—I feel that he understands and forgives us for that hour of passion, though it broke Johnny Haff and started the other on her lifelong search for the key of the barn. For we knew no better then, you and I—we had no light."

Standish raised his head and looked at her with troubled eyes. Her face, at that moment, seemed to mirror all the sorrows of the world.

"What are you thinking of?" he whispered.

She read his face for a moment before replying, and her eyes were full of pity.

"Of your wife," she said.

"Hilda, you can't be mad enough to believe"—his voice shook—"that we can do without each other now?"

Her eyes held him where he stood, but seemed to gather him up in an embrace of the spirit.

"By the pain we are suffering," she said, "I possess you, and you possess me, for all time. That is just why we can never go back to the darkness of damaging other lives for our passing delight, even although—" Her lips trembled piteously. "Help me, dear," she faltered, "for this is our Gethsemane!"

He caught the two hands that she stretched out to him, but she withdrew them. He went white to the lips.

"You mean that we must deny ourselves—all?"

"In this life, as far as our blindness lets us see—yes; to give our light and warmth to others who may need it, and so to purify ourselves for the perfect union, in whatever life it may come—sooner or later, according as we are faithful to love in the highest. That is our way as I see it, dear, with this soul that you have given me."

Gazing at her dumbly, he knew that the tears streaming from those wonderful eyes were not of sorrow. And, suddenly, the bitterness in his heart was swept away by a flood of peace, while new and incredible sources of power were thrown open within him. Again the veil was lifted and he saw, more clearly now, those unknown reaches of his art, trailing eternally in tranquil, sovereign certitude toward the ever unfolding bosom of the Infinite. Could he ever reach them? Came the answer—he would try! And he saw his path fixed forever in the wake of the workers, great and humble, who had seen that vision and held it always in their hearts, having learned, in the anguish of renunciation, the inner meaning of the saying: "Whoso loseth his life shall find it."

[December 1916]

A Son of the Tropics

A story of revolution by the foremost interpreter of Mexican life.
—The Household Magazine

Delayed by a broken bridge and other misadventures of travel, Don Rómulo and Dorotea did not reach the *hacienda*[1] until long after nightfall.

Alejandro, the experienced overseer of La Paloma,[2] Don Rómulo's vast estate, had tactfully organized an outburst of artless enthusiasm which passed off quite admirably by torchlight. There was a mounted escort, there was a band which conflicted stoutly with the clamoring church-bells, there were fireworks which did not always go off, and there was a triumphant arch of white and red camellias.

Dorotea Salgado, who had often felt herself a foreigner in her native land, was stirred for the first time to the roots of her race instinct. If it occurred to her that the cries of welcome had a listless accent, she probably accepted that as an interesting peculiarity, like the echo that bounded from patio to patio in a crystal diminuendo. Everything delighted her, even the feudal promiscuity within the ramparts of her ancestral home, which recalled to her a walled town in Brittany.

Don Rómulo's feelings were different. After one or two emotional tears as a tribute to the occasion, he began to feel profoundly bored. In truth, nothing less than a pricking alarm over his strangely and desperately shrinking revenues would have tempted him to

[1] Estate or plantation.
[2] The Dove, an ironic reference to peace.

revisit his domain of La Paloma after an absence of almost twenty years.

At an early stage of the journey, when Don Rómulo's heart was warm with the thought of re-living his youth through the first impressions of his child, he had recklessly undertaken to ride with his daughter next morning to see the sun rise from a remarkable hill called the Chair of the Devil. Recalling that pledge when she opened her eyes at half-dawn, awakened by a lively duet of trumpeting between a peacock and a burro, Dorotea sprang out of bed, dressed with all the vivacity of her seventeen years, and ran to call her *papá*. Alas! As the shadows of clouds that pass over water are the promises of those who cherish the habit of embracing the pillow until noon. *Papá* was giving music which Dorotea recognized as portending hours of slumber. She did not persist.

Halfheartedly she began to explore the ins-and-outs of the *rancho,*[3] that rambling, low-lying stronghold undulating over the bosom of the earth, a mantle of masonry and baked mud, its roofs of red tile long since disguised in healthy crops of mignonette. From the titanic gate built for sieges, she peered out at the *pueblo*. And out there, beyond the valley waving with ripe grain, rose the Chair of the Devil, that famous hill, clearly recognizable from familiar photographs but looking much nearer and seeming now to be afloat on the bosom of a mystic grey lake.

She sighed. On a chair in the portico of the overseer's house she had seen her new English saddle. How exciting! And yet! The hour was magical for a solitary adventure, and her blood leaped at the summons of the morning.

The *pueblo*, even to her unaccustomed eyes, had a strangely deserted look as she cantered among the straggling huts down toward the open valley. The few women, most of them old, who were carrying water from the rivulet, halted with their great jars on their heads and turned to stare after the daughter of the master, riding alone and fearlessly toward the foothills. They watched her until she was swallowed up in the mist, and long after they watched for her to reappear, but she did not.

Dorotea had imagined that she could arrive at the Chair of the Devil in ten minutes or so; but she was to learn that hills have a trick of retreating as one advances upon them. At the end of half an hour

[3] Group of simple buildings.

her goal still beckoned her from what seemed an undiminished distance; and now stretches of rougher land revealed themselves between. She pushed on, feeling suddenly isolated and very brave. The country grew wilder.

Presently she caught sight of two horsemen on a hill at her right. They were looking down at her. So still they stood against the sky that for one instant she actually experienced "flesh of chicken," but with a return of disdain, she struck her horse with the whip and sped on her way. From the tail of her eye she saw one of the men disappear, and at intervals she could hear the soft pat of hoofs at a steady pace behind her. Suddenly, as she reached the shoulder of a hill, she was almost unhorsed by the rearing of the animal as a hand seized the bridle; and she found herself surrounded by armed men. The sun had climbed high before Don Rómulo found himself sufficiently awake to dip one plump forefinger into the brass cup of holy water nailed to his bed, and therewith sign the blessed cross in two decisive strokes on eyelids and brow. Then, after a few minutes of meditation, he fumbled for his "awakener" and set it ringing. It was one of his habits that the "awakener," a mild form of alarm clock, should be employed to consummate and ratify, rather than to inaugurate, the awakening process. By that usage it served also to summon his *mozo*[4] at the agreeable moment.

Soon all the retainers of the establishment were testifying by more or less ineffectual movements their recognition of the fact the *patrón*[5] was awake. Alejandro, the patient overseer, who had been waiting anxiously for that moment, took an early opportunity of attending upon his feudal lord, with solicitous inquiries as to the quality of his repose and the precise condition of his health.

"I have passed a fatal night," returned Don Rómulo, in a hollow voice, "a night without the benediction of God. Not once did I paste the eyes."

The overseer expressed obsequious concern and enumerated certain traditional remedies for insomnia, at each of which Don Rómulo shrugged his handsome eyebrows with that smile of introspective bitterness which announces that one's case is beyond ordinary aid.

[4] Servant.

[5] Master, boss.

"May you never be condemned to the torments that I pass, good Alejandro," he said kindly; detaching with a silver knife another sherry-gelatine from the tray on his knees and receiving it into his mouth with a sigh.

He did not look at his faithful factotum, for it was one of his morning habits that he should "accustom his eyes to the light," and they had not yet reached the stage of being more than half open.

"No doubt for some excellent purpose of Divine Providence," he went on, "I am a mortal of whom the soul seems elected to suffer and receive displeasures. Perhaps as punishment of sins or trial of patience the why is not for me to question—I am filled with affliction until no more. Nevertheless, I find no one with will to make my path more smooth. As now. Notorious it is that I have in the metropolis various negotiations that ask for my constant attention, also that the air of the country is too strong for my unfortunate organism; yet it seems that to avert disgraceful poverty in my old age I must endure all the anguishes of unearthing myself and coming hither to receive headaches and other disorders, when I have you, Alejandro, for all these things."

His plaintive accent as he concluded, quite out of breath, harrowed the feelings of the elderly Indian. Alejandro's eyes filled with tears and he sank on his knees at the bedside, clasping his strong, brown hands.

"Venerable master," he said in a broken voice, "command your servant what thing he can do so that never again while he lives he may see his beloved master discommoded. May I perish first, one hundred times! If in this old head still remains something of my defunct father's counsels, it is the devotion he recommended to me for his master, your illustrious *papá*—that in peace he may rest—and for you, my own master! Said he, just before he ceased to suffer, 'After God, thy masters,' So I have walked until now, in the sight of God who hears me speak these words."

"It is true, good Alejandro," the master responded graciously, as he wiped some drops of chocolate from his beard. "I know your heart and I value your honesty and affection as did my father—may his soul repose with God! But that is only half the tale you have to tell me, my friend. By the blessed souls! I want to know what has passed with my gains from this, my patrimony, my just increment from the land of my ancestors. Verily I begin to be so reduced that I fear to become a nobody in the capital. The why of this, Alejandro, that I find myself like a pot with the meat taken out?"

"*¡Ay!* God knows how hard I have tried to cover up the truth during these last years, that your Venerable Self might be defended from the anguish of coming hither to have headaches and receive vexations! In all my news to you I have carefully painted all things color of rose."

"Color of rose!" echoed Don Rómulo. "In that case they got themselves well blackened on the way, for certainly no unfortunate sinner was ever submerged in such never-to-end chronicles of calamity as your news has brought me. What floods, what droughts, what failures of crops, what fires of my granaries, what pestilences and losses of my livestock on the hills! Color of rose! What roses or what pumpkins!"

"Praise the Divine Mercy, master, here we have you at last, and doubtless your venerable person can give end to the barbarities that God has permitted to occur in your absence. You shall see who are the faithful ones, and we will defend you to the last drop of our blood. If you had advised me with more anticipation of your coming I would have prepared you a little to receive the truth, but it is certain that our blessed Mother of Guadalupe will not permit that your august person be molested."

Whether or not the eyes of Don Rómulo had properly accustomed themselves to the light, they were now very wide open. Large and black they were, and grandly expressive, like those of a startled fawn. Not less open was his mouth, depriving him of the power of utterance; while Alejandro, who was full of words—in his own phrase, they had been "rotting" in him—continued to pour them out.

"Without doubt, that son of the thousand devils, Rosario, will hear that you have arrived, as he hears all things, but who can believe that he would be so disrespectful as to attack and burn the *rancho* while your mercy is here? Thus he has threatened without shame since a thousand of the youngest and strongest *peones*[6] from all your *ranchos* and some others have joined him in the hills, after stealing all the firearms and many cases of dynamite, not to forget

[6] Members of the landless laboring class, or persons in compulsory servitude.

my clothes and numerous other indispensables, with God knows how many horses, cows, burros, and young women."

"But this is tremendous!" ejaculated Don Rómulo. "Rosario—that name has a sound of malediction in my ears. Is he not proscribed? And what has he to do with my people, this Rosario of the Devil?"

"Miserable of me that I should have to tell your mercy that he, that shameless one who seduces your people with culpable talk of killing all masters and taking their lands, he is a young man of us, born within these walls, who owes you, master, allegiance to the death. Pardon that I say it, he is the creature that Remedios gave to light."

Don Rómulo stared at him.

"Remedios—not the little daughter of my *nana*, the one that was always singing?"

"You have spoken, master."

"She bore a son—but how long ago?"

"Yet he reaches not twenty, but he made himself a large man, and he can read and write."

"Not yet twenty!" Don Rómulo frowned and studied his fingernails. Then he cleared his throat magisterially and said: "Where is Remedios? I will speak with her."

But the overseer shook his head, saying: "It cannot be, master; she died in the year after the year of the great heat."

Don Rómulo bent his head and seemed to observe the pattern of the counterpane, twisting his fingers in his beard. At last he said: "Why did no one inform me of the birth of that little sinner, when both you and the priest undoubtedly conjectured that so I would have wished?"

"As for humble me," returned the overseer, "I would not presume to conjecture the will of my masters in such affairs; as for the reverend priest, he confabulated with your sanctified *señora mamá,*[7] who was then ruling over us—that in peace she may rest!—and she ordained that your honor should not be molested with news of all the disappointments at the *hacienda*. To Remedios she spoke with benign words and made her good faces. The child, as he grew to *muchacho,*[8] was favored by the priest, who taught him to read in

[7] Dear mother.

[8] Youth, a young man.

books, and I would say, with permission, that too much knowledge made him a villain."

"Does he know, this wicked youth, or has he conjectured, that which was confabulated between my mother and the excellent padre?"

"Rest tranquil, master, Remedios was not a parrot, and that assassin of innocence conjectures nothing of nothing."

"He is tall, you say?"

"A Hercules, master; with teeth of catamount and entrails of bull."

Don Rómulo sighed. "What misfortune, Alejandro, that he did not grow up to fear God!" Then he added: "Not a word of this scandal to my daughter. *¡Ay! ¡Ay!* Why did I bring her to this nest of lions? My little lamb, how late she sleeps!"

Alejandro shifted uneasily.

"Not so, master," he stammered. "The birds were not out of their nests before the *señorita* had gone—so those fools came to tell me when it was too late—but I pray God that by now she may be safely returning."

"From where, in the name of all the saints?" ejaculated Don Rómulo.

The old servant spread his hands. "I have given that imbecile of José the Short-Legged, a few good thumps. He saddled a horse for the *señorita* and did not tell me. Who could have told us that it would have occurred to the *señorita* to ride so far into the valley? Rest tranquil, that the blessed Mother of Guadalupe will protect her, and also I have sent out all our men to search everywhere."

With a smothered cry of *"¡Jesucristo!"*[9]—at once an imprecation and a prayer—Don Rómulo scrambled out of bed.

Crowned with their jugs of water from the rivulet, old women and little girls halted with their hands on their hips to stare at the master as he spurred down the valley at a devil's gallop, the sides of his horse already stained with red.

No one followed him. He had flung out a savage order that no one should. Such a cavalcade as might have been mustered from the loyal remnant of his people would have hampered him in his

[9] Jesus Christ!

purpose, which was to come face to face with Rosario, at the first instant permitted by God.

Don Rómulo had not been on a horse for many years, and his muscles were tender and his body was as a full sack of wheat; but he rode as if lifting the goaded beast with him at every stride. And his face was as steady as a mask of fate. He gave no heed to the condition of his crops, overripe, spoiling, for the withheld harvest. All the stagnation and ruin that slipped past with the wind left him unnoting.

Yet his eyes were active. Restlessly, but without expectation, like the eyes of a mechanical figure, they searched for a girlish form unhorsed and lying disabled in some hollow. Once or twice he was deceived by a shadow outline of a bush or a rock, and steered toward it, only to correct the impression without checking speed, and to swerve back with patient vehemence to the chosen road; which carried him toward the Chair of the Devil and the bivouac of bandits beyond. When he divined himself within debatable land, his eyes roved more eagerly and with a living hope, this time in search of any one who might seize him and drag him, with whatsoever indignities, before their chief. And when his horse fell dead, with blood streaming from its mouth, he disengaged his leg, all bruised and wrenched between the saddle and a rock, and stumbled onward, calling two names again and again:

"Dorotea!"

"Rosario!"

The outpost which had distinguished itself by capturing the daughter of the master enriched its fame some hours later by capturing the master himself. Not that the exploit was anything to boast of from a military point of view. Don Rómulo was crawling along on two hands and one knee, dragging his hurt leg behind him and praying for capture. But from a political point of view it was of the highest importance. If the Revolutionary Encampment of the Morning Star needed one thing more than rifles and cartridges, it was a master of whom to make an example before all the world. And here was the one master of all others whom the commander-in-chief, General Rosario, most desired to execute in form.

Half in awe and half in delighted bravado, his captors hoisted him upon a horse, disregarding his appeals for intelligence of his daughter, and convoyed him at a brisk pace to the headquarters of the *comandante*,[10] on the shore of a little lake of sapphire, set in cliffs of pink basalt. Don Rómulo had been wont to bathe there in his boyhood; now the women of the local revolution were placidly washing the shirts and trousers of patriotism in the pellucid shallows.

Seated before a rude table at the mouth of a fern-grown cave, General Rosario was laboriously teaching his fingers the use of an American typewriter stolen from the *hacienda*. Admiring eyes watched him as he perspired over the transcription of a page from Plutarch's *Lives*,[11] pausing at intervals to bestow a piece of sugarcane upon a pet kid which lay across his knees, its palpitating nose ever upturned to him and its legs extended as straight as clutches.

On a box of dynamite a few feet away, a phonograph, under the supervision of a ferocious looking man who had been the barber of the *pueblo*, but was now the lieutenant-general of the army, was rendering a potpourri from *The Prince of Pilsen.*[12] Tula, the barber's daughter, sat on the ground, making dynamite bombs out of doorknobs purloined from the *hacienda.*

She never removed her eyes from Rosario, except to make atrocious faces at the little animal which monopolized his caresses.

"Julius Caesar," he announced suddenly, "had not pursued the wars of Gallia full ten years before he had taken by assault more than eight hundred *pueblos*, subjugated three hundred states, killed a million men, and captured a million more."

The ex-barber, who could not read, squinted at the typewriter and said:

"If thou canst make thy machine answer me where this Don Julio César found a million cartridges growing on the trees let us march there quickly."

But Tula, to cover up her father's jealous temper, questioned softly:

"And this Don Julius César, did he kill many masters, or were they all gringos?"

Rosario made no reply, but after listening for a moment to the mingled sounds of the encampment, he remarked:

[10] Commander.

[11] Also known as *Parallel Lives of the Noble Greeks and Romans*; a collection of short biographies comparing Greek and Roman statesmen, by Plutarch (circa 45-125 A.D.).

[12] Popular 1903 operetta by Gustav Luders (1865-1913).

"The *señorita* Dorotea has ceased to weep."

"The *señorita* has no valor," returned the girl; "the *señorita* is afraid of dynamite." With ostentatious nonchalance she stuffed another doorknob.

Just then came a distant commotion which quickly swelled to a great shouting, in the midst of which a cavalcade dashed up before the cave. And Don Rómulo was presented, a prisoner, at the feet of Rosario. The habitués of the Jockey Club[13] would hardly have recognized their fastidious friend, so disordered was he in person, and so distraught in feature.

"My daughter," he stammered in a hoarse accent, "where is my daughter?"

Rosario, startled by this unlooked for stroke of fortune, studied his captive without replying. He had risen to his feet, holding the kid in his arm. And his heroic proportions struck a sudden awe into the heart of Don Rómulo, as he took in the aspect of that being for whose existence he was responsible, and whom fate seemed to have selected to chastise him.

The son of Remedios had an easy bearing, and his face, the color of unroasted coffee, was cut in precise lines, strong and yet sensitive, while the inward fire of his will was projected outward through a pair of amber-hued eyes, impetuous and dauntless.

"Your honor asks for his daughter," he said. "The *señorita* is here. By favor of the revolution your honor shall see her before he dies."

"Only tell me that she is safe," implored Don Rómulo, ignoring the implication of approaching catastrophe to himself. "Tell me that you have not molested her!"

"The revolution does not molest the *señorita*s," returned Rosario; and his accent caused Don Rómulo, all pale a moment before, to flush beneath his mask of dust to the back of his neck.

Here the ex-barber, who felt that the condemnation of a master should be conducted with more ceremony and volubility, launched into a long and flowery harangue in which he recited the wrongs of the people, dating from the time when their lands had been ravished from them under the placid but infamous regime of

[13] A meeting place for the elite in Mexico City, and a "center of Porfirian wealth and elegance" (Camin and Meyer 60).

Don Porfirio, and themselves reduced to a state of virtual slavery at the mercy of the masters.

Others gathered about the cave to gaze at the master, and the discussion was general. It was explained to him kindly that his conduct had not been worse than that of other masters, and that his execution would be effected without malice and solely for its moral effect on the enemies of the revolution. And they exhorted him respectfully not to take it to heart. Don Rómulo groaned and rolled his eyes at Rosario. And at that moment Dorotea launched herself through the press and into her father's arms.

"*Papá*," she cried, "my brave *papá*, I knew thou wouldst come to take me home. I was not at all afraid, except of the dynamite. By all the saints! They handle it like bread. Do not kick that box, *papá*, lest it explode and injure thy little feet."

Don Rómulo hastened to remove his little feet as far as possible from the box of dynamite, and at the same time sought some remnants of dignity in the eyes of his child.

Misinterpreting his tragical frown, she went on:

"Do not be angry with these, our people. Although they are a little mad, I find they have excellent hearts. I supplicate thee to forgive them. Wilt thou promise me, *papá*, not to punish them severely?"

"I promise thee," sparkled Don Rómulo, raising his voice, as he glanced at the encompassing faces, "that I will not punish them at all. In truth, I forgive them with all my soul."

A murmur of pleasure passed through the ranks of the revolution. The meeting between the *señorita* and her *papá* had touched many sympathies, and an impression was gaining ground that the master was a Christian with a good heart.

"Also I supplicate thee," continued Dorotea, "to let them have a little land. Poor creatures! They have a great desire to grow things for themselves."

"So I will do," exclaimed Don Rómulo, with genial fervor. "I will distribute among these, my faithful people, the lands that were taken from them long ago under the law. Thou shalt see, little daughter mine, that after the harvest is gathered and all things restored to order, each *peón* shall have his piece of land and proper wages for his labor. And with the help of God we will make the Morning Star a paradise for all of good heart."

At this there arose a tumult of amazed cordiality, which enlarged itself as those within hearing passed the news, with variations, to those beyond. But Rosario lifted his arms, with a loud cry sprang upon the little table and upbraided his followers for their infirmity of purpose.

In vehement words he pointed out that the promise just thrown to them had been extorted from the trembling master by well-grounded fear for his own life. He warned them of probable treachery after the harvest, if they should be so misguided as to yield their labor for that operation. He reminded them of the large brotherhood he had preached to them, the longed-for union with all their countrymen then in arms for emancipation and justice. He held up to them the example of a certain Brutus, who, for the cause of liberty, had killed the great master of Rome, Don Julio César; and of another Brutus, his ancestor, who had executed his own sons because they had conspired to restore the banished masters. And, soaring from the past to the future, he sketched in sentences of fire the glory that awaited them, his comrades and himself, on battlefields made sacred by blood shed for liberty.

An oration in the vulgar dialect, often bombastic—often ludicrous in its betrayal of undigested half-knowledge—such was the harangue of Rosario. But it was also much more. Not only did it swing the hearts of the *peones* round again from their lawful lord to their unlawful chief, now with tears, now with laughter, now with exultant cries; but also it stirred to their depths, in spite of their prejudices and their fears, two hearers of the superior caste.

Irresistibly too, the passionate face of Rosario recalled a revered family portrait, that of Beltrán Salgado, Don Rómulo's great-great-grandfather, a statesman, poet, and soldier, who had played a telling role in the overthrow of the Spanish dominion.

The bewildered Dorotea plucked at her father's sleeve, with the words of recognition on her lips. His eyes, agonized, answered her with a swift look which confused her own feelings further. Dorotea seemed lost in something beyond her understanding. She saw her father stagger like a blind man toward the table and heard him cry:

"Hear me, Rosario. If it be the will of God I die for my sins, I must surely die, but not by thy hand, not by thine, son of mine, for that is forbidden by God."

The figure of Rosario was frozen in an arrested gesture, between his feet the typewriter, at his back the sky. He was bent slightly downward toward Don Rómulo, who now sobbed before him—the master, who not only called him "my son," but, more prodigious still, had veritably addressed him, the son of Remedios, as "thou." And whatever ice or fire may have shot through Rosario's veins as he poised there, while the crowd's buzzing wonder hushed into the silence of suspense, perhaps his most poignant feeling was the despairing one of a young Titan disarmed by the gods.

Disarmed and dishonored, his leadership made a mockery, his very blood polluted with tyranny. He thought of his mother in her black shawl. In all the *peón* population of the *hacienda* she had been the only woman of shawl, and he in his childhood had imagined that she was permitted that distinction as a testimony of her peculiar excellence. Now he understood the true reason.

Covering his face with his *serape*,[14] he jumped to the ground, and with head and shoulders bowed low, he tried to escape through the crowd.

They were unwilling to let him go. And in the confusion Don Rómulo laid an entreating hand on his arm.

"All these years, Rosario, I have longed to be blessed with a son," he cried, his face shining with tears; "and now God has given me thee. All that I have shall be thine, with the name of Salgado fixed on thee by law. And thou shalt have an education to fit thee for thy future as a master; and thy life shall be of ease and elegance. Thus thou wilt help me to atone for many injustices and to make my peace with God."

"If your honor makes his peace with God it will be without my help," Rosario returned, in a shaking voice. "How will *I* be a master, or the son of one? I want no life of ease and elegance. What ridicule! No, no."

[14] Narrow woolen blanket, worn as a mantle.

He choked down a convulsion in his throat and dashed the tears from his face with his fists. Then, with an air of resolution, he tightened his belt, saying:

"Rosario has lived of the people, and so he will die. Without favors he made himself something. But now you have made him less than nothing. Master, I give you back your people, in whose faces you have covered me with shame. Let them follow the barber, who has no stomach for fighting, and I think they will return for the harvest and give you much trouble if you do not keep your promises. *Adiós.* This Rosario is well finished."

He plunged through the ranks of his late followers and sprang up the precipitous way, mounting to the Devil's Footstool. All watched him in stupor as he climbed and leaped from rock to rock. When at length he reached the beetling shelf, he seemed to expand himself and gaze comprehensively at earth and sky. Then he was seen to take something from his sash, and, with the gesture of a boy spinning a top, prepare to cast it on the rock at his feet.

Tula, watching from afar with the rest, uttered a loud wail. But the missile danced harmlessly in a spinning curve, and was lost in the lake below.

Impatiently, Rosario pulled another specimen of Tula's handiwork from his sash, and after a doubtful glance at it, threw it clear across the lake.

It exploded against the opposite cliff, tearing a mass of earth and rock with a young tree and agitating the air with angry echoes. The man on the shelf stood motionless until the last splash had subsided. He did not look down at the grouped onlookers, although they included the whole of his little world. And their prayers did not reach his ears.

Once more his hand traveled to his sash. Armed with the third bomb, he paused with bended head, and crossed himself. And not one among the distant spectators, many of whom had fallen on their knees failed to follow his example. Then, with a return of buoyancy, Rosario aimed again at the rock near his feet. And this time he threw with all his might.

The son of Remedios was seen no more. In dust and detonation he vanished from human ken, lost in the bombardment with which the fragments of the Devil's Footstool lashed the lake into bubbles.

[January 1931]

Bibliography

Primary Sources

Short Stories

Mena, María Cristina. "The Gold Vanity Set." *American Magazine* Nov. 1913: 24-8.

—. "John of God, the Water-Carrier." *Century Magazine* Nov. 1913: 39-48.

—. "John of God, the Water-Carrier." 1913. *The Monthly Criterion: A Literary Review* (1927): 312-31.

—. "John of God, the Water-Carrier." 1913. *The Best Short Stories of 1928 and the Yearbook of the American Short Story*. Ed. Edward J. O'Brien. New York: Dodd, 1928. 77-93.

—. "The Emotions of María Concepción." *Century Magazine* Jan. 1914: 348-58.

—. "The Education of Popo." *Century Magazine* Mar. 1914: 653-62.

—. "The Birth of the God of War." *Century Magazine* May 1914: 45-9.

—. "Doña Rita's Rivals." *Century Magazine* Sept. 1914: 641-52.

—. "The Vine Leaf." *Century Magazine* Dec. 1914: 289-92.

—. "The Sorcerer and General Bisco." *Century Magazine* Apr. 1915: 857-66.

—. "Marriage by Miracle." *Century Magazine* Mar. 1916: 726-34.

—. "The Soul of Hilda Brunel." *Cosmopolitan* Dec. 1916: 53+.

Chambers, María Cristina. "A Son of the Tropics." *Household Magazine* Jan. 1931: 4+.

Children's Literature

Chambers, María Cristina. *The Water-Carrier's Secrets*. New York: Oxford UP, 1942.

—. *The Two Eagles*. New York: Oxford UP, 1943.

—. *The Bullfighter's Son*. New York: Oxford UP, 1944.

—. *The Three Kings*. New York: Oxford UP, 1946.

—. *Boy Heroes of Chapultepec, A Story of the Mexican War.* Philadelphia: Winston, 1953.

Articles

—. "Julian Carrillo: The Herald of a Musical Monroe Doctrine." *Century Magazine* Mar. 1915: 753-59.

—. "Afternoons in Italy with D.H. Lawrence." *Texas Quarterly* 7.4 (1964): 114-20.

Letters

Correspondence with *The Century Magazine*

All letters listed below are published with permission from Century Company Records, Rare Books and Manuscript Division, New York Public Library, Astor, Lenox, and Tilden Foundations.

Mena, María Cristina. Letter to Robert Underwood Johnson. 20 March 1913.

—. Letter to Robert Sterling Yard. [March 1913].

—. Letter to Robert Underwood Johnson. 4 April 1913.

—. Letter to Douglas Zabriske Doty. [October 1914].

—. Letter to Douglas Zabriske Doty. [November 1914].

—. Letter to Douglas Zabriske Doty. [November/December 1914].

—. Letter to Douglas Zabriske Doty. [December 1914].

Douglas Zabriske Doty. Letter to María Cristina Mena. 28 September 1914.

—. Letter to María Cristina Mena. 19 November 1914.

—. Letter to María Cristina Mena. 7 December 1914.

Correspondence with D.H. Lawrence

Chambers, María Cristina. Letter to D.H. Lawrence. 9 August 1928. Squires 32-34.

—. Letter to D.H. Lawrence. [11 December 1928]. Squires 34-35.

Lawrence, D.H. "To Maria Chambers." 18 February 1928. Letter 4307 of *The Letters of D.H. Lawrence*. Ed. James T. Boulton and Margaret H. Boulton. Vol. 6. Cambridge: Cambridge UP, 1991. 296-97.

—. "To Maria Chambers." 24 April 1928. Letter 4403, Boulton 377-78.

—. "To Maria Chambers." 25 August 1928. Letter 4613, Boulton 521-22.

Squires, Michael. "Two Newly Discovered Letters to D.H. Lawrence." *D.H. Lawrence Review* 23.1 (1991): 31-35.

Contemporary Sources

"Author Writes Book in Braille for Kids." *Brooklyn Heights Press* 7 May 1959: 131.

Buell, Ellen Lewis. "Mexican Host" in "Mexico—and Points South—for Younger Readers." Rev. of *The Two Eagles*, by María Cristina Chambers. *New York Times* 30 Jan. 1944, sec. 7: 6.

Gordon, Ruth A. Rev. of *The Three Kings*, by María Cristina Chambers. *New York Times* 22 Dec. 1946, sec. 7: 11.

"Heights Woman Recalls a Visit With 'Lady Chatterly's' Author." *Brooklyn Eagle* 23 October 1960: 11.

"Henry K. Chambers, Playwright, Is Dead." *New York Times* 6 Sept. 1935, late city ed.: 17.

Hoehn, Matthew, ed. *Catholic Authors: Contemporary Biographical Sketches: 1930-1947*. Newark: St. Mary's Abbey, 1948. 118-19.

"Mrs. Henry Chambers, 72, Short-Story Writer, Is Dead." *New York Times* 10 Aug. 1965: 29.

Secondary Sources

Acuña, Rodolfo. *Occupied America: A History of Chicanos*. 2nd ed. New York: Harper, 1981.

—. *Occupied America: A History of Chicanos*. 3rd ed. New York: Harper, 1988.

Alexander, John W. "Is Our Art Distinctively American?" *Century Magazine* Apr. 1914: 825-28.

Allen, Paula Gunn. *The Sacred Hoop: Recovering the Feminine in American Indian Traditions*. Boston: Beacon, 1992.

Ammons, Elizabeth. *Conflicting Stories: American Women Writers at the Turn into the Twentieth Century*. New York: Oxford UP, 1992.

Ammons, Elizabeth and Annette White-Parks, eds. *Tricksterism in Turn-of-the-Century American Literature: A Multicultural Perspective*. Hanover: UP of New England, 1994.

Ammons, Elizabeth and Valerie Rohy, eds. *United States Local Color Writers: 1880-1920: An Anthology*. New York: Viking/Penguin, 1997.

Anderson, Benedict. *Imagined Communities: Reflections on the Origin and Spread of Nationalism*. Rev. ed. New York: Verso/New Left Books, 1991.

Anzaldúa, Gloria. *Borderlands/La Frontera: The New Mestiza.* San Francisco: Aunt Lute Books, 1987.

Boulton, James T. and Margaret H. Boulton, eds. *The Letters of D.H. Lawrence.* Vol. 6. Cambridge: Cambridge UP, 1991.

Calderón, Héctor and José David Saldívar, eds. *Criticism in the Borderlands: Studies in Chicano Literature, Culture, and Ideology.* Durham: Duke UP, 1991.

Calvert, Peter. *The Mexican Revolution, 1910-1914: The Diplomacy of Anglo-American Conflict.* Cambridge: Cambridge UP, 1968.

Camín, Héctor Aguilar and Lorenzo Meyer. *In the Shadow of the Mexican Revolution: Contemporary Mexican History, 1910-1989.* Trans. Luis Alberto Fierro. Austin: U of Texas P, 1993.

de la Torre, Adela and Beatríz M. Pesquera, eds. *Building with Our Hands: New Directions in Chicana Studies.* Berkeley: U of California P, 1993.

Echevarría, Roberto González. *Alejo Carpentier: The Pilgrim at Home.* Ithaca: Cornell UP, 1977.

Garza-Falcón-Sánchez, Leticia Magda. "The Chicano: A Literary Response to the Rhetoric of Dominance." Diss. U of Texas at Austin, 1993.

Gunn, Drewey Wayne. *American and British Writers in Mexico, 1556-1973.* Austin: U of Texas P, 1974.

Gunn Allen, Paula. "'Border' Studies: The Intersection of Gender and Color." *Introduction to Scholarship in Modern Languages and Literatures.* Ed. Joseph Gibaldi. 2nd ed. New York: MLA, 1992. 303-19.

Harlow, Barbara. "Sites of Struggle: Immigration, Deportation, Prison, and Exile." *Criticism in the Borderlands.* Calderón and Saldívar 149-63.

Lomas, Clara, ed. *The Rebel: Leonor Villegas de Magnón.* Houston: Arte Público, 1994.

López, Tiffany Ana. "María Cristina Mena: Turn-of-the-Century La Malinche, and Other Tales of Cultural (Re)Construction." Ammons and White-Parks 21-45.

McArthur, F.F. "Unfamiliar Mexico." *Century Magazine* Sept. 1915: 729-36.

Millard, Gertrude B. "The Transformation of Angelita López." *Century Magazine* Aug. 1914: 547-57.

Miller, Julius. "Creole Beauties and Some Passionate Pilgrims." *Century Magazine* Feb. 1914: 558-65.

Minh-ha, Trinh T. *Woman, Native, Other: Writing Postcoloniality and Feminism*. Bloomington: Indiana UP, 1989.

Paredes, Raymond A. "The Evolution of Chicano Literature." *Three American Literatures: Essays in Chicano, Native American, and Asian-American Literature for Teachers of American Literature*. Ed. Houston A. Baker. New York: MLA, 1982. 33-79.

Peterson, Theodore. *Magazines in the Early Twentieth Century*. Urbana: U of Illinois P, 1964.

Pratt, Mary Louise. "The Short Story: The Long and the Short of It." *Poetics* 10 (1981): 175-94.

Rebolledo, Tey Diana. *Women Singing in the Snow: A Cultural Analysis of Chicana Literature*. Tucson: U of Arizona P, 1995.

Rebolledo, Tey Diana and Eliana S. Rivero, eds. *Infinite Divisions: An Anthology of Chicana Literature*. Tucson: U of Arizona P, 1993.

Ross, Edward Alsworth. "American and Immigrant Blood: A Study of the Social Effects of Immigration." *Century Magazine* Dec. 1913: 225-32.

Shuster, W. Morgan. "The Mexican Menace." *Century Magazine* Jan. 1914: 593-602.

Simmen, Edward, ed. *North of the Rio Grande: The Mexican-American Experience in Short Fiction*. New York: Penguin, 1992. 39-84.

Soto, Shirlene. *Emergence of the Modern Mexican Woman: Her Participation in Revolution and Struggle for Equality, 1910-1940*. Denver: Arden, 1990.

Tatum, Charles. *Chicano Literature*. Boston: Twayne, 1982.

"Topics of the Time." *Century Magazine* Sept. 1913: 789-91.

"Topics of the Time." *Century Magazine* Oct. 1913: 951-52.

Turner, John Kenneth. *Barbarous Mexico*. Chicago: Kerr, 1910.

Velásquez Treviño, Gloria Louise. "Cultural Ambivalence in Early Chicana Literature." *European Perspectives on Hispanic Literatures of the United States*. Ed. Genvieve Fabre. Houston: Arte Público, 1988. 140-46.

—. "Cultural Ambivalence in Early Chicana Prose Fiction." Diss. Stanford University, 1985.